ON EDGE

I was waiting for the sun to rise.

Earlier I had watched fishing boats pull out, boxy craft with lobster traps piled on deck, others with nets gathered up like folded wings. It was silent after they left except for the occasional cry of a gull. I sat in my car, the window open to let the cold air keep me awake, as the sky slowly filled with light the same milky color as the sea. I closed my eyes and smelled brine and seaweed, heard waves slap against the pilings.

Then I sensed a wall of body heat near my open window. "Damn," I muttered, blinking in the brightness of the sun on the water.

"Sleeping it off?" A man in a leather jacket rested his arm on the roof of my car. His short-cropped hair was white, but his build was still solid with muscle. He hadn't shaved and looked bone weary, but his eyes were sharp and watchful. Two uniformed officers stood nearby, one with his hand tensed on the butt of the .38 holstered at his side.

"Didn't mean to fall asleep. I wanted to see the sun come up over the water." I shifted and rubbed my stiff leg.

"Missed it. Been up for a while. See you have Illinois plates. What are you doing here?"

"In Maine?"

"In this town. On this harbor."

"Guess I ran out of land."

"Guess you're some kind of smart-ass. Let's see some ID."

I reached for my wallet and pulled out my license, still sticking out from when I debated the definition of "complete stop" with a state trooper in Vermont. A crumpled citation lay on the dashboard to remind me who won the argument.

His eyes flicked between me and my picture. "Chicago, huh?"

"Hog butcher for the world," I told him. "My kind of town."

He handed the license back and I stowed it. When I looked up again his eyes were fixed on the backseat. His casual stance had tightened. "What's that?"

"What?"

"That stain there?" I didn't say anything. He jerked the door open. "Step out of the car, sir. Hands where we can see them."

"All right. Don't get excited." I showed them my palms, but when I turned to get out my right leg wouldn't cooperate.

"Come on, come on." One of the uniforms now had his weapon in both hands, yelling, "*Out* of the car."

"Give me a chance." Without thinking, I reached a hand down to shift my leg. They misunderstood my intentions and yanked me out of the car. The one with the .38 shoved me down across the hood and held me there as someone else snapped on cuffs and patted me down. Gulls called, disturbed by the commotion.

The white-haired cop paced around the car, ducking his head to check out the stains on the backseat. "So, where'd all that blood come from?"

I looked at the sunlight breaking up on the water, followed the course of a gull as it swooped up into the bright

sky. The one with the gun leaned over me. "He asked you a question."

"*Back off,* asshole," I said through my teeth.

He jerked me up abruptly, making red streaks of heat tear across my skull. The barrel of his weapon trembled inches from my chest.

"Neil? Easy," the old man said, locking eyes with the cop holding my collar twisted in his fist. After a moment's standoff, Neil released me and holstered his gun. "Tell us about the blood," the old man said softly.

"It's old. Check it out."

"You're giving us permission to search your car?"

"Be my guest. Can you take the cuffs off? I'm unarmed, I can't run."

He nodded. Neil looked away in disgust as the other uniform, a round-faced kid, took the cuffs off.

"Mind if I sit while you do this?" I asked. Neil ignored me, but the rookie put me into the backseat of one of the cruisers. Then the three of them donned gloves, started the search. They took up the floor mats, went through the shirts and underwear in my duffel bag, looked in the trunk. The rookie got excited when he opened the glove compartment and saw the Glock. The old man slid into the passenger side to examine the gun before putting it back. Then he poked through the ashtray with a pencil and picked up a cup from the floor that bore the logo of a diner on Route 1 where I'd picked up coffee last night. He found the ticket on the dashboard, smoothed it out, and looked at it.

The squad car I was sitting in had seen better days. Foam leaked through tears in the seat and a pine-tree-shaped air freshener didn't counter the stale smell of too many fast-food meals. The town these cops served wasn't flush with tourist dollars. No effort had been made to improve the waterfront with T-shirt shops and ice cream stands. The buildings were weathered and sagging as if the

nor'easters that scoured across the Gulf of Maine over the years had beaten them into a state of resentful submission.

I heard the trunk of the Mustang creak as it was lowered. The old cop opened the cruiser door and squatted down to my eye level. He handed me the cane he'd taken from my car. "What happened to your leg?"

"Workplace injury. Nothing to do with whatever's been keeping you up nights."

"Still want to talk to you. Let's head up to the station house."

"You got coffee there?"

He suppressed a sigh. "I can get you coffee." All the eager tension, that bright, jumping hope he'd been barely holding in check, was gone. He knew as well as I did that whoever they were looking for was still out there.

Three men in camo stood in front of the dispatcher's counter. As we came in, they looked over at us, but the old man ignored them. "Anything?" he asked the dispatcher. Two of the men looked away, disappointed.

"No news, Chief."

The third man scowled at me. Apparently he held me responsible for not being the guy they were looking for.

The chief led the way to a room with a battered table, four wooden chairs, a Coke machine, and coffeemaker. The carafe was dry, rings of brown marking previous high tide marks. The walls were dingy industrial beige, decorated with posters on gun safety and first aid for choking victims. "Neil, keep him company. Bobby? Got a job for you."

I sat. Neil took up position beside the door. "How about we start a fresh pot of coffee?" I suggested.

He acted as if I hadn't spoken. I felt for my cigarettes, but there was a hand-lettered sign taped to the wall: This Is a Smoke-Free Building. I sighed and sat back to wait.

The chief appeared ten minutes later and murmured to Neil, "They didn't find anything out at the old quarry."

"I didn't think they would."

"They want to do the fields up by Northhaven next. Go on out there, keep it under control. Just the fields. Not the old school; the owner hasn't got back to us yet. Don't want anyone charged with trespassing."

"That would be real serious, wouldn't it."

"Neil." There was some kind of warning in his tone, a line being drawn. The back of Neil's neck bloomed with red patches as he stalked out.

"Who's missing?" I asked.

"A kid." The chief pulled a chair out and sat. He waited, giving me an opportunity to break down and confess to something. "What did you say you were doing here?"

"I didn't say."

"So, tell me."

"I have some time off. Thought I'd take a trip. Didn't you mention something about coffee?"

"Brimsport isn't on the beaten path. What brought you here?"

"I was heading east on Route One. I wanted to see the sun rise over the water, so I took the turnoff." I remembered the highway unrolling hypnotically in front of my headlights, the lights flashing over a blurred name on a sign barely glimpsed, but familiar somehow. When the road curved inland I turned onto a road headed toward the water and within two miles saw the name again: Entering Brimsport, Pop. 12,320. Past sleeping houses, down a hill, through a silent, darkened business district, finally rolling to a stop where the road ended.

"Where were you early Wednesday morning?"

"What's today?"

"Friday."

"Let's see." I pulled out my wallet, took out receipts. "This is . . . nope. Here's one from last night. Got gas in . . .

Can you read that?" I passed it over. "Shit. Why do I save all this garbage? I got a receipt from last year here. Okay, I filled up at a Starvin' Marvin in South Bend. Tuesday night, near midnight. And I stopped at this bar after. They probably remember me."

He took the two receipts from me, spread out the wrinkles and read them over carefully. "You have a lot of drugs in your car," he said, finally, his frown thoughtful, like he really wanted to give me a chance to explain.

"Drugs? I don't . . . oh, the Percocet."

"Five bottles, fifty each. That's a lot of Schedule Two controlled substances."

I took the sixth bottle out of my pocket and shook two pills out. "I got extra for the trip, that's all." There didn't seem to be much chance of coffee anytime soon, so I swallowed them dry. I knew it would be a while before they kicked in. Nicotine, now, that wouldn't take long. I could taste the cigarette I couldn't light up in here.

"Look, you're going to have to explain that blood in your car."

"It isn't connected to this kid you got missing."

He put his hands flat on the table and leaned toward me. "Just tell me about it." The eyes fixed on me were an unusual color, almost golden. They seemed to shimmer with a smoldering glow like hot embers.

The young cop with the round face tapped the door-frame. "What?" the old man barked, startled.

"Made those calls, Chief. They know him, all right."

"A sheet? Outstanding warrants?"

"You won't believe this. He works there."

"*What?*"

"He's a cop. There was this shooting. What I heard, that blood in his car? He drove his partner to the hospital."

The old man turned to glare at me. "You had to jerk me around? I'm up all night and you play these fucking games? Why didn't you just say?"

"I'm sorry about this missing kid."

"What about it?"

"I hope he turns up, that's all."

"*She*. Seven years old, missing for over two days now and you show up and play these stupid, these fucking, you *stupid* son of a bitch, *wasting* my time—" He was roaring at me now, his face mottled, and it must have felt good because he looked fully recharged. He stood, shoving the chair back so hard it tipped over. "Get the fuck out of here. Bobby? Run him back to his car. Then get out to Northhaven, make sure things are under control."

"Northhaven?" Bobby seemed startled.

"They're doing the fields up there. We don't have permission on the school grounds yet. The women that live there must be out, they aren't answering their phone. Neil's there but—"

"Got it."

The old man left. Bobby followed behind me as I limped out into the hall.

I settled into the passenger seat of a cruiser. Bobby walked over to a car that had just pulled into the parking lot behind the station, had a word with the driver, then climbed behind the wheel swearing under his breath. "Have to take a little detour." He pulled around the corner onto the main drag and put on his lights. We sped through town, then climbed a hill that rose to the west.

"What's up?"

"Nothing, I hope." He flicked the siren to get a slow-moving car out of the way. "Some of these volunteers get a little overexcited. You're not in any hurry, are you?"

The road left the town behind, running through trees and fields. Soon we came on a dozen cars and pickups parked on the shoulder along a fenced field. Bobby pulled

up between crumbling gateposts that framed a driveway that looked abandoned, grass and moss spilling out of cracks in the pavement. A metal sign that said Private Property—No Hunting was nailed crookedly to a tree beside the drive, its message punctuated with bullet holes.

Men were milling around with the unfocused energy of a pack of hounds waiting to be let loose on a scent. Neil stood frowning over a map spread across the hood of his cruiser, listening to a man in a flak jacket. I thought I picked out the three that had been in the station house, but it was hard to tell. Everyone was wearing plaid and camo.

"Wait in the car." Bobby strolled across the road into the crowd, his hand resting easy on the butt of his .38. I opened the window and lit a cigarette. "What's going on?" I heard Bobby ask amiably.

"Can you explain to us why we aren't in there searching the school grounds?" The guy in the flak jacket jabbed a finger at the gateposts and the driveway that wound into the woods.

Bobby's voice stayed reasonable. "We haven't heard back from the residents yet. We go in without their say-so, it's trespassing."

"You want to wait till they give us *permission*? We got a kid missing. You know what happened before." Some in the crowd nodded, muttering their agreement.

"That's the law, Simons." Bobby smiled ruefully and spread his hands. What can you do?

"Are we going to let some legal technicality hold us back? A child's life hangs in the balance."

"They got a point," Neil said, not quite looking at Bobby. "I think we should check it out. Those women up there are pretty strange."

"Strange? They're fucking perverts," one of the volunteers yelled. There was a rumble of assent.

"This is just like twenty years ago," an angry voice called out. "Whose side are you on, Munro?"

"The same side as you, Alvin. Jesus," Bobby answered, exasperated. "We all want to find her. Let's get moving. We're searching the fields." He yanked the map off the hood of the car and started to fold it up.

Neil flushed. "Hey, that's my map."

Bobby ignored him. "Let's form up a line. I want each of you standing approximately five feet apart. We'll do this in grid formation." He looked around. The guys looked back sullenly, not going anywhere.

"Give me the map, Munro." Neil's voice was thick with fury.

They were standing toe to toe all of a sudden. Neil tore the map, trying to snap it out of Bobby's hand. I reached for the radio.

"We got a situation out at the search site."

"Who is this?"

"Slovo, Chicago PD. I was just at the station. There's a disagreement as to strategy."

A pause. "I'll pass that along to Chief Cobbett." The dispatcher's voice stayed neutral, trained not to convey anything on an open frequency.

Volunteers, led by the flak jacket, started across the road and Bobby called out, "Simons? I'm not kidding. You cross that property line, I'm gonna have to arrest you."

Voices ricocheted across the pasture, passionate and angry, Bobby interrupting with dogged reasonableness. I got out of the cruiser. Behind me, the drive curved upward through the trees, dappled in shadow, peaceful.

I turned and strolled up the drive. Soon the curve hid me from sight of the road and though I could still hear angry voices I felt alone. It was the kind of place that teenagers pick for a party, private and desolate. Faded beer cans nestled in the ditch, half buried in leaves. Fragments of glass glinted on the pavement. A gust of wind caused the limbs of a dead tree to shift and creak. It also brought with it a scent of something out of place here, something I knew

from crack-house stairwells and car trunks and vacant lots, the smell that catches in your throat at your first homicide, the one you never forget. I took a few steps down the narrow path, peering through the shifting shadows. I was ready to write it off when another breeze moved through the branches and it was there again.

The path twisted over a rise and ended in a clearing. Stone blocks showed through the long grass in a circular pattern like some vestige of a ruined civilization. The smell here was sweet and coppery, edged with decay, borne on the gust that stirred the grass. I looked down the slope and saw something dangling from a branch of a maple that grew near the center. As I approached it I could hear the whine of sluggish flies. They rose off flesh, muscles, and tendons wrapped around the shape, trussed with rope and hanging there.

An animal, I thought with relief. Some hunter had been here, dressed out his kill. A fat fly buzzed over to me as I took in the shape of it: too small to be a deer, too big to be a rabbit. It twisted again and I could see the eyes that stared out of the pink flesh, lidless and wide, the whites flecked with red specks, the brown irises clouded over and blank.

All of sudden, like one of those optical illusions, the picture flipped, the shape became something else, something out of place and all too familiar. I stood there, taking it in, then must have turned because I was on the path again, pushing through the branches, trying to move faster than my leg would let me, pushing away the horror that filled my head like a swarm of insects.

B

obby radioed in what I'd found and Neil sent the volunteer search party away without giving them any information. That didn't stop the men exchanging theories as they left. It would be all over town, soon, that something had been found up in these woods.

When Chief Cobbett arrived, he told Bobby to take me back to the station to await questioning. As we drove down the hill and into the town, Bobby kept shaking his head as if it would chase the bad dream away. Neil had insisted on confirming what I told them. When he'd come out of the path there was a splash of puke on one of his highly polished shoes and his face had gone pale as parchment.

About twenty people were clustered on the front steps of the municipal building that housed the police station. As we drove by, more arrived, their faces tight with excitement and anxiety. Bobby circled around the block and pulled up behind the station house. He leaned forward to rest his forehead on the steering wheel.

"You okay?" I asked.

He lifted his head. "Just thinking about Louise. The mother. How's she going to handle this?"

He led me inside and showed me into an interview

room, hesitating at the door. "Chief'll want to talk to you again. Want to know something stupid? I was just so sure this time..."

"This time?"

"I thought we'd find her before it was too late." He smacked a palm hard against the doorframe as he left.

I waited for more than an hour before a man of about fifty with sagging pouches of flesh under blue eyes and an I've-seen-everything air stepped through the door. "Tom Flaherty." He shook my hand and sat across the table from me.

There were big blue letters on the ID clipped to his jacket. "FBI?"

"Bangor office. Chief Cobbett contacted us when Marcy was abducted."

"Something Bobby said made me wonder—"

"Detective Slovo, I don't have a lot of time. Let me ask the questions, okay?" Which he proceeded to do in classic G-man style. When he'd taken me over the discovery of the body three times and was assured he had all the details that could be extracted from me, he left.

Another long wait. I started to doze off. A sarcastic voice in the hall woke me up. There was an electric moment of silence before the chief's voice came in response, wielding the words "ignorant," "incompetent," and "irresponsible" like slaps. When it was over, I caught a flash of Neil striding down the corridor, hands clenched into fists.

The chief came in, his eyes bright and face flushed. "We done?" I asked.

"For now. There's one thing—"

"I won't talk to the press."

"You won't talk to *anyone*. Especially about the state of the body. We need some facts held back."

"Going to be hard to keep it quiet. Something this twisted, the killer's looking for attention. He wants to lead the evening news."

"I don't intend to give him the satisfaction. And you won't either." There was a threat in his words.

The steps outside were jammed and a sound truck had pulled up to the curb. A reporter was interviewing a tall, dark-haired man. He seemed to be speaking as much to the citizens gathered there as to the camera, and they were hanging on his words. Probably the prosecutor, accustomed to playing to an audience. I didn't stay to listen. There was the same charged atmosphere as after a natural disaster— ordinary life interrupted, people with otherwise little in common bonded by a shared tragedy. People stood in doorways, muttering. I started walking, hoping I was headed toward the harbor. They fell silent until I'd passed by.

In the next block I came to a café. A television behind the counter was on and everyone was watching the man speaking to the crowd on the steps. The reporter turned to the camera to say, "Once again, police have announced that the body found this morning has been identified as that of seven-year-old Marcy Knox, missing since Wednesday. Authorities are considering it a homicide, making Marcy the third child abducted and murdered here in recent months. Reporting live from Brimsport, this is Amy Driscoll, WABI-TV5."

I slipped into a booth and took the menu propped behind the napkin dispenser while an anchor promised more coverage at six. A commercial came on. A waitress came up and hovered as I stared at the plastic menu. "Just coffee," I told her. She stalked off.

Four men sitting at a table across from me were looking my way. I recognized them from the search party but when I nodded at them they didn't respond, just kept up the stare. The rest of the people in the room seemed to have caught their hostility like an airborne contagion.

I felt sweat tickle my temples. The waitress thumped a mug of coffee in front of me so hard it splashed over, then ripped the check off her pad and dropped it beside the cup. Before I could ask for directions back to the harbor, she walked away.

The whispers and stares were making me uneasy. I downed the coffee, left some change on the table, and stood. The floor was moving with a pronounced swell, canting to the left. While I waited for the woman working behind the counter to take my money I looked at a street map taped beside the register, a cartoon version of the town with each business depicted whimsically, a smiling sun beaming down from one corner. It was so old the colors had faded to murky shades of green.

The bell over the door jingled and a woman came in and stood beside me. She gave me a flicker of a smile. "That map's way out of date," she said. "Are you looking for something in particular?"

"My car. I left it at the harbor."

"Take a left and follow Main Street around the curve. It will take you to the waterfront." Her eyes were a rich amber tint, almost golden.

"Is it something in the water around here?"

"Excuse me?"

"Your eyes. They're a very unusual color." I reached out to steady myself on the counter.

"Are you okay?"

"I just want to pay my bill so I can get out of here." The woman, busy doing something to a coffeemaker, got busier as soon as I looked her way. I dropped a couple of bucks on my receipt and wiped sweat out of my eyes. "Forget it. Turn right, you said?"

"Left. Are you sure you're okay? Maybe you should sit down."

"I have to go." But my legs apparently liked her suggestion because as soon as I took a couple of steps toward the

door they buckled. She grabbed me and guided me down to the floor. I leaned back against the base of the counter and closed my eyes to make the floor stop spinning. When I opened them I saw a pair of steel-toed work boots approaching across the tile floor. "You know this fella, Ruth?"

"No. I just came in to pick up a sandwich." She put a cool palm against my cheek. "We better get you to the hospital, okay? You're burning up." Her face was close to mine, frowning with concern.

"You have such beautiful eyes," I heard myself say.

When I woke a man was standing by the window, staring out. He turned and saw me watching him. "How are you feeling?"

"Not bad. Kind of tired." I vaguely remembered EMTs asking a lot of questions. Trading my clothes for a gown, getting an IV poked into the back of my hand. Shakes and chills and sweats. Then a procession of improbable visitors: an elderly neighbor, a homeless guy from Lower Wacker Drive, an IA detective standing at the end of my bed, chewing a toothpick. I thought I saw that golden-eyed woman from the café again, but I wasn't sure. My grandmother showed up to ask me questions that sounded like accusations: Was I eating right? Had I been to church lately? When was I going to get my hair cut?

"Do you know where you are?" the man at the window asked.

"Eastern Maine Regional Medical Center. Says so on the sheets. Property of."

He smiled then, showing even white teeth. "I came by yesterday, but you weren't exactly lucid."

"I saw you talking to the press. You with the state's attorney's office?"

"We have district attorneys in this state."

"Oh. Any progress on the case?"

His smile faded. "It's going nowhere. Even with assistance from the FBI, state police, the best forensic expertise in New England, the killers are still out there."

"Killers? More than one?"

He stared down at a view I couldn't see, then turned to face me. "What happened to Marcy, what happened to all three of those little girls, is part of a long history of violence and perversion here."

"No kidding." There was something off about this guy. The prosecutors I knew saved their theatrics for the courtroom.

"You've had a lot of experience with crimes against children. What did you make of the crime scene?"

"I don't believe I caught your name."

He sat on the edge of the bed, drew a card out of his wallet. "You may have heard of me. I left law enforcement to devote my life to missing and exploited children."

Mike McGavin, executive director, the Innocents Foundation, the card said, along with a Brimsport P.O. box, a toll-free number, and a URL. "Nice try. I can't talk about it." I held the card out but he ignored it. "Sorry you wasted your time."

"It wasn't wasted. I was here anyway, visiting Marcy's mother. Louise was out of her mind when Marcy went missing. She seemed calmer after they found her body. You see that in parents sometimes. But early this morning she slit her wrists. A neighbor found her just in time."

He rose to leave, his eyes fixed on mine. "I know about you. The cases you've worked. Call me when you're ready to talk."

The name tag the doctor had pinned to his lab coat said he was Dr. Hari Chakravarty. He was a short, dark brown

DRESSED TO KILL

The smell here was sweet and coppery, edged with decay, borne on the gust that stirred the grass. I looked down the slope and saw something dangling from a branch of a maple that grew near the center of the clearing. As I approached it I could hear the whine of sluggish flies.

An animal, I thought with relief. Some hunter had been here, dressed out his kill. A fat fly buzzed over to me as I took in the shape of it: too small to be a deer, too big to be a rabbit. It twisted again and I could see the eyes that stared out of the pink flesh, lidless and wide.

All of a sudden, like one of those optical illusions, the picture flipped, the shape became something else. I stood there, taking it in, then must have turned because I was on the path again, pushing through the branches, trying to move faster than my leg would let me, pushing away the horror that filled my head like a swarm of insects. . . .

ACKNOWLEDGMENTS

Brimsport can't be found on any map. The town, along with its inhabitants and the events depicted in this book, are entirely the products of my imagination. However, an epidemic of investigations into what came to be called satanic ritual abuse did begin in 1984 with the McMartin day care case, followed within a month by a massive criminal investigation in the tiny town of Jordan, Minnesota. Kenneth V. Lanning, an FBI analyst, examined the records of over three hundred reported cases and concluded in 1992 that none could be substantiated. His *Investigator's Guide to Allegations of "Ritual" Child Abuse*, published by the bureau's Behavioral Sciences Unit, remains the most lucid and evenhanded exploration of the phenomenon from a law enforcement perspective. Debbie Nathan and Michael R. Snedeker's book *Satan's Silence: Ritual Abuse and the Making of a Modern American Witch Hunt* (Basic, 1995) is the best in-depth treatment of the subject. I also found Jeffrey S. Victor's sociological approach in *Satanic Panic: The Creation of a Contemporary Legend* (Open Court, 1993) helpful.

I'm deeply grateful to Dan Mandel for his unwavering support, to Katie Hall for taking a leap of faith, and to Kate Miciak for her persistence and deep understanding of the craft. The mistakes I've made are in spite of their best efforts to set me straight.

Published by
Dell Publishing
a division of
Random House, Inc.
1540 Broadway
New York, New York 10036

Copyright © 2002 by Barbara Fister
Cover design by Craig DeCamps

Dell® is a registered trademark of Random House, Inc., and the
colophon is a trademark of Random House, Inc.

ISBN: 0-440-23751-3

Manufactured in the United States of America

Published simultaneously in Canada

December 2002

10   9   8   7   6   5   4   3   2   1
OPM

ON EDGE

BARBARA FISTER

DELL BOOKS

man with a handlebar mustache, thick eyebrows over sad brown eyes, and a thatch of wiry hair. He stared at me for a minute, eyes wide with fake surprise. "My God, you aren't talking your head off for a change. The rubbish you've been spouting."

"What did I say?"

"Nothing I could make out." He unhooked the chart off the bed and read it over, frowning and unconsciously sharpening the points of his mustache with two fingers.

His accent wasn't right. The Indian doctors I knew either spoke with American accents or in a singsong Indian-English. "Where are you from?" I asked, and he glared up at me from the chart.

"I'm so bloody sick of that question." He hung the chart up crossly. "I was brought up in Swindon. That's in England, in case you need a geography lesson. If you must have the whole story, my parents came to Swindon from Madras, by way of Uganda."

"How'd you end up here?"

He yanked my covers back to examine my hip. "Got fed up with the National Health, came over here to do some research and study, ended up board-certified in orthopedics and family practice, being something of a genius, and then found out my job offers were limited. It came down to this godforsaken outpost of civilization, someplace in Alabama, or Pikeville, Kentucky." He frowned and poked the inflamed scar tissue. "Sorry, did that hurt? D'ye know, I've always regretted not choosing Pikeville."

"How soon can I check out of here?"

He was suddenly furious. "Are you trying to kill yourself or are you merely stupid? You're recovering from a serious injury, you git. Helen!" he roared out at a nurse who had crept by in the hallway on crepe-soled shoes. She backed up and looked in the door, wearing the expression of a bored martyr. "Mash us some tea would you, love? I'm that parched."

"Not in my job description, Hari."

"Miserable cow," he muttered as she whisked away. "I hate this place. Look, sunshine. You'd started a nasty infection. We caught it in time, but we'll keep you here another night to make sure that infection's under control. After that, we'll see." He checked his watch, ran a hand through his hair. "Your brother Steve wants you to get in touch. He's called so often it's annoying the nurses. Shall I see about getting you something to eat?"

"That's okay. I'm kind of tired."

"Rest, then." He squeezed my wrist gently and then he left.

When I woke again, the sun was low in the west. I pulled the IV line out of the catheter in the back of my hand, loosely knotted the tubing, and hit the reset button on the machine when it started to beep. Then I dressed and found my way out a back door.

It was cool outside, the scent of rain in the air. I sat on a retaining wall facing the parking lot and lit a cigarette, watching a trio of seagulls squabble over the remains of something spilling out of a fast-food bag.

The door opened and the woman I'd seen at the café leaned out. "Oh, there you are. Are you supposed to be up?" She came over to sit beside me.

"They have this thing about smoking in hospitals." One of the gulls seized a half of a hamburger bun and spread his wings. The other two birds mugged him before he could take off. "Did you come by last night?" I asked. She shook her head. "I thought I saw you. Actually, I was pretty out of it."

"I heard. Hari said you were speaking some foreign language. Russian?"

"Ukrainian. I was having this long conversation with

my grandmother, which was kind of odd because she's been dead for four years."

"You speak Ukrainian?"

"Had to around her. She didn't know hardly any English."

I knew what was coming next. It always did. "Say something in Ukrainian."

"Ti diisno krasivaia zhinka."

"What's it mean?"

"You have something on your nose."

"Funny." She made a face at me, but rubbed her nose just in case. "Listen, Hari says you'll have to stay put for a while. There's a summer place on Hunter's Point that's available. You interested?"

"Maybe. I don't know how long I'll be here."

"The owners are willing to rent it by the week. Cheap, too." She caught my puzzled look. "I checked. You can move in as soon as you're discharged."

"Why'd you—"

"You'll love this house. It's right on the water."

A car pulled up in the lot and the gulls grabbed for bun fragments and fries before scattering. She waved. "Hey, Dad."

Chief Cobbett climbed out of the car. Her father. That explained the eyes. They looked a lot sexier on her, though. "Ruth." He gave me a suspicious frown. "I thought you were sick, Slovo."

"I'm better."

"You tell him about the house?" he asked his daughter. She nodded.

"What is this, a conspiracy?" I asked, only half joking.

"You're not supposed to travel," Ruth said defensively. "I heard Hari say so."

"I'd just as soon you stick around awhile, seeing as you got yourself involved in this thing," Cobbett added.

"Look, I don't mind answering a few questions, but I don't want people thinking I'm part of this. Like, this guy shows up in my room, executive director of some foundation for missing kids."

Cobbett's face clenched like a fist. "McGavin. An interfering, incompetent, media-hungry jerk. Watch out for him. He's trouble." He looked toward the back door, suddenly preoccupied.

"You going to make it home for dinner tonight?" Ruth asked him.

He reached out to squeeze her shoulder gently. "Don't count on it."

"You won't be able to talk to Louise Knox. Her wrists aren't too bad, but they're keeping her sedated."

"Good. She's got enough to deal with." He avoided the question in her eyes, then blurted out, "That pathologist from Augusta's here for the autopsy. Don't wait up. I got a ton of stuff to do at the office." He gave her an empty smile and went inside.

"I'm worried about him," Ruth said softly. The scent of approaching rain was growing stronger on the breeze that stirred around us. "He's working too hard for a man his age. I don't think he's had a good night's rest since this started." We sat together until rain started to freckle the ground at our feet.

CHAPTER 3

Sorry to put you to trouble on your day off," I said to Bobby as we drove away from the hospital in his Jeep. I had a sackful of pills, an appointment card for physical therapy, and a slew of instructions from the doctor.

"'Day off' doesn't mean much these days. You'd do the same for a fellow cop."

On the main drag every third storefront was empty, the dusty windows turned opaque in the autumn sunlight. A derelict mill loomed behind the shops, exposed rafters looking like the ribs of a giant carcass. In the distance I saw an unfinished modern structure, a swoop of poured concrete topped with twisted rebar. "You live here long?" I asked Bobby.

"Born and raised in Brimsport."

"The name of this town's familiar. Is it famous for something?"

"Been in the news a lot lately."

"No. Something else." The memory teased like a fly buzzing around my head, but I couldn't pin it down.

Bobby slowed, watching a woman push a stroller down the sidewalk, plastic grocery sacks hanging from the handles. Four teenaged boys were walking close behind her.

Bobby pulled up to the curb and powered the window down. "Hey, Meg. How's it going?"

The toddler in the stroller, who had curly hair and café-au-lait skin, kicked his feet happily, but she looked tense.

"What do you want, Munro?"

Bobby called out to the four teens, "You fellows need something?"

They shrugged and looked at each other. "Naw," one said. They walked on.

"Give you a hand with those bags?" Bobby asked Meg.

"I don't need any help." We watched her push the stroller up to a dented Nova. Bobby pulled out and cruised slowly past the teens who were elbowing each other and laughing. One flipped us the bird when we were a safe distance away.

"Dumb kids," Bobby mumbled. He turned onto a road that ran along the shore, and added, "Meg was a year behind me in school. Dropped out when she was fifteen, ran away to Boston. Nobody heard from her for ages till she turned up with that baby. She's living out at Northhaven with another lady."

I remembered the men at the search talking about perverts. "These are the women that Neil said were strange?"

"People don't approve of their lifestyle, and that baby being mixed race doesn't help. They don't do any harm, but it's a small town. People have their prejudices."

"These women know anything about Marcy?"

"Nope. Their trailer is way the hell on the other side of the property. Didn't hear or see a thing."

Bobby turned onto a road marked with a No Outlet sign. After driving a mile through thick woods, we turned onto a winding gravel drive. He pulled up next to a green pickup truck. A collie paced in its bed, waving its plume of a tail, barking.

"Not bad!" Bobby said, taking in the huge three-story

house clad in silvery cedar shakes perched over the water. He grabbed my duffel bag and started for the steps. Someone had driven my car from the harbor and parked it beside a three-car garage.

I climbed onto the porch and went through a kitchen, following voices into a vast living room lined with windows. The room was cold and everything had been draped in dust covers. A man wearing a polo shirt and jeans that looked pressed was folding a cloth he'd taken off a couch. "I didn't have time to finish getting the place ready." His hesitant speech was almost a stutter. "I moved a bed into the study for you. You won't have to climb the stairs." He glanced at me and looked away quickly.

"Name's Slovo," I said, sticking a hand out.

"Will Sylvester." He wiped his hand on his pants before taking mine. "Caretaker for this property."

"Is that your collie in the truck?"

 • "Chewbacca, yeah."

"Beautiful animal."

His shy smile flickered like an involuntary muscle twitch.

F og rolled in as night fell. I sat on the porch listening to the waves wash around the rocks. Every now and then I'd hear some small animal patter through leaf litter or tree branches rustling. Bobby left after exploring the place, impressed by the six bedrooms upstairs and the servant's quarters tucked under the eaves. Will Sylvester disappeared soon afterward, his collie hanging out of the side of his truck.

I'd grown up on Chicago's West Side in a cramped third-floor walk-up. My current digs on Kedzie Street were no improvement, a room with a view of a trash-strewn alley. Investigations had taken me into luxurious lakeshore condos,

where the stiffs looked just as surprised at being dead as
some DB on the street. I wasn't intimidated by the huge
house I was renting, just not very comfortable.

And I was trying to figure out why Joe Cobbett wanted
me here.

Three children abducted and murdered. I thought of
Marcy Knox's body, then Cobbett's face, the dark circles
under his eyes, his skin ashy from lack of sleep. I knew how
he felt. Maybe he knew I'd investigated cases like this,
thought I could help.

Maybe he just wanted to keep an eye on me.

The wooden chair I sat in had wide, flat arms perfectly
designed to hold a drink. I'd discovered that someone had
thoughtfully stocked the kitchen with a dozen eggs, a loaf
of bread, cans of soup. Not thoughtful enough to provide
alcohol, though. I rose and limped around the porch, down
the steps, and across the gravel to where my car was
parked. Hari Chakravarty's list of orders included no driving. But there was a medicinal argument to be made for a
short trip to the nearest liquor store.

I climbed in and started the engine. The headlights lit
a patch of woods swirling with mist, giving the impression
of things sliding into the dark just out of view. As I re-
versed, the car thumped and wobbled like a lame thing. I
switched off the engine, killed the lights, and found a flashlight at the back of the glove compartment underneath my
Glock and a pile of road maps. The rear right tire was flat.

"Fuck!" I roared. Something invisible exploded out of a
bush and went winging away into the woods. My heart
hammered in the quiet that followed. Then a light moved
half a mile to my left, blurred by the fog. It moved closer,
disappeared, then bobbed over a rise, becoming twin headlights as it approached. I switched off the flashlight, tossed
it back into the glove compartment, and picked up the
Glock. A Honda drew up and two people got out.

"You looking for something?" I called out.

"Slovo? What are you doing out here?" It was Ruth.

I slid the gun into the back of my waistband and made my way to the steps. "My car has a flat."

"Where were you planning to go?" She pulled two sacks out of the Honda, handed one to her companion.

"Nowhere important. Let's go inside."

"You're not supposed to be driving."

"Does Hari give you a copy of all his medical orders, or just mine?" I led the way up the steps, opened the door to the kitchen, and waved them in.

"Ooh, aren't we in a cranky mood. This is Bryn Greenwood, your neighbor and a good friend of mine."

Greenwood set his sack on the kitchen table next to Ruth's. "I rent the place next door. Want me to change that tire for you?" After some polite back-and-forth I surrendered the keys and told him where he could find the flashlight. He loped out. Ruth started to unpack pretzels, chips and salsa, a can of coffee. From the other sack I pulled a six-pack of Rolling Rock.

"Want one?" I asked her.

"We shouldn't stay. You need your rest. Hari says—"

"It's getting old, hearing you tell me what Hari says." I handed her a can, then popped one for myself. "I could use some company. It's creepy out here. Way too quiet."

"There are all kinds of sounds if you pay attention. The waves, the trees rustling. Sometimes you can hear the bell buoy at the end of the point."

"I'm used to the city. Trains, sirens, screams in the night. I don't know how I'll get to sleep tonight."

She grinned. "When I lived in New York I had an apartment over a subway line. You could feel the building shake whenever there was a train. I missed it when I left."

"What were you doing in New York?"

"Went to NYU. Then worked as a science writer. Did

press releases for a research hospital, some freelance journalism. Got a story in the Science Tuesday section of the *Times* once. I joined the staff of the local paper about a year ago."

"Not the same league as the *Times*."

"Hardly. It's a weekly. And it's dreadful."

"Why did you move back to Brimsport?"

"I thought my dad needed company." There's always something when a person is lying. With her it was the way she tossed her hair back and looked away. "What about you?"

"Been with the Chicago PD for fourteen years."

"I meant, what brought you to Brimsport?"

"A flip of the coin. Turned up heads, so I took I-Ninety eastbound. If it had been tails, I'd be in Seattle."

She was about to ask another question when Greenwood came to the door. "Uh, I didn't change that tire after all."

"Don't worry about it."

"See, you got two flat tires. I think they were slashed."

I put my beer down and went out to look. Three-inch gashes in the rear right and the front left tires. I worked the flashlight beam around the ground but the gravel didn't tell me anything.

"Must have happened since this morning," Greenwood speculated. "One of the cops drove it out here from the harbor. I gave him a ride back to the station. I work there, doing computer support for all the municipal offices."

"You have much vandalism out this way?"

"Never had any problem, but I've only lived here since March. You going to report this to the cops?"

I thought of the long hours they had been putting in lately. "Nah. Not worth the time it would take to fill out the paperwork."

We went back inside. Over beer and chips, Bryn and Ruth told me how they had met in New York three years ago. Bryn had sent her an E-mail correcting a small technical mistake she'd made in an article on search engines. She contacted him when researching another computer-related story and after a few meetings they became good friends. The dot-com he worked for in Silicon Alley folded and Ruth told him the town of Brimsport had an opening for a tech-support specialist.

"I've always lived in the city," he said. "I'd never even been to Maine. It's a big change. But I was paying over a thousand a month for an apartment the size of a closet. For half that rent I can live in a castle up here."

"Is your place as fancy as this one?"

"This is okay, but mine's a castle. Really."

"No moat," Ruth objected. "No drawbridge."

"But it has towers and crenellations. A parapet you could use to pour boiling oil on your enemies. Some eccentric built it a hundred years ago after reading too many romances. The roof leaks and you'll freeze your ass off in the winter. But I'm king of my very own castle."

"Speaking of cold..." Ruth said, eyeing the woodstove. She got up, opened the stove door, took a sheet of newspaper from a stack near the stove, and bunched it up. "Sheesh, weren't you ever in the Boy Scouts?"

"Er, no."

She added kindling and lit the paper under it. "I wasn't in Boy Scouts either," Greenwood confessed. "I have a lot to learn before I'm a real Mainer."

"You'll never be a Mainer, Bryn. You've only been here six months. I've lived here since I was nine and they still consider me an outsider." Ruth brushed her hands off and picked up the bag of pretzels. "I was born in Brooklyn. Dad put in twenty years with the NYPD before we moved here."

I took the bag from her. "That's an adjustment, going from the biggest police force in the country to a place this size."

"And from detective to police chief. The department was a mess when he got here. He doesn't like administration much."

"I hate paperwork," I said. "I hate forms. I hate telling

people what to do almost as much as I hate being told." I was beginning to hate the bag that wouldn't open, too.

"Better not apply for a position as chief of police, then."

"Wouldn't want it. Too much desk time."

"I can't see you behind a desk," Ruth admitted, studying me.

"He doesn't even look like a cop," Bryn added. "His hair's too long, he has that scruffy beard. And he looks kind of stoned."

"Hey. My eyes are made that way. I can't help it."

"Highly inappropriate for a law enforcement professional."

"Inappropriate? What's that word supposed to mean?" The bag still wouldn't give, so I grasped both sides and yanked. "It was all over my performance review last year, said I had a problem with—*fuck*! You mother*fucking* piece of shit!" The bag had split in two, sending pretzels flying all over the room.

"A problem with anger?" Bryn murmured to Ruth.

"A problem with inappropriate language," she suggested.

I ignored them and reached for another beer. A car crunched on the gravel outside. Hari came to the door with a paper sack in one hand. He looked at me, pained. "You really shouldn't be drinking that."

"Fuck you."

Ruth found the broom closet while Hari pulled a bottle out of his paper sack. "I meant, Slovo, you headstrong prat, why waste your time with that piss-awful lager when I brought some excellent whiskey. Hand us a glass, would you? It's been a very long day."

Ruth swept up the pretzels and shook her head when Hari offered her what he called a jar. "I'm driving."

"Don't be silly, darling," Hari said. "You have friends on the force. They'd look the other way."

"Not if I smashed up someone else's car they wouldn't."

"Can you drop me at my place?" Bryn asked, and she nodded.

"Thanks for coming by," I said. "And bringing all the stuff."

"See you, Slovo." She smiled, her cheeks flushed. "And Hari, watch yourself. Seriously."

CHAPTER 4

But Hari was in no mood to be serious about anything. After they left, he poured two generous glasses of single malt scotch and threw more wood into the stove. "Fantastic place, this, innit?"

"Too big."

"Rotten mood you're in, even with visitors to cheer you up. Greenwood's a bit of a weed, but Ruth's a treat. Lovely legs, nice bum." Hari took a contemplative sip of whiskey. "Her tits aren't much good, though. There's a woman at the hospital canteen who has splendid knockers. Now, if I could assemble a woman out of spare parts—"

"You're making me kind of sick, Hari."

He made one of his abrupt shifts in mood, from mellow to malicious. "Don't go all over PC, Slovo. Abstinence makes me spiteful. I suppose you have a woman?"

"You make it sound like property."

"Good God, a feminist pig? All very well for you to talk, I expect you have no trouble getting laid." He swallowed some whiskey, looking increasingly gloomy. "Women here won't put out for me, I'm too short, too dark-skinned, too foreign. I'm forced to practice medicine in this bigoted hellhole and then they treat me as less than human.

Reduced to whores and hand jobs. Christ." He took a gulp, then added, "Who is Robin, by the way?"

"What?"

"Robin. You kept saying that name when you were raving."

"No one. Somebody at work."

The phone rang. I went over to unhook it from the wall, wondering who had this number. "Kostya? God, I've been trying to reach you forever."

"Oh, shit," I said without thinking.

"I've been going crazy here. What's the matter with you?"

"Sorry. Look—"

"You could have a little consideration. You take off with no word to anybody, just a stupid note about flipping a coin. I don't know where you've gone, the police keep asking me where you are, your lawyer wants to know what the hell's going on—"

"You're making way too big a deal out of this."

"—and then I get a call that you're in this hospital in *Maine,* for Christ's sake, and your leg's all infected. God, Kostya, I could kill you sometimes."

"I said I'm sorry, Steve. Jesus."

"I'm doing my best to take care of you after you almost die thanks to that stupid job of yours, but you run off like a lunatic and land in the hospital again. What the hell's wrong with you?"

I took a breath. "I just . . . I had to get away for a while."

"From what? This family of yours? You didn't even have the courtesy to return my calls. I was concerned."

"You worry too much."

"I'm gonna worry about my kid brother, I can't help it." His voice was thick. "Kostya, I wish you'd get some help."

"Don't start that again."

"Okay, okay, forget I said it. At least tell me this: You doing all right?"

"I'm doing fine. I know I should have called you back. I just—Steve, I need some time to figure things out."

"Yeah, okay. But until you do that, do me a favor and keep in touch, willya?"

After we said good-bye, I hung up the phone and waited for Hari to make some smart remark. But when I turned around he wasn't there.

I lit a cigarette and had smoked half of it by the time he strolled back in the room. "Gave myself a tour while you were tied up on the phone." He slumped back into his chair by the stove. "Amazing house."

"It's the fucking Taj Mahal. I don't know what the hell I'm doing here."

"Recovering from a gunshot wound, remember? Which reminds me, mustn't forget your physical therapy appointment tomorrow."

"I don't think I can make it. My car's got problems."

"You're not supposed to be driving, you clot. We'll organize a ride for you. You won't get out of it that easily, sunshine." He reached for the bottle and topped up our glasses. "I understand you've investigated child homicides before."

"Where'd you hear that?"

"I don't know how police who deal with these things routinely avoid going right round the bend. How do you manage?"

"Same way doctors do, I suppose."

"Ah, yes. Maintain that famous professional distance. If you do it right I suppose it's just perishable evidence to bag and tag, not a child at all."

"No. It's never like that."

"Sorry. That was a stupid thing to say." His dark eyes filled with pain and bewilderment. "I gave all three of those girls their immunizations, treated their ear infections and colds, kept charts on their growth to show their mums. And performed their autopsies. I hate this place. There's something wrong with this town."

As if his words had tripped a switch, I heard the man at the search saying *twenty years ago*. And all at once I knew why I'd heard of Brimsport. "There was a big child sex abuse scandal here."

"Almost twenty years ago now. I wasn't here then, but supposedly a large number of children were ritualistically abused in secret. Or not, depending on who you talk to."

"Lot of that going around then. Jordan, Minnesota. The McMartin Preschool thing. There was a day-care case in Chicago. A whole epidemic."

"In Brimsport it began in 1984 with a five-year-old acting out suspiciously. A kindergarten teacher reported it to social services, and they brought in police. With the help of therapists, the details began to emerge: organized groups of adults using children in orgies, child pornography being filmed, satanic cult members using kids in rituals. It could be anyone. The man next door, the priest in the church, the woman who ran the bakery."

"But it was all bullshit, right? I mean, there might have been abuse going on in isolated instances, but the big sex rings, the conspiracies—was anyone convicted here?"

"No one was even brought to trial. Dozens of arrests were made, but the investigation was out of control and the accusations were growing so bizarre that the DA finally dropped all charges. The police chief was dismissed and Cobbett was brought in to pick up the pieces. But a great many people still believe that a conspiracy had existed, that evil went unpunished."

"Hard to understand how so many people bought into stuff like that."

"It was a combination of things. Therapists who coaxed improbable stories out of children and then insisted they must be believed because not believing would be a betrayal.

Police officials who were trying to find some pattern in the violence they saw every day. Prosecutors on a crusade, journalists bent on telling the big one. And, of course, children at the center of it all, some of them genuinely abused and others abused by the process. It must have baffled those kids, the stories they had to tell, all growing out of the sickest fantasies of the adults who were supposedly trying to help them. I suppose you could call it mass hypnosis. Or a mass sexual fantasy."

"I went to an in-service on interviewing child witnesses last year. The instructor used interview transcripts from the day-care case to show what not to do. I remember wondering if it messed the kids up, the leading questions they were asked, the things they were told had happened to them. It was pretty twisted."

"To be fair, Brimsport's chief of police honestly believed he had uncovered a terrible crime. Mike McGavin saw himself at the center of some gigantic struggle between the powers of light and darkness."

"McGavin? That guy visited me in the hospital. He was the police chief?"

"Right, before he started his foundation and dedicated his life to the cause." Hari set his glass down and tented his fingertips. "Interrogation techniques are fascinating. The relationship of the interrogator and the interrogated, it gets quite intense, doesn't it? Kind of like sex, come to think of it. Two people moving toward some climax using a sensual mode of communication, where every gesture, every tone, every glance carries so much meaning, the interrogator using those subtle cues to draw his subject into an emotionally dependent state, to make him say what has to be said."

"You want the truth."

"But you *know* the truth, you just need for the other to speak it. Haven't you ever got a confession from an innocent man?"

"Well, sure. You get these whackos who read the story in the paper and come in to confess and all you do is let them say 'I did it in the library with the candelabra' when it was done in the basement with a chain saw. You know they're for real when they give you some detail that isn't public."

"Set aside the whackos. What about the guy who says *I didn't do it, I wasn't even there.* The two of you are alone in a little room. You scare him, then you turn the tables and get friendly, get his loyalties all mixed up, keep him awake for hours asking the same questions over and over, you make his head spin, you make him crack. But." He held up a finger. "Turns out, he wasn't there. He didn't do it."

I flashed on a suspect in a gang shooting once, cocky at first, then terrified, finally wetting his pants and sobbing, grateful to cop to any unsolved crime I put in front of him.

Hari pounced, gleefully. "You've done it yourself, haven't you?"

"It happens."

"Well it happened here, and on a massive scale. Children were persuaded they had been involved in deviant acts and, led on by the police, they invented even more. Their parents and teachers confessed to things that never happened and implicated their friends and neighbors. Mike McGavin has followers today because people want to believe these three murders fit a pattern of evil he uncovered years ago. You can see the zeal in their eyes, their hunger for more."

"You're making it sound as if they want these murders to happen."

He sat forward excitedly. "When McGavin told them there was a secret, satanic ring operating in their town, abusing innocent children, it provided a moral focus for their pointless, depressingly mundane lives. That sense of importance has come back with these murders. Their little community is once again the site of a cosmic struggle and they can be on the side of the angels."

"Great. Cosmic struggle. Exhibitionist killers love being part of that."

"Is that what he is?"

"Just an impression from the scene. I don't know anything about this case."

"I do. More than I want to. Bethany Lowell was the first." Hari's voice had flattened. "Six years old, snatched from her yard about a week before Christmas. She was playing outdoors within sight of the kitchen. Her mother got tied up in a phone call and when she looked again, Bethany was gone. The police suspected a parental abduction. Her parents were separated, not amicably. The father had a solid alibi, once they located him, but it took time. The real search didn't start until the next day. She was found two weeks later under the floor of an abandoned farmhouse twelve miles from here. Suffocated. She was naked, wrapped in a couple of garbage bags."

He pressed a finger and thumb against his eyes, then reached for the bottle again. I noticed when he set it down it was already two-thirds gone. "Second victim was Ashley Underhill. Why are children given such peculiar names in this country?"

"We don't need to talk about this, Hari."

"'S'all right. There aren't many people I can talk to in this town. Ashley was nine years old. Last June she went out to play after supper and never came home. She was found the next day in a shallow grave, about three miles away from her house." He gulped whiskey and went on, "She had been sexually assaulted. She had also, ah, sorry. She'd been cut. Mutilated. Cause of death was exsanguination. Bled to death." He stood up abruptly. "Just a . . . I have to get some air," he muttered, and banged out. I saw his shape through the windows, pacing along the porch, stopping to lean on the railing, hunched into the wind.

Hari returned, windblown and embarrassed. "Dunno why it's getting to me. Haven't been sleeping too well since..." He threw himself back in his chair. "Right, then. The one you found, Marcy Knox."

"It's getting late. Maybe we should call it a night."

"You want to stop now? Let this stew and fester until we get drunk again?" His tone was teetering between dark irony and fury as he sloshed whiskey into his glass and did the honors for me. "No, we'll get right through the entire museum of horrors." He gave a weird hiccup of a giggle. "It's quite a tour. Each time, it's worse, see."

"Take it easy, Hari."

He shot me a burning look. "I *knew* these kids. I delivered Marcy, as a matter of fact. It wasn't easy, the stupid woman had decided on a home birth and things got complicated. She came in hemorrhaging badly, the baby obviously in fetal distress. Never delivered a baby on my own before, and this was a regular case study in OB disaster."

He put his glass down and leaned forward, gripping his temples between his palms. "Her mother wasn't clever and didn't have a job other than motherhood, which she did badly enough. She hadn't been brought up very well herself, and was only seventeen when she got knocked up. Louise wanted to be a good mother, though. She even read books about parenting, probably the only books she ever read in her life. I don't know why she bothered. Marcy was destined to be a fat, stupid girl who'd end up just like her mum, miserable and poor and kind to children but not able to take care of them sensibly." He reached for his glass. "Louise had been trying to get Marcy to stay in bed through the night. The kid had grown used to climbing in with her mum if she woke up scared, in the dark. Louise asked me about it and I said she should be firm, don't let Marcy keep setting the rules, make her go right back to her own room and Louise did what I said, that night, she sent her away...."

He emptied his glass in a shuddering gulp. "So little Marcy went back to her bed, all alone, and he came hunting to the back of the house and forced the window and took her into the night and raped her, raped her every way he could." He took a gasping breath, his eyes wide and glassy. "And when he was finished he must have looked down and seen an animal so he did what you do . . . Dressed her out like an animal. Skinned and all."

CHAPTER 5

I didn't get much rest that night. A little after 3:00 A.M. I heard a noise outside so I took the Glock and went to check. A stiff breeze was blowing and a buoy clanged monotonously, but no one was there. I went back to bed and finally slept. It seemed only minutes later when someone started banging on the door.

Cobbett looked me over critically when I let him in. "You get any sleep?"

"Not enough. Some idiot kept ringing a bell out there all night."

"No, see, there's a bell buoy..." He realized I was pulling his chain. "Hear you had some vandalism out here yesterday."

"Couple of tires slashed, is all."

"Numbskull kids. Nothing much for them to do around here beyond sniffing glue and getting drunk." He headed for the coffeemaker on the counter. "Ruth said you and Hari were starting a binge when she left." He filled the carafe with water and poured it in.

"Hari. Shit. What time is it?" Before passing out cold, he had complained about having to make early rounds.

"I saw his car parked by the hospital, don't worry." He opened the coffee, scooped some into a filter, and punched the button on. "Gonna lose his job if he keeps drinking like this."

"He told me about the murders. The three little girls."

"Dammit, if he's going to spout off every time he gets hammered—"

"It wasn't like that. He was pretty distraught. He said Marcy... there was sexual assault?"

"Vaginal, anal, and oral. No fluids recovered, but they found a couple of pubic hairs in her mouth. Cause of death was asphyxia by manual strangulation. Hyoid bone was crushed."

"The way the body was, the condition—"

"Done with a small, sharp knife or scalpel, post-mortem. Some hesitation marks. Doesn't look like an experienced hunter's work, for what it's worth."

"Did you find... the rest of the remains?"

"No. Not even blood. He did all that somewhere else. Look, it's important you don't tell anyone about what you saw in the woods. Only a handful of people were allowed on the scene: Bobby Munro, Neil Forester, the forensic techs from the state Criminal Investigation Division that processed it. Sabine Forché from the CID; she's assigned to this full-time. And Tom Flaherty, the FBI agent you met. I've kept it back from most of my own officers. A town this size, word can get out. And people here would go berserk if they knew how it was."

Cobbett filled two mugs and sat down heavily, making a face when I reached for my cigarettes. "Going to kill yourself with those things."

"It's on my list for Lent this year. This isn't your typical serial. The three MOs are different—the abduction, the cause of death, the places they're found."

"There is some evidence that ties them together. All three victims had traces of an opiate in their blood. And with the first two, there's another link. Forty-eight hours before Bethany and Ashley were kidnapped, the perp stole something of religious significance from a church. Forty-eight hours after the kidnapping, it was returned with something extra, something belonging to the child. Like it's all just a practical joke."

"What were the things he stole?"

"Bethany Lowell was abducted three days before Christmas. Two days before it happened, the Baby Jesus was taken from the nativity scene in front of the Episcopal church. The paper ran an editorial about the Christmas spirit and everyone hoped the kid that had done it on a dare would put it back. On Christmas Eve, Bethany's doll was found in the manger. The doll's clothes were gone. Instead it had, what do they call 'em? Swaddling clothes. Made from the victim's torn-up underwear. You can imagine; we hadn't found Bethany yet and this..." He sighed angrily. "June, we get a complaint from the Catholic church. They're missing a little plaster Christ Child, located in an alcove with a rack of those candles in front of it like they do. A statue wearing a fancy cloth dress."

"The Infant of Prague." He looked at me. "Where I went to school the nuns had one. Dressed it in different robes depending on the liturgical season."

"Same deal here. And I'm thinking, another Baby Jesus? What the fuck's going on here? Two days later we get the call: Another little girl is missing."

"Did the public put it together?"

"Not until McGavin told a reporter about it."

"Just what the killer wanted. Publicity."

"Him and McGavin both. Press made a big thing out of it, got some ugly feelings stirred up. People in this town, they're scared, they want this solved. And it's not the first time. See, back in 1984—"

"McGavin's big child abuse investigation."

"People didn't know what to think when the investigation ended without trials or convictions, and now...they don't have much faith in the system. They're angry, looking for someone to blame, anyone. Ashley's folks hadn't called it in right away. They're not the greatest parents in the world, didn't pay much attention until it was too late. There was a scene at their house the next day, people yelling, a scuffle. Their front window got smashed. We staked out the church, thinking he'd return the Infant of Whatsit, only he's shrewd, sets up a pattern to get us going and then works a variation. Two days after Ashley's taken, the statue turns up in the cemetery, dressed in the victim's T-shirt, wearing her underpants around its neck."

"This only happened with the first two? There wasn't a missing Baby Jesus this time out? With Marcy?"

"No. Everyone's on guard, volunteers keeping watch at the churches and the cemetery. Maybe he couldn't find a Baby Jesus to joke around with. Didn't matter a damn, we had another abduction anyway."

"Got any solid suspects?"

"A car was sighted near Marcy's house the night of the abduction. Black Ford pickup with a topper, left headlight out, rear bumper hanging loose. We've been talking to a couple that own a vehicle of that description. Social Services removed Ardis Burke's children in 1984, during the big scandal. They were sexually abused by her boyfriend, but she was complicit. This was apparently one situation McGavin got right in spite of himself, but his investigation was shoddy and when the prosecutor finally put an end to it, she got off, along with a lot of people who were being falsely accused. Kids weren't returned, though. She's had several boyfriends since, all bottom feeders. Guy she's with now is a drifter who showed up a couple of years ago."

"They look good."

"They're morons. We have to follow up, but it's a waste of time. Whoever's doing this is smart. He plans carefully and doesn't make mistakes. This is the most frustrating case of my career. And I've never had one that mattered so much."

A sleepy fly bumped up against a window. "There's someone else we're looking at," Cobbett added. "Got an anonymous tip two days ago. Will Sylvester, the caretaker for this property, was investigated for molesting his daughter six years ago. She was in first grade at the time."

I pictured the man in the polo shirt and pressed jeans, his voice stuttering with shyness. "Talk to him yet?"

"He denies the whole thing. Comes across as a guy who got caught in a pissing match with an estranged spouse. Only I spoke with the lead investigator in Auburn, where this happened. She thinks there was something in it. Sylvester moved here late last fall, a few weeks before the first abduction. Lives alone, takes care of vacant properties, doesn't seem to have any friends. If you happen to notice anything—"

"I'll keep an eye out."

He bristled. "Don't get ideas. You're a cop; you might pick up on something other people would miss. But I don't need someone from Chicago—"

I felt tired. "It's your case, Cobbett, and I'm on leave. I'm not looking to get involved in a murder investigation. Believe me, I would rather someone else had found that child's body. I'd sleep better at night."

In the silence that followed, the fly buzzed and thumped against the glass. Cobbett swatted at it ineffectually. It bumbled into a corner of the window and subsided.

"I have to get back to the station." He sounded old and tired. When he pulled the door open to leave the bluebottle launched itself into a drunken flight, zigzagged past him, and disappeared outside.

CHAPTER 6

I poured another cup of coffee and started calling garages. The first one I reached said they couldn't get to my car until next week. The second one said he'd send out a truck, but then called back and canceled without explanation. Before I could try a third, the phone rang: Bryn Greenwood, offering to take me to my physical therapy appointment on his way in to work.

He dropped me at the front of the medical center and told me to call the cop shop for a ride home when I was finished. Inside, a receptionist pointed me down the hall where a man gave me a standard pep talk, went over my records from the PT clinic in Chicago, then turned me over to a therapist who looked sixteen. She put me through the routine, her voice brimming with giggly cheerfulness even when I was gasping and almost in tears. "Come on, let's try it again."

"Are you sure this is wise? It doesn't feel right."

She gave me one of those "you big baby" pouts. When it was finally over I rested with ice packs around my hip. As my aching muscles went numb, I listened to the radio nattering away, some local call-in show discussing whether or not the authorities were doing enough to protect Brimsport's children. The popular answer seemed to be no.

The therapist came in to remove the ice packs and told me I was done till next time. Without saying it, she implied that I was a wimp and a spineless slacker, but she would whip me into shape. Next time.

I decided to prove my manhood by walking the few blocks to the station. As I reached the front steps someone came up from behind me and gave my arm a friendly squeeze as he passed. Mike McGavin. "Good to see you up and around. Let's have coffee sometime." He trotted up the steps.

Inside, the dispatcher looked up. "Can I help you, Detective Slovo?"

"Bryn Greenwood around?"

"I'll let him know you're here. If you want to have a seat—" She pointed to a waiting room to the right. Someone distracted her with a question and I went down the hall to the left.

McGavin perched on the edge of the table in the staff room, talking with a uniform—Neil Forester, the hothead who'd pointed his gun at me that first day. Forester frowned and came out into the hall, radiating that barely suppressed potential for violence that some cops mistake for authority. "What are you doing here?"

"Waiting for a ride from Greenwood. Any coffee in the machine?"

"The waiting room's down this way." He took my elbow with a bruising grip and marched me past the dispatcher's counter into an alcove lined with plastic chairs. Two small, dirty children were burrowing through a tote bag, throwing toys out on the floor at the feet of a woman who was reading a magazine. A ferret-faced man was working at a lighter, trying to put a flame to the cigarette drooping from his lips.

Forester shoved me into a chair. "Wait till you're called."

"Where's all this hostility coming from? Jesus."

His face grew red. "I find you sneaking around like that again, I'll throw your ass right out the door. And you. Lyle." The ferret-faced man raised his eyebrows, the picture of innocent bewilderment. "You know damn well you can't smoke in here."

"Aw, jeez. I'm supposed to sit here for hours while you grill Ardis and I can't even have a cigarette?"

"You want to smoke, do it outside." Forester stalked off.

"Neil's gonna give himself a stroke one of these days," the woman muttered, nudging a wailing child with her foot. "Hush, Tyler."

"What'd you do to piss him off?" The man clicked ineffectually at the lighter. He was in his thirties, his skin pale and pockmarked with acne scars. He had nervous fingers and his eyes were bright and spacey. Crank, I guessed. Or maybe coke.

"Beats me." I found some matches for him in my pocket, then lit up to keep him company.

"Fucking police state around here. They got my girlfriend in there right now, been grilling the both of us, making threats. Asking if they can search our house. I says to them, sure, you show me a warrant."

"Gotta stand up for your rights."

The woman rose and carried the sobbing Tyler down the hall to buy a candy bar from a vending machine, the other child scrambling after. "Damn straight. My lady friend, they took her three kids away from her, gave 'em away to total strangers. All over some bullshit they couldn't even prove in court. This was years ago, and they still come around bugging her about it. Don't believe I seen you here before."

"I was passing through town when I got sick. Leg got infected."

"What brings you to the station?"

"They, uh . . . they found a bunch of pills in my car. It's kind of complicated."

"Oh, yeah?" A knowing grin broke out on his face.

"I just needed something to help with the pain, you know?" I dropped my voice. "If I could only score some percs . . ."

"That's what you like, percs?"

"The doc here, he says I got a problem. Stuff he gives me is fucking useless."

"Doctors." He shook his head disgustedly.

"Look, you don't . . . No, never mind."

"What?"

I closed my eyes. "I can't think straight anymore. Stupid, talking in here. Cops everywhere."

"Getting to you, huh?"

"Shit, I don't have friends here. Don't know my way around."

He looked down at the linoleum, prodded a grubby spot with his boot. "I got friends. There's a place down by the waterfront. Clyde's. Drop by tonight, around ten. Maybe we can do a little business. Hey, baby!"

A gaunt woman with sharp planes in her face slumped against the corner of the alcove, rubbing a thin arm. She was at least ten years older than Lyle and chemical treatments over the years had turned her hair into something synthetic. "C'mere, sugar." Lyle stood and scooped her to him for a kiss.

Cobbett stood behind them, making an involuntary grimace of disgust. "I can explain about them pills," I said before he could speak. "I had a prescription. Okay, I changed the numbers on it, but it's not like I was going to distribute."

"Don't be such a hard-ass, Chief," Lyle leered.

"Let's go," Cobbett said to me, jerking a finger to show the way. We could hear them laughing as he followed me into his office. "What the hell are you up to?"

•

"That's the couple whose pickup truck was spotted the night Marcy was abducted, right? Lyle thinks I'm in the market for drugs. He wants to do business tonight at Clyde's. We set up a bust, you could nail him for intent and have probable cause for a search. Who knows what you might turn up while you're tossing his place?"

He stared at me. "How'd you get Lyle to trust you?"

"Just a matter of empathy, getting on the same wavelength. And inventing a few details to move things along. It's worked for me before."

"Is that how you got the best clear rate in Chicago?"

"Where'd you hear that?"

Ignoring my question, he hunted through the mess on his desk and pulled out a manila envelope. "That cop in Auburn, the one that investigated Will Sylvester for molesting his daughter? She sent copies of her case notes. Sylvester looks good for these murders. Only he was real careful when I had him in the box, wouldn't give me anything I could use. I've been wondering how to approach him. Any chance you could—what did you call it? Get on his wavelength, get him to open up?"

"I could try. But what about Lyle?"

"Don't worry about that. The state narcotics squad can handle it."

"But—"

The phone rang. He set the envelope aside and reached for it. "Cobbett. Oh, right. Be there in a minute." He put the phone down. "Look, Slovo. You have a hell of a record. Great clear rate, all that experience investigating child homicides. Maybe you'll be able to get inside Sylvester's head and tell me what's going on in there. Being in on a drug bust—I'm not so comfortable with that. Given your situation in Chicago."

His words hit me like a sucker punch. "You think I—?"

"Until your Internal Affairs people finish their investigation, I don't think anything. I'm late for a meeting. I'll let Greenwood know you're here." He rose and left.

For a moment there, I'd forgotten about the shooting. Forgot my career was going all to hell and the only thing I wanted to do with my life might be over forever. For a while, I'd been back on the job.

I forced myself to breathe slowly and evenly until my heart stopped slamming inside my chest. I scanned the jumble of papers on Cobbett's desk. Ardis Burke's file from the 1984 investigation lay open on top. Underneath it, a familiar star-shaped logo caught my eye. I pulled the clipped-together fax out from the stack of papers and flipped through it. My CPD jacket, with a confidential memo from my lieutenant. "Concerning Det. Konstantin Slovo . . ."

I tossed it back on the desk, dislodging a piece of paper. An incident report on a lawn ornament boosted from the grounds of the Brimsport Historical Museum. A sticky note was attached: "Complainant wants to know if progress." I read through it, then looked at the date. The report was taken on Thursday. Marcy Knox had been abducted early Wednesday morning. I thought for a moment, and then reached for the phone.

"Yes?" The voice was loud and querulous. Elderly and hard of hearing.

"Mr. Pensely?" I read the name off the badly typed report. "I'm calling from the police department."

"It's about time! Have you found her?"

"Found her?"

"Our Diana."

"Uh . . . Diana?"

"The statue. Isn't that what you're calling about?"

"The lawn ornament that was stolen."

"Lawn ornament." He snorted. "Makes it sound like a vulgar garden gnome. Have you found her?"

Bryn Greenwood came in. I held up a hand for him to wait. "I take it the statue's still missing?"

"Of course. Well, I assume so. I visit the museum almost every day, but with my arthritis I can't always go into the garden."

"That's fine, Mr. Pensely. I'm wondering if the statue might have been stolen before Thursday, say as early as Monday morning."

"That's possible." He said it grudgingly. "I gave a tour of the grounds on Sunday afternoon—the Brimsport Women's Club—and the statue was in its place then, but no tours have been scheduled since."

"So as far as anyone knows, the theft could have occurred anytime after the Women's Club went through? I'd like to take another look. Could you meet me at the museum in, say, fifteen minutes?"

"I suppose I could."

"Mr. Pensely, one other thing. Don't go into the garden until we arrive."

Bryn was grinning as I hung up. "What was that about?"

"Can you spare some time? I need to run by this museum."

"All right, but what for?"

"I'll tell you in the car." I folded the incident report into my pocket.

Heading across town I explained.

"So it might be another prank," Bryn summed up. "What's it a statue of?"

"Some lady." I unfolded the report and read from it. "'Marble figurine of a woman, classical in style.' What did he call it? Oh, yeah, Diana."

"Huh." He shot me a glance. "I guess you could call that a religious figure—if you count Roman goddesses."

"Is that what it is?"

"Goddess of the hunt."

I looked out the window at the pleasant houses and tree-lined streets, feeling suddenly cold.

Pensely squinted at us. "Can I help you?" His tone strongly suggested that was unlikely.

"Detective Slovo." I flashed my CPD shield. Pensely peered at it through bottle-thick glasses and I quickly stowed it in my pocket. "My associate, Mr. Greenwood. Can you show us where the statue was?"

"Is that what police use for plainclothes these days?"

He was looking down at my Converse high-tops with their duct-tape repairs. "We just came off a narcotics assignment, didn't have time to change."

Bryn had a coughing fit while the old man processed that. Then he led us on a walkway that circled around the Victorian house into an overgrown garden. We made our way across a shaggy lawn past flowerbeds full of dead stalks toward an odd structure at the bottom of the slope. "How well-known is this statue?" I asked him.

"We show it on tours. And an art historian came to study it once."

"What does it look like? The theft report wasn't that descriptive."

"It's not much over two feet in height, pre-Raphaelite in style. She has long tresses, quite beautifully carved, and is carrying a bow and a rabbit to signify the hunt." He gestured toward the rock structure. "The grotto was built at the turn of the century as an English-style folly. The statue is meant to stand on a ledge there." We were approaching a pile of mossy stones ringed by five Greek columns.

"The place doesn't seem very secure. Is the statue valuable?"

"Tastes change and what is valuable in one era—" His

next words were shrill with surprise. "Good Lord, it's back."

I heard Greenwood grunt behind me as if he'd been punched. I limped closer to the little figure perched on a plinth of rock. I took a breath. "We need to call it in."

"Yes, but—I don't understand." Pensely peered up at it through his thick glasses. He reached out a hand and I grabbed it.

"Don't touch anything. We need to call it in."

A cascade of black, tangled curls spilled over the carved marble tresses. Over the head of the statue a scalp had been secured with a floppy white bow. At her feet, near the marble rabbit dangling from her marble hand, was a large jar. Pink and gray shapes pressed up against the glass, floating in a cloudy liquid.

I heard a gulping sound behind me and turned to see Greenwood staggering away. He tripped and fell to his knees. "Jesus," I heard him gasp. "Oh, Jesus."

CHAPTER 7

The museum grounds were cordoned off and uniforms were stationed in front to fend off the curious. Cobbett sent officers out to canvass the neighbors to see if they had noticed anything suspicious in the past week. Flaherty, the FBI agent from Bangor, showed up with a stocky woman wearing a Maine State CID windbreaker. She beckoned Cobbett to join a huddle by the grotto as white-suited technicians arrived to process the scene. Only a few techs and detectives were allowed near the grotto, but there were whispers and heads being shaken and I had the impression the details were working their way loose among the police.

Cobbett questioned us once the scene was secured; then Tom Flaherty took a turn. It was late afternoon when Bryn and I left. The police had made few discoveries. They surmised the killer had parked in an alley that ran behind the museum and cut his way through a wire fence to gain access. Photos of Marcy Knox were compared to the scalp found on the statue, but the state lab would have to use a sample of Marcy's hair taken from a hairbrush at her house to be certain it was a match. The floppy white bow was made of a cut-up pair of girl's underwear, the size and brand that Marcy had been wearing. No one could say for sure what was in the jar, but it appeared to be viscera.

A crowd had gathered on the other side of the yellow tape, townsfolk watching the police work with that weird intensity you see at bad accidents, a combination of horror and ravenous excitement. The ones in front parted reluctantly to let us through to Bryn's pickup. Reporters came hurrying up as we climbed in. Bryn flinched as they rapped on the windows and yelled out questions. He pushed Built to Spill into his deck and filled the Ranger's cab with pounding music as we pulled away.

"Want to come in for a minute?" I asked Bryn when we reached my place. He followed me inside and tried to start a fire while I found Hari's whiskey and poured us each a drink. He finally got a blaze going and sat hunched toward the warmth, holding his whiskey in both hands. The amber liquid in the glass trembled. "Kind of fell apart out there today. Finding the statue with that hair and all the . . . I guess you've seen worse. Probably used to it."

"You don't get used to it."

"I have a sister. She had black hair, curly, like that. She ran away when she was fourteen. Don't know what happened to her."

"Ah, jeez. I'm sorry."

He took a sip of whiskey and grimaced. "Know why I applied for this job? I heard what happened to Bethany Lowell and it kind of haunted me. Six years old, how could somebody . . . Anyway, when Ruth called and told me this position was open I thought maybe I could help. Not that I'd solve the crime or anything, but I know computers, I know networks. God, this sounds really dumb."

I didn't say anything.

"I mean, the jobs I had before? I'd put in twelve- or

fourteen-hour days, but none of it mattered. This *matters*. If they find the killer it won't be anything I did, but at least I've contributed something. Not much, but something." He swirled the liquor around in his glass, then took a gulp and choked. When he finished coughing he said, "I'm not used to this stuff. Too strong for me."

"There's beer in the fridge."

He set the glass down. "Nah. I made a change in the network configuration today. Think I'll drive over to the cop shop and make sure things are working."

I was scrambling some eggs for supper when Joe Cobbett drove up. He came to the door holding a manila envelope. "Want something to eat?" I asked.

"No, thanks. Just dropping off those case notes from Auburn." He set the envelope on the table.

"I'll look them over tonight. Help yourself to coffee."

"No, I have to get going." But he stood there, rubbing his palm across the back of a chair.

"What's on your mind, Cobbett?"

"Look, I didn't have a chance to say this earlier today. What happened in Chicago was the kind of mistake we all have nightmares about."

I put the eggs on a plate and spooned salsa over them.

"'Mistake' is the wrong word," he said after the pause I was supposed to fill. "It was a tragedy. Hell, I'm just saying anybody who wears a gun to work knows there may come a time they'll have to make a split-second decision—"

"You notice, when a cop plugs someone who's holding a cell phone or a wallet, everyone says he was making a split-second decision? I didn't decide anything that night. Whoever opened fire on us made the decisions, not me."

"I don't know all the details—"

"You don't know shit. My supper's getting cold."
He left.

After I ate, I read through the case notes. When I finished, I went out onto the porch to smoke a couple of cigarettes and listen to the night noises, letting my mind empty of everything. I went back inside, took a legal pad from the study, and outlined what I knew about the three murders in three columns. I reread the notes from the Auburn investigation, then slipped them back in their envelope and sat, thinking.

When I switched off the kitchen light it was near midnight. I took the last of the whiskey with me into the bathroom. I stripped and sat on the edge of the tub, soaked a towel under the hot tap, and wrapped it around my hip. Between the morning's PT session and the hours sitting over papers, the joint had grown stiff and sore. After a half hour of hot compresses, I pulled on my shorts and limped out to the refrigerator. I popped a Rolling Rock and took a long drink. When I shut the door the refrigerator light was extinguished, but there was still faint yellow light playing against the far wall. I checked the woodstove, but it was cold to the touch. The flickering light came from outside. I opened the door to the porch.

My car looked as if someone with Martha Stewart tendencies had decided to convert an unsightly old Mustang into a lantern. Cheerful yellow flames played on the front seats, lighting up the windows. "Use the rest," I heard a male voice call out. The flames died down, then bloomed with a whoosh.

"Hey!" A face illuminated by the flare-up ducked out of sight. I started forward, but a spidery silhouette raced in front of the car to hurl a jerry can in my direction. It hit the porch and clanged down the steps as two figures scampered down the driveway. Car doors slammed and tires shrieked against the gravel.

I called 911. By the time a fire truck arrived, the heat had blown the gas tank and there wasn't much left but thick, stinking smoke and a few flames flickering inside the burnt-out shell.

Bobby Munro pulled up in his cruiser as firemen played water onto the roof of the nearby garage in case any sparks had landed there. "There were two of them," I said as he walked over to the car for a look. "They poured gasoline on the seats. Didn't see them clear enough to make an ID."

"Don't suppose you'll collect any insurance. Book value must have been near zero."

I felt a pang of nostalgia. "It may not have had much monetary worth, but it was a great car." Once the firemen were satisfied the garage was in no immediate danger, they started soaking the smoking wreck with their hose. I realized I was barefoot, still in my boxers. "Shit, it's freezing out here. Let's go inside."

I went to pull some clothes on. When I got back into the kitchen, kindling was beginning to crackle in the woodstove. "I started some coffee for Brimsport's Bravest," Bobby said. "Hope you don't mind." When it finished dripping, he filled four mugs and took them outside.

"Looks like you could use some caffeine, too," I told him when he returned.

"Been on duty since eight this morning." He sat at the kitchen table and idly picked up my legal pad. "These your notes? You can't spell for shit, Slovo." I took the pad away from him. "Interesting ideas, though. You figure it's the public response that motivates him?"

"It could be a factor."

"If that's what turns his crank, he's probably having multiple orgasms as we speak. The press got hold of it that there were human remains with the statue. Reporters are swarming all over the place. Mike McGavin's on his soapbox, saying this is connected to those sex rings he went after years ago. His only problem is he can't seem to decide whether the authorities are part of the conspiracy or just fuck ups. Either way, it riles everyone up."

"That's why my car got torched?"

He shrugged. "Probably just kids acting up. But the mood out there is ugly. People want an arrest and McGavin's grandstanding just makes it worse."

"You grew up here. Do you remember McGavin's big investigation?"

"Not real well. Some officers came to our house once, asked questions. I wasn't interested in much except fishing back then. Spent all my time outdoors. Should have been a game warden instead of a cop."

"A place like this must be great for hunting and fishing."

"I was never much for hunting, but there's some incredible trout streams."

One of the firemen came to the door, bringing a whiff of burnt rubber and electrical wiring with him. "Fire's out." He set their empty mugs on the table, nodding his thanks to Bobby. "Shame about your car." He shot me a sideways look and ducked out the door.

Bobby yawned prodigiously. "Too dark to see anything out there now. Somebody will come out to take a look tomorrow morning, after the briefing. Tom Flaherty gets us all together every morning to share information on the case."

"What's he like to work with?"

"He's all right for a feeb. Worked for the Boston PD for years before he joined the feds. I'm not sure how he ended up in Bangor, but he knows what he's doing. We also got a woman from the state Criminal Investigation Division working with us."

"I think I saw her with Flaherty out at the historical museum."

"She's smart and tough as nails. Few years back she nailed a carjacker on I-Ninety-five. They say she took his head clean off with a shotgun. Not a lady you want to mess with." He yawned again. "God, I'm tired. Not sleeping too good lately. Don't guess I will until we catch this guy."

I lay in the dark, listening to the old house creak. Before dawn leaked into the sky I gave up and went out on the porch to smoke the last of my cigarettes. When it was light I walked around the charred remains of my car.

Neil Forester drove up at around nine followed by a man who introduced himself as the municipal fire inspector. "Ehyup, arson," he said, peering into the wreck. "I'll report it to the state fire marshal."

"The vehicle wasn't worth more than two thousand, was it?" Forester asked, looking at a form on a clipboard. I shook my head. "Class D offense, then. Criminal mischief." He nodded vaguely to the fire inspector, who was taking his leave. The cop filled in more blanks, then took a few steps away from me, scanning the gravel.

"You might lift something from the jerry can," I said, "but there's nothing to see out here. I already checked."

"You're the expert."

"I'm just saying don't waste your time. You got more important things to do."

"Great. You're giving out assignments now?"

"What's your problem, Forester?"

"You won't have that bloodstain to remind you anymore." He jerked his chin at the blackened springs in the back of the car. "Remind you of the night you shot your own partner in the back."

"Cobbett tell you that?"

"Three bullets, wasn't it? And then you ran out on the investigation. Were they asking too many questions? Wondering about a guy with a record like yours? How old were you when they picked you up for muling drugs? Twelve?"

"How'd . . . how'd you hear about that?"

He bared his teeth in a smile. "The dealer you worked for was tied to a chair with his head battered in. Blood all over the place and you were just sitting there, cool as could be."

"How'd you hear this shit?"

"You're such a piece of work, Slovo. Hanging out with scum since you were a little kid."

"You sanctimonious son of a bitch. He was a good man."

"He was a lowlife criminal. You made deliveries for him."

"He took care of me, of course I helped him out. They cut off his ears and broke all his fingers. His face, I couldn't even recognize him. Rainy was good to me. You can go fuck yourself, Forester."

"We're keeping your IAD informed. You won't be able to run away from it this time. They're closing in on you." He had moved in close, but something in my eyes made him take a step back. He held my gaze for a moment, then looked away, sauntered to his cruiser and left.

I only told funny stories about my childhood. My partner got a kick out of it when I showed her the places I'd hung out when I ran the streets, introduced her to the oddballs I knew back then, once flashy dressers with big rings and gold chains, now skaggy addicts and drunks wearing three layers of moth-eaten sweaters, full of nostalgic tales of the good old days. I made people laugh, telling them about the scrapes I got into, the lies I told to get out of them. They were pretty hilarious, my stories.

But some of them, the ones I couldn't make funny, I pushed them back, way deep into the dark, and didn't think about them at all. Not ever. When I thought about Rainy he was just a small-time operator with a graying ponytail and bum legs, a colorful character I once knew, not the bloody wreck in the chair, not the guy who helped me out when no one else was in my corner.

Only now something inside had cracked wide open and those stories came swarming out of the dark. They were all around me now, inescapable. Closing in.

CHAPTER 8

I heard the phone ringing inside the house. It rang a dozen times, then stopped.

I couldn't make my mind up to move. While I stood there, a pickup pulled up. Will Sylvester's collie lolloped over to me to sniff the perimeter of the wreck with great interest. "Too bad about your car," Sylvester said.

"It wasn't worth anything." A breeze moved through the broken windows and flecks of ash rose inside the car like a swarm of small gray moths. "My tires got slashed too. I don't know why they're doing this."

"Well, people . . . there's no telling." He hesitated. "You want me to call a scrap yard to get it towed out of here?"

"I'll take care of it."

"I'll be going, then. You need anything, my phone number's on the fridge." His dog, busily snuffling at the ashes, tore itself away reluctantly when Sylvester whistled for him.

I went inside and lay on the couch in the living room, memorizing the cracks in the plaster ceiling until the light started to fade and I couldn't see them anymore. At around six, Hari called. "Fancy some company, sunshine? My neighbor's been having a bonkathon with his new girlfriend. Another evening of that and I'll go barking mad. Thought I'd pick up a pizza and something to drink—"

"Not tonight, Hari."

"You sound a bit down. What's the trouble?"

"Nothing." Thunder growled in the dark sky outside.

His cheer was relentless. "Tell Uncle Nosy."

"I'm just tired."

"Having trouble sleeping, eh? Not surprising, after a trauma. I'll bring something to help. Anything else I can get you while I'm at it?"

"Cigarettes."

"All right. Shan't be long." He must have been feeling sorry for me. Normally he'd go off on a rant about my smoking.

But when I opened the door forty-five minutes later it was Ruth who held the pizza box, raindrops caught in her hair like tiny jewels. She came in, bringing a perfume of moss and damp earth in her wake. "Hari got tied up with some emergency, so he asked me to bring this out. There's a gorgeous storm brewing up. Can we eat in the living room? I want to watch the lightning over the water."

She switched on lamps, laid a fire, went into the kitchen to find a corkscrew and some glasses for the wine she had pulled out of her shoulder bag. She poured two glasses and sank onto the couch beside me. "I'm sorry about your car. Not very hospitable of us locals, setting fire to it like that." She slipped her feet out of her shoes and tucked them up under her. "At least you can't take a notion to flip a coin again and take off for, say, Newfoundland."

"If your father's wondering, I wasn't planning to run off." Lightning bathed the room in cold light, followed three seconds later by the rumble of thunder rolling across the water like the report of distant cannons. "You should go before this storm breaks," I added.

"I'd rather watch it from here with you. Hey. What is it?"

I heard her glass clink down, felt her hand on my arm. "I'm in a lot of trouble at home. The CPD's getting ready to can me."

"Says who?"

"Says Forester, for one."

She stared at me. "Neil? What's he got to do with it?"

"He was out here this morning. Chicago faxed all my records here and in return the Brimsport PD keeps them informed so the IAD will have a current address when it's time to issue an extradition order or whatever. I'm sure your father told you all about how I killed my partner."

"Dad said he died in the shooting, that's all."

"She. Robin Freeling. One of my snitches had something for us, so I set up a meet. When we got there someone opened fire on us. I took a .357 slug in my hip. The snitch took one in the head. Robin was hit with three bullets from a Beretta. Same make as my service pistol. The IAD says it was crossfire."

"Oh, no."

"But they're wrong. I returned fire, sure, but I had standard-issue ammunition in my gun. Hollowpoints. The bullets that killed her were full metal jackets. I saw the exit wounds. You could tell—"

"Were the bullets recovered?"

"Yeah. FMJs, but there's nothing to match them to. I dropped my gun when I fell. It was gone before the cops got to the scene. Unless it turns up, it's my word against theirs."

"But if you didn't do it—"

"They lost a cop. Someone needs to pay for it and I've made enemies over the years. They'll find a way to make this shit stick."

"Whatever happened to innocent until proven guilty?" She was nettled when I laughed. "What's funny?"

"Nothing. Sorry. Been feeling kind of strange today.

Forester knew things about me. Stuff I hadn't thought about in a long time."

"Neil? He's an idiot. What does he know about anything?"

"He knows I have a juvie record." Another wash of blue light flooded the room, followed by a sharp crack of thunder. "You live on the streets young, you can get into a lot of trouble."

"How did he know? Aren't those records sealed?"

She had a point. It wasn't in the faxed CPD jacket that was lying on Cobbett's desk, and the cover memo from my lieutenant hadn't mentioned Rainy. "He must have talked to someone there. Someone who remembered. There was a homicide investigation."

A gust of wind slammed into the house and rattled the windows, then rain began to pound down. The lights blinked out, came on again, then went dark. The only illumination in the big room came from the flames in the fireplace. "Are there any candles around?" Ruth asked.

"I think I saw some in a drawer." We went out to the kitchen. Ruth found a box of stubby emergency candles and soon had a dozen candles in saucers flickering on the low table in the living room. I picked up my glass. Ruth took a bite from a slice of pizza. "Mm. Cold, but it still tastes good. Why did you leave home so young?"

"My mother was abusive." The word sounded too clinical, like something off a social services report. "Five boys to feed and no money and it was all on her because my father died right after I was born. She was always getting angry and knocking us around. Me especially. The others, it was like kicking the cat when you're in a bad mood, no big thing. She'd beat the tar out of me."

Ruth rubbed a little sauce off her upper lip. "You must have been the youngest, right? How did your brothers react to that?"

"They'd slip out and shoot hoops or whatever until it

was over. Sometimes the neighbors complained and these cops would come. One would talk to my mother and the other one, his name was O'Mally, he'd take me into the living room and ask me questions. I wouldn't tell him shit, but I could see he knew what was going on. These social workers came by sometimes, after, but they never found anything. The apartment was always clean. They really liked that, how clean everything was." Ruth gave me a pained grin.

"After my brother Steve left for the army it got a lot worse, like she was . . . I don't know. There was something wrong with her. It was getting scary. One night she was really mad and she backed me into the radiator, and I tried to get away but she grabbed my wrists and held me there—Shit. I'm sorry, Ruth, I shouldn't . . . Why am I talking so much?"

"It's fine, Slovo."

"I took off after that. Lived on the streets. There were other kids out there, standing around waiting for business, you know, but I didn't . . . I was only twelve, I didn't know anything. One night I noticed the lights were on at Rainy's place. Rainy was this cripple that ran a video rental place. He had two big old mutts that I liked a lot, real friendly dogs. I went in and said I could cook and clean, I could help out with the business, only I needed a place to stay. He laughed at me but said okay."

Ruth took another slice of pizza. "You should have some of this. It's good."

"I can't stand anchovies. They look too much like those bugs with all the legs."

"So pick 'em off."

I took a piece, held it near a candle, carefully removed all the anchovies and folded them into a napkin so I wouldn't have to see them, making her laugh. "Anyway, I stayed with Rainy for a while. First time in my life I felt safe, which is funny because turns out he didn't rent many videos, he made his money dealing. I helped him out and nobody looked twice at me because I was just a kid and everyone was used to seeing me running around the streets. It was great being with Rainy. We joked around all the time. Only he expanded the business and it got him in trouble with some competitors."

"What happened?"

"They killed him." I finished the slice of pizza and wiped my fingers with a crumpled napkin. "Beat his head in."

"How old were you when this happened?"

"Almost thirteen. I wasn't with Rainy that long, just a few months."

"You must have been pretty upset."

"The cops took me in for questioning but I wouldn't cooperate until Tim showed up. Tim O'Mally, the one that used to come to our house. He got me to talk. I was doing okay until I remembered I had to let the dogs out and Tim said they killed the dogs, too." I laughed. It seemed stupid to get all worked up about the dogs when Rainy had been killed so brutally. But I remembered how it had felt, that raw burst of pain. I felt Ruth take my hand and I cleared my throat. "Later on, I asked Tim was he married. And he said no, not lately. And I told him I could cook and keep his place clean if he'd let me stay with him. But he said I couldn't."

"Bet that hurt."

"I thought, you know, he'd been real nice, but of course he couldn't. I figured that out later, you couldn't do that every time you found a kid in trouble, right? Where'd you put 'em all? Like those old ladies with all the cats. Anyway, they sent me to a group home for a while. They had a lot of rules. I really hated it there. Then they found out my grandmother would take me in. I didn't even know I had a grandmother."

"Did that work out all right?"

"We got along fine, even though she was real old and didn't speak much English. She got confused about some things, like what I was supposed to do for an education, so Tim took me to his old school and this nun gave me something to read and I totally bombed it. I'd skipped out all the time, I was basically illiterate. I felt so bad, letting Tim down like that, but she said they'd find a way. Sister Veronica was always saying shit like that, they'd find a way, or a path would be revealed. Crazy nuns. They wouldn't give up on me. You wouldn't believe how dumb I was, and being so far behind I had to be real careful not to get in fights and stuff. But these nuns tutored me after school. This one, she was French Canadian, she always called me 'wild child.' I forget how she said it in French but then she'd say it in English and laugh and give me these weird-tasting candies."

"And she got you up to speed?"

"Yeah. Barely, but enough to take the exam, get into the academy. Because that's what I wanted to do, real bad."

"Because of Tim."

"If it wasn't for him . . . in my line of work, I'm always dealing with the kind of person I would have been if he hadn't stepped in. He saved my life. That's why I wanted to be a cop. I wanted to prove to him it was worth it, all the time he spent. He used to come get me on weekends, we'd go do stuff together. Work on his car, watch a baseball game on TV. Sometimes he had to work, but he'd let me ride along. He never missed a weekend."

"He sounds like a neat guy."

"He was the greatest. He kept telling me I'd make a good cop one day. Some afternoons I'd hop the bus down to Harrison and bring him stuff I heard on the streets. He would tell me to go do my homework, get outta here Slovo, go study, but he liked having me there. He even kept a picture of me on his desk, like I was family. All that effort he made, and now I'm going to get canned."

"You must have a lawyer. What does he think?"

"Probably that he has a jackass for a client. Haven't talked to him since I left Chicago. I gotta call him."

"You have contacts at work who could tell you what's going on? What about Tim?"

"He died four years ago."

"I'm sorry. You have any friends in the media? A reporter can ask questions you couldn't."

"There's someone at the *Trib* who owes me a few favors." I reached for her hand, took it in both of mine and ran my thumbs across her knuckles before letting it go. She went over to the fireplace to poke at the dying fire as I refilled our glasses. Just as she coaxed some flames out of the remains of the wood, the lights came back on.

We sat together, sipping our wine. There was a commotion at the door as Hari burst in, harassed and disheveled. "Your drugs." He tossed an amber bottle to me, followed by a pack of cigarettes.

"You're a true humanitarian, Hari."

"Can't believe I'm supporting that disgusting addiction of yours." He crammed a slice of pizza into his mouth and mumbled around it, "Mm, lovely. Had all you want? I'll take the rest, then." He closed the box and scooped it up.

"I thought you were going to stay here tonight."

"Too busy. I won't get away from the hospital for hours. Cheerio, good children. If you can't be good, be careful." He tucked the box under his arm and strode out.

"I should go too," Ruth said.

"Thanks, Ruth."

"For what?" She took my hand and kissed my knuckles. "I'll call you tomorrow."

After she left I took the bottle of wine out on the porch and lit a cigarette. The clouds had rolled out with the storm and there was a hint of winter in the breeze. I finished the bottle out there, under a sky full of stars, brighter than they ever were in Chicago.

Inside, I read the label on the pill bottle and then took

twice as many as I was supposed to. I was never good at following instructions. Lying in bed, I felt something tremulous but pleasant as I drifted off into a white, cottony wooziness. It took me a while to identify what it was.

Hope. Something I hadn't felt in a long time.

CHAPTER 9

I was plunged in sleep as murky as a swamp when the window near the bed exploded into a thousand fragments, and pieces of wood and plaster and glass flew around the room. A second blast slammed into the wall and I rolled into the crevice between the bed and the wall with my arms wrapped around my head, then scrabbled behind me with one arm, groping blindly for the Glock tucked between the bed frame and the springs. There was shouting and feet pounding and darting light as flashlights slashed across the room, nailing me against the wall. I found the gun at last but arms yanked me upright and I lost it. Something crashed down hard on my head and the room went even darker and very still.

When I woke the darkness smelled of wet wool and cat piss. I didn't have anything between me and the chill air but my undershirt and shorts and whatever it was they had over my head. My head throbbed, pain stabbing into my eyes when I moved. "Shhh." Someone was close by, warning others to silence. I felt him tugging at the ropes that bound my hands to the arms of a chair, then at ropes that bound my feet. "Okay," a voice whispered. "They'll hold."

"They're too tight," I tried to say, but it came out a string of unfocused vowels.

"Shut up." I heard feet shuffling, things being shoved around, voices muttering. Then, someone must have thrown on a light switch because the darkness turned a different shade of black. "Wait," someone muttered, and there was more shuffling. "Where's the . . . oh, gimme that. Right, let's . . ." Someone behind me pulled the wool hood off my head. I couldn't focus on the shapes at the edge of the corona of white light. "Wow, the Untouchables," I said. "Seen it on *Nick at Nite*."

"Shut up." The barrel of the shotgun moved up from my chest to prod under my chin, forcing it up before it withdrew.

"Jesus, would you look at that," someone hissed, "fucking St. Sebastian."

"Hey!" A sharp command.

That was at least three voices so far, the one with the gun, the one with the Catholic education, and the one who was in charge. I tried to put them away for later, but I wasn't sure there would be any later.

"Konstantin Slovo, Detective in the Chicago Police Department, currently on suspension," the one in charge intoned. "Three complaints of unnecessary force filed by civilians, one of them substantiated resulting in two weeks disciplinary action without pay. Juvie narcotics record, a drug habit that continued into adulthood. Suspected at times of possession with intent, assault, evidence tampering, perjury. Under investigation for murdering a fellow officer in an ambush."

"Medical leave," I corrected him. "Not suspension, it's a medical leave. And I didn't kill anybody."

"The suspension will be official any day now. You're a piece of work, Slovo." The voice wasn't Forester's, but they were his words, that last phrase. I peered into the brightness, looking for him. "A piece of work," whoever it was said again, liking the sound of it.

"Yeah, well, you're a piece of shit," I returned. The

shotgun barrel crashed against the side of my head. Somebody said something, but I couldn't hear it over the blood pounding in my head.

Water splashed against my face. "Pay attention. You investigated several crimes involving children, you were the local expert, and then you suddenly stopped. Why was that?"

"Huh?"

"Don't be stupid, Slovo. We want answers." The shotgun moved a little, sketched some uncertainty under my chin.

"Chill, will you? I stopped . . . what happened, see, I don't have kids. The others did and they all thought it wouldn't bother me as much. Well, fuck that, it bothered me plenty and after this one, this baby they found in pieces in the park, I said forget it, I did my share."

"Maybe. Maybe you just had a hard time keeping your urges under control. You had one last winter again. Lauren Alvarez. Was it good, working on a case with a child victim again? You ever masturbate over the corpse of a kid, Slovo?"

"What? Jesus, that's a sick—"

"We know why you stopped. You lost control, they were going to find out."

"Hell are you talking about?"

"But you couldn't stop, could you? We know about the one in the park. What about the other victims, Slovo? How many children have you killed?"

"I never killed any kids. You fucked up in the head or what?" The gun barrel moved sharply and I cringed.

"You were here in Brimsport when Marcy disappeared."

"No. I was down the highway, I can prove it. There's a bartender in South Bend that'll vouch for me."

"You were here when Ashley Underhill and Bethany Lowell disappeared."

"Bullshit."

"You have a lot of innocent blood on your hands, Slovo." The voice of the Man in Charge sounded pleased, as if he was getting to the part he liked best. "You're going to suffer eternal damnation. You're going to undergo tortures far worse than those you inflicted on those innocent children, you're going to be in pain that never ends. We want you to think about the evil you've done, we want to watch you hurt, hurt like those innocent lambs did, hear you beg for mercy just like they begged you, you sick monster."

"This is crazy. I wasn't anywhere near here."

I could hear the papers shuffle again. "Bethany Lowell was taken December twenty-second, at which time you were on suspension without pay for two weeks. No one knew where you'd gone."

"I was in a cabin in Minnesota, up in Otter Tail County. A friend gave me the keys to his summer place. Chancey Bluefoot, he tends bar at Donovan's, down in the Loop. Check it out, he'll corroborate."

"Ashley Underhill disappeared on June twelfth. You took a vacation that ran from June eleventh to June seventeenth. You weren't seen in Chicago during that time."

I tried to clear my buzzing head, figure out those dates. Shouldn't be too hard, I didn't take vacations very often. "I was seen in Las Vegas, though. Stayed at the, the, shit, I can't remember what it was called now, you got this all fucked up. Give me time to remember the place, I can prove it to you, I wasn't here."

"With your record, going well back into childhood, why should we believe anything you say?"

"You ever heard of evidence? What you got, it's bullshit."

"Who were you working with here in Brimsport? We know you aren't working alone. Give us some names."

"Are you a little slow? I didn't have anything to do with it."

"That's enough. He had his chance." The Man in Charge was through with me. Then a fist smashed into my stomach and I folded over. My chest felt full of stabbing pains as if I were on a bed of nails. The next blow snapped my head back. "Don't, please," I said, not clearly because my mouth was full of blood.

"The fingers, now," someone whispered. "Let's do the fingers."

Somebody pinched my left ear tenderly. "Sure? Fingers first?"

"Hey, no, *no*." I bunched my hands into fists. They'd moved in carefully, one of them adjusting the light to keep their faces in darkness. One pried my fingers out and held my hand flat while someone else took hold of my little finger. I heard the crack. They paused to stuff a cloth into my mouth and tape it over. Then they spread my hand out again and broke the finger next to it and I passed out.

When I was aware again, the lights were growing dim and someone was swearing. "Battery's about gone," a voice I hadn't heard before said. "Let's go." The bright light was doused. Flashlights played across the ground. I caught glimpses: concrete floor covered with dirt. Some rusty rebar, a twist of electrical conduit, old and corroded. From the way the sounds bounced around, it was a big space.

"What about him?"

"Leave him. Let him be an example."

"What is that anyway? Sticking out of his forehead?"

Fingers came through the flashlight beam and reached toward me, blood flooded down into my eyes. "Jesus," the one said, delighted.

"Glass," the other voice said. "Piece of the window. Let's go." And I heard their whispers recede.

But then I heard footsteps coming back. A light was snapped on to shine into my eyes again.

"You're dirt, Slovo. You're a disgusting, scum-eating piece of toxic waste." It was making my blood run cold, this low-pitched, hissing, singsong voice, quivering with excitement. "You make me sick, you make me so sick, people like you deserve to die slowly, painfully, get taken to pieces by dogs." He was working my head back and forth, twisting

my hair in his fingers. "You whoremongering, sick, rotten
bastard. Look at you bleeding and pissing in your pants,
you miserable pervert." Then he let me go and the light
went sweeping up the vast space before it was shut off, and
then I felt him thrusting close to me, fumbling, urgent, and
I knew I'd feel the barrel of a gun against my head any moment. I'd seen guys get crazy like this, plan an operation,
then lose it at the last moment in an ecstasy of adrenaline,
pop someone just for the thrill of it. I found garbled syllables of a prayer my grandmother used to say chanting in my
head over and over, like when she rocked and crossed herself in front of the icon in her bedroom, *hospodi pomilui,
hospodi pomilui.* Ropes of something slimy and hot
splashed against my face, and I fought down nausea. I
couldn't vomit with the cloth in my mouth: I'd choke in it
and die.

I heard him give a shuddering sigh, and then he
stepped back and whacked me hard against the side of my
head with the flashlight. Icy water sluiced over my head
and shoulders and ran down my chest, pooling around me
in the chair. "Bastard, bastard. Perverted fucking bastard."
He flung the bucket away, clanging into the wide, empty
space. His footsteps retreated and I was left alone in the
darkness.

The cold, that was the main thing. The water seemed to
have burned through to the bone, and I shivered like I had
epilepsy. After a time I felt the numbness spreading from
my feet until all of me was numb, and that was better. It replaced the pains with a hard, rigid emptiness that ached
hollowly, coupled with a strange lightness in my head.
Things floated through the emptiness, like the realization
that this was like what happened to Rainy.

For a time I was back in Otter Tail County, reaching

for the blankets but always dropping them because my fingers were numb and I started to get scared because there was an icy wind blowing off the frozen lake and if I didn't get warm it was going to kill me. I was in this freezing cottage because in a white-hot rage I'd beat the shit out of a man, lost it completely when he reacted to the picture I showed him of his own daughter, the picture we had pinned on the wall to remind us to find the bastard that did it. He'd looked at it and laughed and instead of blowing his head off like I wanted to do I used my gun to coldcock him and then I grabbed his hair and pounded his face into the floor until the others pulled me off. Only while I was hammering his head against the linoleum, making him pay for that little girl, it turned out it was me who was getting hammered, and when I could catch a glimpse through the blood in my eyes I saw my mother bending over me.

I heard noises sometimes, small animals scuffling and slithering around, but it all seemed remote, not something to worry about, not in this strange, cold, floating darkness. I wondered why those men had picked me up and worked me over, and I couldn't get past the way Forester looked at me, excited as he trained his gun on me when I sat in my car on the harbor, Robin's blood staining the backseat. Closing in, he'd said, they were closing in.

Then I'd start to drift again. I'd hear that voice telling me that I was going to burn in hell, a hissing voice calling me a pervert, a piece of shit, worthless, my lieutenant or Robin's father or my mother leaning into my face to say it, or that last one, a shape in the dark, full of hate and excitement.

Something strange started happening to the ceiling of the vast, gray room. Part of it kept changing color, first pearly and then marbled gray and white, pale light leaking down the walls. Twisted metal rods writhed around the light patch like claws. The rustling noises turned out to be cats, dozens of cats, slinking around the shadowy edges, darting across the floor near my feet, bony and feral. They seemed to be waiting for something and when they heard a noise beyond my hearing their heads would swivel, they would tense and shrink and vanish into the shadows.

The changing color was sky. A hole in the roof. Later a gull drifted by, riding an air current, head tipped as if checking me out. The sun streamed almost vertically through the hole, and when I opened my eyes again it was getting dark. With a sky that clear, it would be cold. I wouldn't make it through another night.

When I saw the light stabbing through the shadows I thought the guys with the shotgun had come back for more. Beams of light, footsteps, loud male voices, they were back. I couldn't see well, but sounds etched themselves into my consciousness with extreme clarity, dipped in an acid bath of fear.

But then I heard Cobbett's voice. "It's just like—ah, fuck. The bastards." And there were lights flickering around me and through a haze Bobby reached toward me.

"Oh, God. He's cold."

"Christ—"

"Wait, I think—there's a pulse. It's awful weak."

"He's hypothermic. We have to get him out of here."

"You're going to be all right," someone said, hands reaching for me.

CHAPTER 10

How are you feeling?" Ruth asked.

I thought about it for a minute. Three fingers on my right hand were splinted and taped together. They looked like sausages that had started to go bad, but my head was swimming with opiates and I wasn't feeling any pain. "I'm okay. Did they cut my ears?"

"Your ears are fine." She smiled, puzzled.

Those eyes, God, they were something. And I was so happy that I still had my ears. I let my eyes close for a minute. When I opened them again I gave her a dopey grin. "You should get some rest, Ruth. You look tired."

"You think you can talk now?" It was another woman's voice, from the other side of the bed, but I couldn't see who it was.

"I'll be back." Ruth gave my arm a gentle squeeze and rose.

The other woman turned Ruth's chair, sat astride it, and leaned on her folded arms, her short, dark hair a ragged frame around her face, her eyes piercing and hard. "Sabine Forché, Maine State Police." She set a pocket-sized tape recorder on the bed, stated the date and time and our names. "We need to know what happened out there. How'd it start?"

"I was asleep. I had taken a couple of sleeping pills, so I was really zonked. First thing I know, there's a shotgun blast taking out the window and then they're firing again, just over my head. And then they were all over me."

"How many?"

"I'd guess five or six, but...it was dark and they knocked me out before I knew what the hell was happening. When I heard the shots I rolled to the side, tried to get a nine-millimeter I had tucked away there—oh, great, they probably took it."

"We found a Glock under the bed." She smiled briefly, an amazing transformation that you'd miss if you blinked. "What next?"

I told her what I could remember. She reacted only once. "St. Sebastian?"

"I had these shards of glass and splinters of wood sticking into me from the shotgun blast. Like the dude with the arrows, this saint—"

"I know who St. Sebastian is." She gave me that blitzkrieg smile again.

When I got to the part where the man said "You're a piece of work," I stumbled to a stop. She frowned. "What? Tell me."

"They knew stuff about my work history. Like, last December I got suspended—"

"I know, Chicago faxed your jacket here. Maybe a cop or a civilian in the office mentioned it in public and it was overheard."

"They had facts no one would mention casually. Like the exact date I took vacation. I think they had a copy of that fax; I could hear them shuffling the pages. One of the cops tipped them off." She was frowning, her dark eyes working on something behind the scenes, and then told me to go on.

When I had finished, she probed for details—if the hands had any distinguishing features, whether I'd caught a glimpse of clothing. "Anything else?"

"I was kind of drifting. I just remember cats everywhere, the cold. Where was I, anyway?"

"An unfinished cooling tower. They started to build a nuclear reactor here years ago, but the project was halted by a lawsuit." She snapped off the recorder, slipped it into her pocket, and stood up.

Beyond her I could see the window and I blinked. "What's going on? Another storm coming in?"

"They're saying clear tonight."

"Why's it so dark?"

"It's nearly eight. This time of year the days get short."

"Ruth's been here all day?"

"Ever since they found you last night. And she spent most of the previous day helping with the search after Will Sylvester reported your place had been shot up. What devotion. Enough to make you gag. I'll get you a statement to look over tomorrow. You going to be able to sign anything?"

I looked at the splints. "Maybe an X."

"Good enough. Bobby tells me you're illiterate anyway."

She left and I dozed off, coming back to find Ruth sitting beside me again. "Jeez, Ruth. Go home."

"I could use some sleep," she admitted. "Haven't had much since...when was it, Tuesday? You weren't the only one that got hurt that night. Those women who live together at Northhaven—their trailer was set on fire."

I remembered a woman pushing a stroller, four teens following her down the street. "One of them has a baby."

"Meg. She got out with her little boy, but Amanda, her partner—she was badly burned, had to be airlifted to a hospital in Portland. Oh, and some concerned citizens shot out most of the windows at Ardis Burke's house. These murders have everyone worked up. People are looking for scapegoats."

"I need to talk to your father."

"I'll tell him. For now, take it easy." She stood, then bent down for a lingering kiss. "I like you, Slovo," she whispered.

"Have I ever mentioned you have beautiful eyes?"

She gave me a lopsided grin and left.

I n those slow, dead hours when the clock seems stuck just after 4:00 A.M., I woke myself out of a confusing dream with a groan. "Man," I muttered.

"Easy," Hari murmured from the shadows.

"What are you doing here, middle of the night?"

He didn't answer for a while. Then he said softly, "I wish you hadn't got hurt, Slovo." It was too dark to see his face clearly.

"You'll feel better soon," he said, as a shape appeared in the doorway. He took a syringe from the nurse and slid the needle into my arm, then pressed a square of gauze against it. He stood there, looking down at the pale bit of gauze, his eyes in shadow, until I faded out.

I n the morning Cobbett came in and sat in the chair by the bed, hunched over a steaming cardboard cup that he held by the edges. He looked haggard and about a decade older than when I'd last seen him. "What is it you want to tell me?"

"Neil Forester is in with the people that attacked me. He may not have been there that night, but he provided them with information."

He didn't seem surprised. "What makes you think so?"

"When they had me tied up, they ran this bullshit theory that I did the murders. Somebody noticed I wasn't in Chicago on the key dates, when the three girls disappeared. Looks bad, okay, but I got solid alibis for those times."

"I know you do. I noticed those dates, too. I had that

receipt you gave me from South Bend, they confirmed you were there. You made quite an impression, in fact."

"This drunk kept trying to start a fight. I just wanted him to leave me alone."

"You could have been in seriously deep shit, drawing your weapon in a bar like that. I talked to someone in Chicago who remembered you borrowed a cabin from a friend when you got suspended, it checked out. The Vegas thing took a little longer."

"Forester must have given them a copy of my CPD jacket. When he came out to do the paperwork on my car that morning, he said I was 'a piece of work.' The one leading the charge out there, he used the exact same phrase, twice. The setup in the cooling tower was like some trouble I got involved in as a juvenile, which Forester knew about, I have no idea how."

"Maybe from Mike McGavin. McGavin wanted to be sure I knew about the IAD investigation and threw in your youthful indiscretions as a bonus."

"How the hell did he—"

"Who knows? He has connections all over the country."

"Forester was talking to McGavin at the station house on Monday. Your cop is leaking information. That's dangerous."

"I fired Neil's ass this morning. Yesterday I'm talking to a dirtball who might have been involved in your assault. And he lets drop the fact that Marcy was . . . he knows details about the scene nobody should know. For a minute there I thought maybe we had the bastard." He crumpled his empty coffee cup in his fist. "Find out his wife told him, she heard it from Neil's wife. Neil knew damn well how important it was to keep that stuff quiet. He says he'll sue over some due-process bullshit, but I don't care. He's jeopardizing my investigation."

Cobbett stood and dropped his cup into the trash can.

"Say, on another matter." He studied the fine print on the IV bag. "Whatever's going on between you and Ruth, it's none of my business. But she got out of a bad marriage not long ago. She was pretty racked up about it. Just . . . be careful, will you?"

I pulled the phone over after Cobbett left. Sylvester's answering machine told me to leave a message. "Uh, Will? It's Slovo. I understand you called the police and got the search for me started. I'm sure glad you did. Those guys that took me were really . . . well, let's just say they had it in for me. I'm sorry about the mess they made at the house. The owners won't be too happy about it, huh? This is getting kind of long. I just wanted to say thanks." I let the tape run some extra seconds before I hung up, hoping he'd take that silence as an urge to talk some more.

Next, I punched in a number and got the usual adenoidal tape recording: "Can't take your call right now. Leave a message." Beep.

"Clay? It's Slovo. Pick up." I knew he was there. He was always there. I'd known Clayton Zemanski since seventh grade, when he was a fat, asthmatic child with a streak of weird brilliance that didn't save him from being despised and tortured by the other kids. Now he was a fat, asthmatic adult with a PI's license and a thriving business. His social awkwardness and hypochondria developed into full-fledged agoraphobia, but the fact that he never leaves his loft in an old building on South Wabash doesn't do his business any harm. He can find almost anything on the Internet and on the rare occasion that his hacking skills fail him, he gets on the phone and talks people out of all kinds of confidential information. It isn't charm, he just has an uncanny ability to lie with conviction.

"Slovo? No shit. I hear you're in a world of trouble with

the PD. We're talking profound scatology, man." Clayton has a pedantic way of talking due to having read too many books over the years, but his asthma makes him sound breathless, like a geeky teenager wound up with his own brilliance.

"Yeah, whatever. I need you to run someone down for me."

A keyboard started to clack. "Came to the right place. Card number and expiration date?"

"Hey, you owe me. I risked my career for you and spent a whole night doing it."

"You coulda done it in no time if you did it my way. All you had to do was reformat that partition on the hard drive. And anyway, that was years ago. Am I gonna pay for that one little favor the rest of my life?"

"Yes. His name's William Sylvester. Goes by Will." I gave him all the details I could remember from the skimpy file Cobbett had given me. "See what you can turn up. Personal history, news stories about the incident, any priors. Can you get medical records?"

He bristled. "I can get anything."

"See if he was ever prescribed oxycodone or a painkiller like that. I need this soon, Clay. Like tomorrow."

His sigh sounded like a truck with faulty pneumatic brakes.

CHAPTER 11

Lunch arrived on a tray. I ate some lasagna, drank the coffee, wished I had a cigarette. An orderly took the tray away. I stared at the view through the window for a while, then pulled the phone over again.

My lawyer was as irritated as I expected him to be. He offered to resign if I wanted different counsel and seemed disappointed I didn't take him up on it. He went over the procedural steps we would take when I got suspended. He reminded me that he had been successful defending officers before the Police Board in the past, but they all had one thing in common: They wanted to keep their jobs. He wasn't sure I did.

After I persuaded my lawyer I was still interested in a career in law enforcement, I called a cop I'd worked with at Area 4 Headquarters for nearly ten years. Donny Zarelli seemed happier to hear from me. "What gives, Slovo? You had a sudden craving for lobster? How you doing, buddy?"

"Not great. Back in the hospital. How's things at the shop?"

"The usual. Bunch of ag assaults, couple shootings, just gang shit. Oh, and we got a serial rapist. Four women attacked, all in the same block. Ton of overtime authorized and not one fucking lead. Sorry to hear you're in the hospital again."

"My lawyer thinks a suspension's in the works."

"Robin's dad has been agitating for it. I don't get his attitude. You and Bill were pretty tight."

"He needs someone to hate right now."

"There's going to be a meeting about it on Monday. I'll speak up for you of course, but Bill Freeling still has a lot of juice with the superintendent. How things work around here. Politics."

"Is there anything new on the shooting? Any progress at all?"

"Afraid not."

"No leads on my gun?"

"Not that I've heard. Course, I've been tied up with this rape all week. It's making me crazy."

"You say they've all been in the same block?"

"You know that restaurant up on Ashland that's, like, Ethiopian or one of them? Had camels on the sign, the plastic palm trees? That block. Four-story brick apartment buildings, he follows them in, attacks them on the stairs."

"You know if the guys talked to Abe Dreyfus? He lives right across the street in that home for the elderly. Abe hardly sleeps and he notices everything."

"Offhand, I don't know."

"He's a Holocaust survivor, he gets nervous when people he doesn't know show up at his door, and he won't talk to uniforms. It might be worth going back to him, even if he didn't say much the first time."

"Hang on. Just a . . ." I heard the phone clunk down, some papers shuffling, a barked question. "Right. I got the report here. Jamison talked to him. Nothing much here."

"Oh. That's another thing. Abe's kind of racist."

"A racist Holocaust survivor?"

"He can't get used to the way the neighborhood has

changed. But he's observant and if he's in the right mood he'll make a good witness. Send a white plainclothes to talk to him. A woman. He likes women."

"I'll give it a shot. Look, anything I can do for you? Name it."

"Do what you can at that meeting. And if there's anything new on the shooting...It shouldn't have happened to Robin."

"You know that Puerto Rican joint where she used to get her coffee?" His voice dropped. "I walk by there, I have to cross the street. Can't handle it."

I pushed a finger and thumb against my closed eyes until a checkerboard of bright squares floated in front of them. Then I punched in another number. I could hear the familiar chaos of the *Chicago Tribune* city desk in the background as Maura finished a conversation with a colleague, then said impatiently into the phone, "Yeah. Doyle here."

"Hey, Maura."

"Slovo! Where the fuck are you?"

"In Maine. I just...I got fed up with things, so I left. Look, they're going to suspend me. I think it's the first step in getting me fired."

"Whoa, whoa. Where in Maine?"

"It's on the coast, a place called Brimsport."

"Isn't that where they had that big sex ring scandal years ago? What are you doing there?"

"I'm in the hospital."

"What for?" Rapid-fire questions, Maura's usual style. I could see her scribbling notes, hunched over with her hair in her eyes.

"An infection. Then I got out for a while and...man, it's a long story. I just need to know if you'd heard anything. About Robin. What they have on me."

"Tell me the long story first, then I'll tell you what I know."

I'd known Maura for years. She couldn't be shaken when her curiosity was up. I finally was able to bring it back to what I wanted to know. I heard her flip notebook pages. "Okay, everyone's been up in arms over you just taking off like you did. Also, I heard from a source in the PD there's a retired sergeant you worked under in Narcotics who's claiming you used drugs on the job."

"So, he went through my desk once and found a couple of white crosses, big deal. He didn't even report it. And that was ten years ago."

"He's reporting it now. Somebody must have dug pretty deep to dig him up. Bill Freeling's turning up the heat big-time. What's he got against you?"

"He's hurting bad. I'm the one took his daughter into that situation. It was my snitch we were meeting that night. Shit, I wish my gun would turn up."

"Whoa, hold it. Your gun?"

Maura goes after the details like a pit bull. I was relieved when Hari came to examine me and I had an excuse to hang up.

Dusk had fallen and the dinner trays had come and gone. I drifted into a dream about being interrogated by cops in that room where they brought me after Rainy was murdered. They kept asking me questions about Robin, questions that didn't make any sense. Then, in one of those sudden scene changes you get in dreams, I was in an orange jumpsuit and shackles at the Cook County Criminal Court and my lieutenant was in the witness box pointing at me, saying something I couldn't make out except that I knew it wasn't true.

"It's a goddamn lie," I said and woke myself up.

"Excuse me?" An old man with a clipboard was peering at the door number, checking something on a list. The room was full of shadows jumping in the blue, flickering light of the television.

"Who are you?"

"Jim Donohue. I'm a deacon at St. Catherine's. I'm sorry it took me so long to see you, but you weren't on my list. They didn't put your religion down when you were admitted, is why."

I found the switch for the light over the bed. "I'm not real religious." My roommate was lying flat on his back, dead to the world, every now and then a snore leaking out of him. I noticed another figure standing by the door, leaning against the doorjamb, hands in his pockets.

McGavin pushed away from the wall, came over with his hand extended. Seeing my broken fingers, he put it back in his pocket and rocked on his heels a little. "Gave Jim a ride down here. I've been wanting to have that conversation with you and we never got around to it. Shame what happened to you."

"Yeah, well. Shit happens."

"It's not surprising. People here are deeply frustrated. The system has failed them."

"I'm not impressed with their version of justice. They pronounced me guilty without any evidence. Guess getting solid evidence was your problem, too."

"We had more than enough evidence. Children don't lie about those things." The words flowed easily as if he had them memorized. "There was an organized ring of sexual predators operating in this town, people who conspired together to corrupt the innocence of young children. It was big and had deep roots and I did everything I could to put an end to it. But people couldn't handle it. They pretended it never happened. Can you imagine what it was like, going through that degradation, being rescued from it, and then having people say you lied?"

"Kids are suggestible. You can't always tell—"

"There's no way they could have made that stuff up." There was an edge to his voice now. "Children were routinely abused and a number of townsfolk participated in it. But because people in places of power were cowards and worse, they all got away with it."

"The work of the devil, Mr. Slovo," the deacon contributed solemnly. "It may be fashionable in these godless times to believe that there is no such thing, but Satan still walks among us."

"Chasing Satan isn't my job. Cops don't decide what's right and wrong, we go by the rules of evidence and the criminal code." I decided to rattle McGavin's cage. "If anybody got away with child abuse here, it was because the cops working the case opened it too wide, lost their focus, forgot to follow the evidence."

He stopped with his head tilted as if listening to a faint sound only he could hear. Then he drew up a chair to sit beside the bed facing me, his hands clasped in front of him, like a priest getting ready to hear a confession. "Some cases mark a turning point in a cop's life. I learned a lot about human nature when I worked that case. I learned that the average citizen is more interested in his safe, comfortable life than in the truth." He spoke quietly, almost in a whisper. "That those in power exert it only to maintain it. And I learned that some cops are so hardened, so jaded by what they've seen on the streets, they no longer know what side they're on. What drives me, what makes me tick, is seeing good triumph over evil. You think that's funny?"

"It's not that simple. You want simple, you should have joined the priesthood."

He leaned forward suddenly, fixing me with a gaze that was almost hypnotic. "Without belief, it's too easy to slide into despair and confusion. You know what I'm talking about. All those cases you worked, all that violence done to children."

"I work Violent Crimes. Sometimes the violence is on kids."

"No one else could deal with it, but you made them your specialty, those brutalized children." The voice was gentle, but it slid into me as easily as a sharp knife. Part of me admired his technique—the guy was good—but another part of me just wanted to get some distance from the intensity of his face. "Nothing fazed you, did it? Until that baby was found in the park. What happened then, Slovo? Why didn't you make any progress, why was that case never solved? Was it starting to show, the way you really felt?"

"I've heard this somewhere before. The guys who did this to me friends of yours, McGavin?" The accusation slipped out, too angry.

He moved in a little closer, like a boxer finding an advantage. "Your brother Charles has a sheet, four raps for prostitution."

"*What?* No."

"He never told you? In San Francisco. He was fifteen the first time they brought him in. A runaway, like you. You were even younger—twelve, wasn't it, when you left home?"

"I think it's time you guys took off." I pushed the nurse's button, pushed it again for good measure.

"You grew up abused, took to the streets while you were still a child, did what you had to do to get by. The things you go through that young, they stay with you." He squeezed my forearm, sent some intense message with his eyes, wanting something from me and promising some kind of absolution for it. "Talk to me," he whispered. "Help me understand."

"Take your hand off me."

"Son, we're trying to help," the deacon said. "There is a way, you have a choice. The Church is there for you."

I tore my eyes away from McGavin's gaze, a new anger

jittering through me. "Look, no offense, Deacon, but the Catholic Church is *not* there for me, okay?"

"But you are Catholic?" He looked down at his clipboard, suddenly confused, as if somebody made a mistake and he was wasting his time on a Buddhist. The nurse arrived at the door and stood there, perplexed.

"Are you asking do I believe that stuff? No, I don't. It doesn't make sense, praying to this guy that got tortured and killed and promised he was coming back but never shows. Two thousand years? Figure it out already. It ain't gonna happen. But I was raised Catholic, sure. My mother used to take us to church on Sunday, show the world what a regular family we were." I sketched a big sign of the cross to prove it. "I don't need those lies, okay? Just leave me alone."

McGavin shook his head wearily; the deacon's eyes had grown wide with horror. He recovered himself to mumble that he would pray for me and then they left.

The nurse was looking at me warily. "Did you need something?"

"Guess not. Sorry."

I switched off my light and lay there, too wired to sleep. McGavin had found a way to get under my skin. The guy was charismatic, compelling, and totally confident of his version of the truth. And I was certain that even if he hadn't literally been present, he was standing in those shadows behind that bright corona of light, putting me on trial and finding me guilty of something monstrous.

CHAPTER 12

And how is the devil worshipper this morning?" Hari asked cheerily. "I hear you were visited by a delegation from the forces of Goodness and Light, but you perversely threw in your lot with the Prince of Darkness."

"McGavin came by with some old fart, if that's what you mean."

"Clever, the way you frightened them off, if a trifle heavy-handed. We had to give your neighbor a bed in another room. His family was most disturbed to discover he was bunking with a Satanist. Shouldn't wonder if they sue the hospital."

"All I said was Christianity seemed kind of illogical."

"It wasn't that, it was the gesture you made."

"Huh? I didn't . . . I just crossed myself." I showed him and he shrank back in mock horror. "What?"

"You did it backwards. The sign of Satan."

"What are you—? Wait a minute, wait a minute. It's the Eastern way. You cross over to the right side before you go to the left. Regular Catholics touch their left shoulder first. We went to a Uniate church."

"What on earth is Uniate? It sounds sinister."

"No, it's just a different rite. See, when the Poles took over the Ukraine way back when, all the Ukrainians were

Orthodox, right? Like the Russians next door. And the Poles said, Hey, we're in charge now, get Catholic. And the Ukrainians, being kinda stubborn, said Up yours, we like doing it our way. And the compromise they came to was that we would be Catholics, but didn't have to change the way we did things. So we cross ourselves the Orthodox way and our priests can get married. But we're Catholic."

"I've never heard of this before."

"Probably don't have lots of Ukrainians in England."

"They're not that plentiful in Maine, either, apparently."

Sabine Forché came in, followed by Tom Flaherty. "He sure had me fooled. Looks like a regular guy," she complained.

"Goes to show, though. These evil bastards are everywhere, infiltrating the police force, seducing the chief's daughter, leading a secret life. You done with this pervert? We want to interrogate him some."

Hari looked around. "Where are your rubber hoses?"

"Damn," Forché said. "Knew I forgot something when I left for work this morning."

"I'll come back later to pick up the pieces." Hari left.

"Actually, we have a plan to spring you." Flaherty leaned close. "We talked your landlord into letting you move back to your millionaire cottage by promising extra security, two armed officers there every night."

"How can you afford to do that?"

"Me and Flaherty been staying in this dump of a motel," Forché explained. "While you got six bedrooms just going to waste. Okay, let's cut to the chase. What was McGavin doing here last night?"

I gave them a blow-by-blow account. "He might have run a lousy investigation, but I can see how he got people to confess to things they didn't do back when he was chief. He's sort of ... hypnotic."

"What was he after?" Forché asked.

"Same thing as his buddies in the cooling tower."

"Allegedly," Forché corrected automatically.

"Allegedly, shit. He was definitely in on that, and he doesn't mind me knowing. That business about how I quit investigating crimes against children? They used the exact same line of questioning in the cooling tower. What's with this guy? He was a cop in a nowhere jurisdiction, off the job for years now, but he's got connections in San Francisco willing to run my brother's sheet for him? And where's he get all the money? Those clothes of his are expensive."

"He made a fortune as a consultant." Flaherty spat the word. "Gave him connections in law enforcement all over the country. And he's a hell of a fund-raiser; that foundation of his brings in tons of money."

"Don't forget his book," Forché added. "He did all the talk shows. It was on the best-seller list for weeks."

"Maybe I should read it."

"You sure you can handle it? It has a lot of big words."

"Shut up."

"What do you want to read that crap for?" Flaherty winced. "It's not worth it. He's just a pain in the ass, using this case to grandstand."

I remembered the feeling I had when McGavin fixed his eyes on me and urged me to confess to crimes he somehow made me feel responsible for. I opened my mouth to argue, but gave it up.

It was strange, driving down the main drag: Mike's Fresh Seafood, McGuire's Tavern, old men with suspenders sitting on a bench in front of the post office. It felt as if the storefronts were all false, a set for a scary movie. The Stepford Good Ol' Boys.

Flaherty pulled up to the curb in front of the Brimsport IGA. The swooping shape of the unfinished cooling tower stood up against the hillside across the water. He followed my gaze, then said, "I need to get a few things."

"Sure. I'll wait in the car."

He nodded and got out. In the harbor at the bottom of the hill, boats bobbed at their moorings, the water glinting like broken glass. I checked out the glove compartment: some papers and maps, an empty fifteen-round clip for a .45, a penlight, an old gas bill, and a letter from a church in Bangor listing Flaherty's charitable giving for the year, a big fat zero. Underneath everything a crumpled pack of Chesterfields holding one bent cigarette, fossilized with age. I opened the window and lit it.

I sat back feeling a little dizzy from the first puffs, knocked some ash into the gutter. When I looked up, a familiar figure was coming up the sidewalk. Forester had a fixed look on his face and it seemed as if he would pass me without a word, but he swung around, and said, "Happy now, Slovo? Fucked me over, you son of a bitch."

"There's this rule cops follow, Forester. You don't share confidential information that's critical to an investigation."

He gripped the door frame and leaned toward me. "You're going to pay for this."

"Back off, Neil. I don't want to get into anything with you, but the fact is you compromised a case and you handed my personnel records over to some bottom-dwelling fanatics and they came close to killing me. You got fired because you fucked up."

"At least I didn't kill my partner." His knuckles grew white. "Let me tell you something, asshole. My family served and protected this town for three generations. Cobbett thinks he's a big shot, coming up here from the city, always treating me like—he's full of shit. It's all an excuse to kick me out because I happen to think he's fucking up the investigation. If Mike McGavin was still in charge, we wouldn't be waiting around for another kid to get killed."

"McGavin was an incompetent cop. And your spilling the beans about the crime scene puts you in the same league."

He looked ready to pull me out through the window and kick the shit out of me, but backed off when Flaherty came out of the store. "Do yourself a favor and get lost, Forester," he said, putting a sack of groceries in the back-seat and leaning against the car.

"You're gonna be sorry." Forester looked at me.

"Yeah, right. We've heard from your lawyer." As Flaherty spoke, his voice low and almost lazy, three teens walking down the sidewalk stopped to watch. "He'd tell you it isn't wise to publicly threaten people who just got out of the hospital. Especially given you might be implicated in the assault that put him there."

Forester barked an incredulous laugh and appealed to a couple coming out of the grocery. "Where does he get off, a fed from Bangor sent here to push us around? Look whose side he takes." The couple's eyes slid from Forester to me; their faces were stiff with suspicion.

Flaherty sauntered past Forester and got in the car. We pulled out and rode in silence. "Know something?" he finally said as he turned onto Hunter's Point. "I'm really looking forward to nailing the bastard that killed those girls."

"I bet."

"Because then I can go home. This place gives me the creeps."

There were three cars parked at the house beside my charred Mustang. I picked up my cane and followed Flaherty inside. He set the sack of groceries on the kitchen table as Bryn came in from the living room, winding up a loop of cable. Bryn winced when he saw me. "It looks worse than it feels," I told him.

"I got your satellite office set up," Bryn said to Flaherty. He led the way into the living room, where furniture had been moved from a corner of the room, replaced by two utilitarian banquet tables holding two computers, a printer/fax, and telephones. A box held neatly labeled folders—copies of the case files.

"Dibs on the bedroom with the balcony," Forché said, trotting down the staircase from the second floor.

"I beg your pardon?" Flaherty acted out a double-take. "Need I point out you are outranked, Forché?"

"Bite me. I already put my stuff in there. You get our network connection up and running yet?" she asked Bryn. They huddled over him as he showed them how to log on. I headed toward the study. The window had been reglazed and the wall patched. It smelled of fresh paint. Someone had rearranged the furniture in here, too.

"Hi," Ruth said, looking up from the old mahogany desk where she was working on a laptop computer. She was dressed in a baggy pullover, the long sleeves shoved up to her elbows, her hair pinned on top of her head. "Hope you don't mind having company. I got Bryn to run a modem line in here while he was at it."

I sat on the bed. "You look good."

"Slept twelve hours straight. I got a call from the editor of *Uncover* magazine yesterday. I did a story for them once. He asked me to write another article."

"Great. What about?"

"The old Brimsport case and all those cases like it that were happening at the same time. I talked to Dad about it. He said to go ahead if I wanted to, so I'm taking a week's vacation to get started on the research." She nodded toward a stack of printouts and files. "I'm a little nervous. I haven't written anything all year except dumb features for the local paper."

Her face was framed by tendrils of hair escaping from the pinned-up bundle. There was a hint of a shape under that shapeless sweater that made me want to run my hands up under it, caress her breasts, press my body against hers, feel her wrap her legs around me.... I told my imagination to take a hike, but my body wasn't listening.

"I'm heading back to town," Bryn called out.

"We're leaving too," Flaherty added, poking his head around the doorframe. He looked around at the room and raised an eyebrow. "Very cozy."

We heard the door close behind them, the cars start up and drive away. "Maybe I can lend a hand with your research," I told Ruth, feeling oddly breathless.

"Pleasure before business." She came over to the bed and gave me a kiss, then reached down to unsnap my jeans.

"Are you sure?" I asked.

She was. Her pants slipped to the floor, followed by the sweater. She had pale skin, flawless except for some freckles across her shoulders and a small birthmark just above her right breast in the shape of a little starfish. Her mound was the same color as the locks falling loose around her face. She laughed as I got down to my shorts, a jazzy pair patterned with chili peppers, then as they joined the pile of clothes on the floor she gave me a gentle nudge backward, knelt over me and began to run her tongue delicately across my skin so that I was held suspended over some ocean of delight. Then, learning her signals, I discovered what made her tremble and sigh until she was breathing hard and quivering with readiness. "Wait," I said. She opened her eyes to look down at me, those amber depths opaque with self-absorption. "In my wallet."

She reached for my jeans, pulled out the wallet and, straddling me, searched for the little square packet. Her skin was flushed with pleasure, her motions so languorous and yet infused with tension held just barely in check. As I held her hips she guided me into her, and we moved together until I felt her tightening around me, gasping, and I let go at last, that sweet moment of release.

She lay on top of me, spent, then slipped over to my side, resting her head on my chest. I nuzzled her hair and rested my palm against the roundness of her hip. Our bodies fit perfectly together, her curves nestling into my angles. "Good thing you had a condom handy, Slovo. I didn't know you were so practical."

"I never was a Boy Scout but I always liked that slogan of theirs." She ran a finger along my incredibly shrinking organ, making it twitch hopefully before subsiding.

Ruth traced the scar tissue on my hip, then doodled with a fingertip across my chest between the cuts left from the shotgun blast. "*L'enfant sauvage.*"

"Hey, that's what that nun used to call me. How do you say that again?" I tried it out a few times and Ruth laughed at my mangled attempt at French.

"Enough. I better get some clothes on."

"Ruth?" She tilted her head to look up at me. There was something in her eyes, some form of warning, a line being drawn. "That was great," I finished lamely.

She grinned and slipped the sweater over her head, gathered her jeans, and headed for the shower.

CHAPTER 13

While she was in the shower, I got the box of files from the new office in the living room. We settled down to a quiet afternoon of research. Ruth had printed off a stack of articles and was going through them with a yellow highlighter. I skimmed through the case files of the three murders, then borrowed Ruth's laptop and logged onto her Nexis account, perusing stories about McGavin's investigation, cutting and pasting anything that looked interesting into a notepad file for her. In the late afternoon, Ruth yawned. "I'm falling asleep. I'll put on some coffee." She got up and headed for the kitchen.

I looked away from the article I had just pulled up and found myself thinking of my partner, seeing her sitting across from me in that crowded squad room, oblivious to the ringing phones and the clattering keyboards as she went over some stubborn case. Robin would comb her fingers through her hair as she read, and then she would look up and stare right through me as she worked an idea out and then her eyes would sharpen as they focused on something out on the far horizon, and her lips would part as she saw it at last, the thing we'd missed all this time—

It seemed so real for a moment, Robin there, about to speak, and then it vanished. My chest ached a little, some splinter of loss lodged deep inside. I took a deep breath and pinched the skin between my eyes before looking back at the computer. And that was when a name on the screen suddenly came into focus. As if it was the thing she was about to say to me: Hey, what about this guy?

Julian Flyte. He was one of several small kids who had been questioned about a summer art program that the police alleged was a cover for systematic sexual exploitation. He was articulate for a five-year-old and a quote from him conveyed the nightmarish nature of the case, handy for reporters short on facts.

Why was his name so familiar?

I did a full text search with his name and scanned through the sixteen headlines that came up. All but one had dates in the mideighties. But that one explained a teasing idea half-formed in my mind. It was a recent piece from a Boston paper about a rich kid who got off when a rape charge was dismissed. The story covered a half dozen similar cases, one of them from several years ago involving a freshman at Harvard, the son of the well-known author and lecturer J. B. Flyte. The freshman had been accused of rape, but the charges were dropped.

I'd seen Julian Flyte's name in the case files. Cobbett knew about his starring role in McGavin's investigation and, when he learned Flyte had moved back to the area not long before the first abduction, the chief apparently was curious enough to run him through the system. In addition to the rape charge in Cambridge, there had been possession busts in Boston and Brookline, neither of them resulting in a conviction. Flyte had voluntarily come in for questioning, but as soon as Cobbett asked about the rape, his lawyer had ended it, firmly. But Cobbett's question told me what was left out of the newspaper story: The rape charges that had been dropped involved a thirteen-year-old girl.

So Julian Flyte was now an adult with sexual tastes that may have been shaped by that early encounter with sexual abuse—whether the abuse was at the hands of the art program teachers or thanks to McGavin's imagination and all the media attention. Could coaxing testimony about deviant sexual acts from a five-year-old child lay down land mines in his psyche that would trip off years later?

I pulled the phone over and called Cobbett. He wasn't available, but the dispatcher connected me to Bobby. "We're kind of busy down here. What do you need?"

"A guy named Flyte was questioned after the first homicide. Do you know if he's been looked at since? I was just looking over some old news accounts. He was accused of raping a thirteen-year-old a few years ago."

"Down in Massachusetts. The charges were dropped."

"He also was a star witness for McGavin during his sex-ring investigation, back when he was five. From what I've seen in the press reports, his testimony led to arrests of at least three teachers and implicated several other adults. I was thinking that someone who was made to believe he had been abused and who has a history of sexual violence against young girls might be worth a look."

"We looked. The rape in Cambridge was statutory, not violent. Okay, the girl was young, but so was he, and it was consensual. I'm not saying I like it, but it happens. And if being involved in that investigation as a child was enough to make people nuts, we'd have a town full of seriously fucked-up individuals." You do, I almost said, but this was his hometown and he seemed uncharacteristically touchy today.

As I hung up, Ruth returned with mugs of coffee and I told her what I'd learned. "Dad interviewed him?"

"He tried. The kid's lawyer wouldn't let him answer many questions." I reached for the box of case files and flipped through them until I found the interview transcript. "I'm going to see if a friend back home can find more information on this guy."

"How will a friend in Chicago find information about a person in Maine?"

I logged onto my E-mail account. "He's really good with computers. He does me occasional favors after I helped him out once. There was this big child pornography bust when he was just getting started and the CPD seized his computers even though he wasn't involved. But there was some stuff on a hard drive to do with a divorce case he was working for a police lieutenant's wife which I agreed to delete for him." I typed out a message with Flyte's vitals and asked Clayton to find out anything he could, including what Flyte was up to on the dates of the three abductions. Phone records or charge card purchases at local businesses could confirm whether he was in the area. I sent the message, then packed up the case files and returned them to the other room.

Back in the study, Ruth was hunched over her work, lost in concentration. I lifted her hair and nuzzled her neck. "Hey, quit that. Your housemates are back."

Their voices rattled in the quiet house. "The fuck're you talking about?" Flaherty said. "I leaned, okay?"

"You should have leaned harder." Forché was storming around the kitchen, banging into things, slamming doors. "Give me one of them beers. I'll drink it in the shower." We heard her climbing the stairs, a door slam, the shower start up.

Flaherty, Sam Adams bottle in hand, stuck his head around the door. "The security forces have arrived."

"We heard," Ruth said.

"Yeah, well." He tipped the bottle up and drank half the beer in three thirsty gulps. He frowned in concentration, then belched and relaxed. "The good news is, we have a suspect in custody for the assault on you, Slovo. The bad news is he's small fry and he won't give us anything bigger. Got old, trying to get anywhere with him. Hours of it. And then I get nothing but grief out of Forché all the way home. Hey, Ruth, I'm making a chowder, why don't you join us?"

"I usually fix something for my dad."

"Give him a call. I'll make enough to go around."

Ruth went out to help Flaherty and I went back to my file of news clips, but the pulsing anger that came with the memory of the shotgun blasts, those hands grabbing at me, made it hard to focus. I closed my eyes and massaged my temples. When I opened them again Forché was in the room, bending over the trash can by the desk. She gave me an evil leer. "Congratulations." She pulled out the used rubber with a crumpled Kleenex and waggled it obscenely.

"Fuck off, Forché."

"Hey, I'm happy for you. You had that look guys get when they need to get laid. We arrested one of the dirtbags that beat you up. Tom 'Kid-Gloves' Flaherty failed to gain his cooperation." She dropped the rubber back into the trash from shoulder height, making bombing sound effects as it dropped.

"So, what were you doing while he was screwing up the interview?"

"Lucky me, I was watching through the glass. All because I bumped the perp a little when we made the arrest. Took a few stitches, so big deal." She shrugged. "Asshole resisted arrest."

"Happens. How'd you find this guy anyway?"

"He had a few too many last night and started bragging about breaking some pervert's fingers. It got back to us. Should have let me take a turn with him. I need another beer." She stalked off.

More voices joined the clamor. I saved my notes, disentangled myself from the laptop, and limped out into the kitchen. Bobby was sitting at the table next to a freckled woman with a healthy, outdoor look about her, familiar from the counter at the cop shop. "Hi. You're the dispatcher, right?"

"Irene Lacey," she said. "Good to see you up and around."

"You sure you should be out of bed?" Bobby sounded doubtful.

"I'm fine." Cobbett looked like he was the one that should be in bed. His skin was sagging and he could use a shave. "Good work, that arrest," I told the chief to cheer him up, but ruined it by adding, "Anything new in the homicide investigation?"

Cobbett seemed to be drifting off to sleep with his eyes open so Bobby finally said, "Well, Lyle's disappeared."

"Oh, great. More vigilante stuff? Someone got to him?"

"Yes, but not a vigilante." Forché was by the stove, sniffing at the chowder. "An undercover vice cop had a meet set up with him to buy some shit. Lyle didn't show. Come to find out the local heavies objected to him breaking into their business, told him to take his entrepreneurial impulses elsewhere. Not in so many words."

"No, what we hear they actually said was they would pull his nuts off with a pair of pliers and stuff them down his throat." Flaherty frowned. "More salt?"

Forché tasted from the spoon he proffered. "Nope, perfect."

They filled bowls with creamy chowder, thick with clams and chunks of potato, butter beading on the surface under a sprinkling of paprika. The aroma made me suddenly ravenous. "What about Ardis, did she book too?" I asked.

"No. Lyle left his lady behind."

"Think she'll be any more forthcoming without him around?"

Forché opened her mouth to speak, but Cobbett growled, "About what? She doesn't know anything about those murders."

I looked at the gloom in his face and changed the subject. "Say, I noticed you interviewed one of the key witnesses in McGavin's case. Guy named Julian Flyte." Bobby gave me a "not again" look.

Cobbett nodded. "Yeah. He was only a kid at the time. Somehow the press got hold of him. Once that happened, he became an important part of McGavin's strategy."

"What do you mean?" Forché asked.

Cobbett shrugged. "McGavin used the press to give credibility to his investigation. The more times people read about it in the papers, the more they would assume it all really happened. And it meant the people involved would be invested, too. Hard to say, 'Gee, I was just making it all up' after you're on record in *The New York Times*. Think how embarrassing that would be." He took a roll and wrenched it in two. "I wonder about parents that would let reporters ask their five-year-old how it felt to be sexually abused." He looked down at his bread in his hands as if wondering how it got there.

"This five-year-old grew up and went off to college and raped a kid," I said. "Thirteen years old. He moved back here just before these murders started. Do we know where he was when Marcy went missing?"

Cobbett's eyes weren't sleepy anymore, they were sharp as razor wire. "No, we don't. We didn't ask him. See, his family has money. People like Ardis who can't afford a lawyer have to spend hours not telling us anything, whereas rich folks like Julian Flyte don't even have to listen to the question." I had to look away, his face was so full of frustrated bitterness. "The same family that falls all over itself telling the world about how their five-year-old was sodomized by a half dozen adults over the course of a summer withholds comment when we're trying to figure out who raped and butchered three little girls. That's pretty fucking hilarious."

An uncomfortable silence settled on the room. "Flyte wasn't abused, though, was he?" Ruth said finally. "The stories he told, weren't they the product of suggestion?"

"Of course." Cobbett carefully set the mutilated bread on the edge of his plate. "Sorry, sweetheart. I'm so goddamned tired I hardly know what I'm saying."

"The prosecutor wants us to focus on locating Lyle Penny at the moment," Flaherty said from the stove where he was refilling his bowl.

"There's still no evidence against Ardis and Lyle beyond that witness seeing their car near the house the night Marcy was abducted, right?" Nobody corrected me. "I'm with Cobbett, it's a waste of time. Lyle's too stupid, and Ardis's interest in kids is only in how they can be exploited to satisfy the men in her life. This isn't their crime. First of all, your guy's smart, he has a lot of patience and plans things out to the smallest detail. He's someone who's been involved in an investigation in the past. Someone who knows a lot about police procedure, but carries a grudge against law enforcement, who feels a need to make fools of us in some public way. Someone who knows firsthand how powerful public opinion is, who whips people up so that they will come to participate in the violence. He's just as motivated by their reaction as he is by the crime itself, and it drives him to make it worse each time to up the ante. It's a cycle that's going to keep accelerating until the town goes up in flames. Or he's caught."

"This is amazing." Flaherty dropped his jaw. "What's his name? You got his address handy? We'll run right over after supper and nab him."

"I don't know who it is, I'm just saying that's the profile."

"Oh, a *profile*. Hold on, you forgot the part about torturing animals as a kid."

"Yeah, and what about the bed-wetting?" Forché complained. "He's doing a profile and he didn't put in bed-wetting? What kind of a behavioral scientist are you, Slovo?"

"It's just what I got out of looking at the files," I mumbled, embarrassed. "I know it doesn't help." But I couldn't help thinking that Will Sylvester had never been convicted of abusing his child, but he'd lost his job, his place in the community, his family. How much anger was there, inside that quiet shell?

After dinner, as Ruth was getting her coat, Cobbett

pulled me aside. "I've been thinking about your description of the killer. What you said could be on the money and Sylvester fits. Is there any chance you can get somewhere with him soon?"

"I'm making a move tomorrow. I'll let you know how it goes."

"Good. If you can't get close, that's the breaks. But if he's working in a cycle and the next one will be even worse—" He broke off, unable to finish the sentence.

CHAPTER 14

In the morning I opened the closet that held the hot water heater, adjusted a valve in the gas line, and then called Will Sylvester to report the hot water was on the blink. He promised he'd be by sometime in the late morning to fix it.

I tried to use one of the computers Bryn had set up to check my E-mail, but couldn't get past the logon screen. When Ruth arrived, I borrowed her laptop. Clayton had sent two attachments. I clicked on the first, a skimpy dossier on Sylvester. Contrary to Clay's boasts, he couldn't get everything, but he did find out that Sylvester had a misdemeanor drug rap from college days, and that he'd had knee surgery in his early twenties for which he'd been prescribed Darvocet. There was also a brief story from the *Lewiston Sun-Journal* that reported he'd lost his job as a high school teacher after his wife's accusations came out. The second attachment was much more substantial.

"You might be interested in this, Ruth. Looks as if Julian Flyte's brush with fame as a tyke was what got his father's career off the ground. While escorting his little boy on the talk show circuit, Daddy got to know people in showbiz. Which maybe caused some strains; Julian's parents divorced when he was nine. Where's Tally's Harbor?"

"Twelve miles down the coast." She came to sit beside me on the bed.

"That's where he grew up. After the divorce, Julian lived there with his mother and visited his famous father now and then when Dad wasn't too busy motivating people. Went off to Harvard but didn't finish, got incompletes in everything that he didn't flunk that first year, then dropped out. I guess wasting time with all those cops and shit after the rape charge, it interfered with his studies. But looks like he supported himself with a little genteel drug dealing among the college crowd."

"One of the benefits of going to a good school. You make such useful career connections." She rubbed my thigh.

I scrolled down. "Mostly party drugs, although towards the end he was supplying skag to the ultrahip. He got busted a couple of times but whaddya know, nothing ever came of it. His daddy can afford very expensive lawyers. He moved back to Tally's Harbor about a year ago, after his last bust."

"Just in time for the murders. How did your friend get this stuff, anyway?"

"Mostly from the Net. The drug busts, that came from a call to law enforcement."

"They gave a PI that information over the phone?"

"He may have created a convincing context for the phone call."

"In other words, he lied."

"Right," I mumbled indistinctly, her lips against mine, then detached myself from her long enough to set the laptop on the floor, out of harm's way.

Ruth was just tucking her shirt into her jeans, her hair falling around her face, when the door to the kitchen opened. "Oh, jeez. I totally forgot the caretaker was coming by." She threw me my shirt. "Hurry up and dress." She burrowed in her purse, found a hairbrush.

"You know what I really need?" I said, pulling the shirt on obediently. "I'm out of smokes. Could you pick some up for me?"

"It's a rotten habit."

"I know, but . . . I got a lot of stress in my life, you know? Please, Ruth?"

She frowned at me but I could tell she was weakening. "Okay, but will you think about quitting?"

"Sure."

"I mean really, Slovo."

"Well . . . I tried before, it was awful. I went nuts."

"It's so unhealthy. And it smells bad."

"Yeah, but . . . it smells bad?"

"And your mouth tastes pretty grungy."

"Man. Okay, I'll think about it. Jeez."

I heard her greet Will as she went out to her car, exchange some small talk. Then I heard him moving around by the little closet off the bathroom where the hot water heater was. I picked up my cane and went to join him, catching sight of myself in the bathroom mirror as I passed. The bruise on my left cheek was beginning to sport a green-and-yellow rim and the gash on my forehead was still red and puckered. I hobbled over to where he was kneeling on the floor, his head deep in the closet examining the inner workings of the hot water heater. I bent to see what he was up to, resting my hand near the copper gas line, and casually turned the valve I'd shut. "Hey, Will."

"How you doing?" He didn't look up.

"Not too bad. Wanted to thank you."

He stuck an arm around to the back of the gadget, concentrating on something back there, not looking at me. "What for?"

"Calling it in. Getting the search started."

"That's all right. Don't see anything wrong here. I'll try relighting the pilot." It lit and the gas whooshed to life. "Huh. Seems to be working now. Let me know if..." He looked at me at last and his words died away.

"Yeah, I know, I'm a mess, right? Those guys, they got a little carried away. You want a cup of coffee? There's some ready in the kitchen."

"I don't know, I really should be going."

"So many mansions, so little time, huh?" I started out in front of him, making a show of leaning on my cane and struggling along. "Sure you won't join me? Truth is, I get kind of spooked out here when no one's with me. So if you could stay, uh...you know, just till Ruth gets back. Unless you really have to go." I got two mugs onto the counter from the cupboard. "Goddamn it. Sorry, I can't..."

"Here, I got it," he murmured. He poured two cups, set them on the table.

"Thanks, Will." I pulled a chair out and eased myself into it, making a show of adjusting my leg. "Funny thing was, those guys were so sure I deserved what they were doing to me. They thought I killed those girls. Three of 'em now, Marcy being the most recent. You know the girls I'm talking about?" He nodded, sipped at the coffee, keeping his eyes averted. "They needed someone to blame. You could tell, it made them feel good to do something about it," I said. He looked over at me, his face closed and tight. "People think you hurt a child, they can get ugly. Real ugly."

He stared down into his coffee.

"Because they think, a *kid*, you know? Makes them want to tear you apart. But you didn't actually hurt your daughter, did you?"

"How did you hear about that?" It was almost a whimper.

"Did you hurt her, Will?"

His mouth looked as tight as his rigid shoulders. "No," he said at last, the syllable sounding deep in his chest.

"That's what I figured. I see this all the time. Messy divorce, your wife wanted to hang something on you."

"Someone makes a complaint like that, doesn't matter whether they can prove anything or not, your life is ruined. I haven't seen my daughter now in...not even a picture. Nothing." He had grown pale under his weathered tan. It made him seem gray and years older. "She's twelve now. I can't even imagine what she looks like. I don't even know where they live."

"Doesn't seem fair, does it?"

"They had me in for questioning. Hours and hours. I hate cops." The last words came out in a growl. He looked at me then, challengingly.

"They just wanted a confession."

"But I didn't do it."

"Let me tell you how this works. Those cops probably pushed you just to see if you'd cave, you know? I mean, people lie, they lie to you all the time, you gotta push 'em some, it's part of the job. You didn't cave, though, that's a real good thing, Will. They had to let you go, right?"

"She said...see, they said my daughter was, told them I...but that's..." Sylvester was wound so tight I thought he might break the mug between his hands. "I didn't hurt her." It was the only thing he seemed to be able to get out whole.

"I interviewed a suspect once. Turned out he had fucked his daughter for, like, years." Interesting effect: Sylvester ducked his head down over his coffee mug, resting it between the palms of his hands, gripping his temples. "Funny thing was, the guy loved this kid. The sex, I don't know. Maybe it just felt right to him, maybe he thought she liked it too, no harm done. I mean, sex is kind of funny, people have different attitudes. Guy went to prison, though." Sylvester made another funny noise. "Whoa, take it easy. You didn't hurt your daughter. And you didn't lose your cool with the cops. So you're all right."

"I lost my job. I haven't seen my kid in six years. I'm all right?" He laid his hands flat against each other, like the praying hands picture. They were shaking. "Nobody here knew, nobody looked at me like that, they didn't...but now this, you had to go and...*why couldn't you leave it alone?*" He was suddenly on his feet, his chair shoved back so abruptly it tipped over, and he was standing there, crouched like a spring wound into a dangerous coil. I stood too and he shoved me on the chest with both hands, making me step back, then shoved harder and I hit the closet door behind me with a clatter and teetered there, nearly losing my balance.

He stared at me, horrified. "Oh, my God, I'm—are you all right? I didn't—"

"I'm okay. Look, I'm sorry, I'm sorry about your daughter. Cool it, all right? Calm down."

He rubbed his face with both hands, hard. "Oh, man."

"It's okay. I won't tell anybody."

He reached for his toolbox, a dazed look in his eyes. "I really have to go...."

"Thanks for the, you know, the water heater. And hey, any time you want to talk—I understand what you're going through."

He headed for the door, a little clumsy as he tried to open it. I listened to the sound of his pickup dying away into the distance. Then I went back to the bedroom and made a phone call.

The dispatcher put me on hold. Ruth came in and handed me a pack of cigarettes. "What happened to Sylvester?" she asked. I stared at her stupidly. "I thought he'd be here. Did he fix the hot water heater?"

"Oh, yeah. He had to leave. Some other job."

"Who are you calling?"

"Your father asked me to check up on something." She raised her eyebrows questioningly but when I didn't explain she turned away.

"What now?" Cobbett growled, preoccupied.

"That information? That, uh, that stuff you wanted me to look into? I got something you might be interested in."

"Hell you talking about?"

"We talked about it yesterday."

"Sylvester?" He was suddenly alert. "I'll send someone over to pick you up."

CHAPTER 15

I sat across the desk from Cobbett, a cup of bitter coffee in my hand. "Sylvester wants to talk, but he's scared. I think I can get him to confide."

"How long will it take?"

"I'm not sure. He seems pretty close to breaking point. Thought I'd let him stew today, follow up tomorrow and—"

The phone rang. He picked it up and his face grew blank as he listened. "They're here now?" he asked. "Right. But not me. Bobby and Forché will do the interview. Get hold of Flaherty."

He put the phone down, shaking his head. "This case just gets weirder. Ardis Burke is here with McGavin. She's got something to tell us."

Flaherty, Cobbett, and I stood outside the interview room watching through the window as Bobby and Forché started the interview. Ardis looked different. When I'd seen her before, Lyle's hand groping her ass, she seemed hard and sassy and full of insolent pride. Now she sat in a wooden chair pulled tight into herself, her face drained of everything but wariness. Smoke trailed up from a cigarette that trembled in one hand. She was staring at the edge of the table in front of her. Voices came across the system, sounding tinny.

"So, what's it about?" Bobby asked. He lounged in a chair, tipping it onto its back legs and jiggling one foot. Forché kept her eyes fixed on the woman.

"Ardis has some information she wants to share." McGavin glanced at the mirrored window, aware of his audience.

"Ms. Burke?" Forché's voice was a low, intimate murmur, and her eyes stayed on the woman until she looked back. "Mr. McGavin isn't a lawyer. He can't give you legal advice."

"Don't want a lawyer."

"I'm here in the capacity of a friend." McGavin reached over and touched her arm, but she had her gaze fixed on the table again.

"How long you been friends?" Bobby managed to put a world of implications into the words.

"I think it would be more appropriate to treat her with dignity, Munro, instead of clowning around," McGavin shot back. "This isn't easy for her."

"What's he up to?" Flaherty muttered, his eyes fixed on the scene on the other side of the glass.

"Do you want Mr. McGavin to be here?" Forché asked Ardis.

Ardis took a toke on the cigarette and let the smoke leak out of her mouth before she answered. "Sure."

"Okay. What do you want to tell us?"

Ardis didn't speak, and McGavin sat forward. "I'd like to lay some ground rules here. She has some information you need. She wants to come forward, but she needs to be assured that you'll take into account her cooperation."

"Mr. McGavin?" For a moment Forché sounded like herself again. "You are not competent to give legal advice. We're here to talk to Ms. Burke. I'd appreciate it if you'd bear that in mind." Their eyes locked for a moment before she turned her attention back to the woman across from her, her voice gentler. "Take your time."

Ardis's eyes flicked up at Forché again, but she finished smoking the cigarette before she spoke. I sensed

Cobbett's muscles straining with impatience as he stood motionless beside me.

"They'll kill me," she said at last, that raspy voice coming out reluctantly. "Be better off in jail."

"Who'll kill you, Ms. Burke?"

She pulled another cigarette out, scraped a match and lit it. After a few puffs she put a palm over her face and seemed to shrink into herself even more.

We all waited.

"Okay," she said at last. "Here you go. There's a lot of people involved, it ain't just me and Lyle. I can give you names."

"Involved in what?" Bobby's chair thumped upright.

"Them girls. All of it."

"Whoa, Ms. Burke?" Forché leaned across the table, her tone kind. "Hold on. We need to make you aware of your rights before you say more."

"Shit, who cares about that? You think I'll have rights when they come after me?"

"I'm required to, it's the law. You have the right to remain silent. You don't have to talk to us, understand? Because what you say can and will be used against you in a court of law." Ardis waved her cigarette, pushing it all away, trying to speak, but Forché kept on, her voice growing harder. "You have the right to an attorney." Forché went through it, asking her if she understood. At the end she glanced at Bobby, and said, "We're going to have you sign a form, Ms. Burke."

"Whatever," Ardis muttered, and Bobby rose. "You can call me Ardis," she added, shooting a furtive glance at Forché, who gave her a quick smile.

Bobby came out, shut the door behind him, and exploded. "This is ridiculous. Woman's scared out of her mind."

"Is McGavin telling her she'll get a deal if she talks?" Cobbett was choking in his own fury. "Someone better set her straight: This is a murder investigation. It isn't some witch hunt where you get off if you turn enough people in."

"You want to tell her, boss?"

"It wouldn't be wise for me to be in the same room with McGavin right now. Get 'em separated. Get Forché alone with that woman and get McGavin the fuck out of here."

"Think she'll talk without him?"

"At least we stand a chance of finding out what she really has on her mind."

Bobby went back in and had her sign the form. Then he said, "Time to bow out, McGavin. We need to speak with Ms. Burke alone."

"I'm here to support her."

"I think she can handle it. You okay with this, Ms. Burke?"

Ardis looked over at Forché anxiously, biting her lower lip.

"This isn't easy, Bobby," McGavin insisted. "You, of all people, should realize that."

The color rose from Bobby's collar, flooded patchily into his cheeks. "Ms. Burke, you can talk with Detective Forché, here, one-on-one if you like. Just you and Sabine."

"You were old enough, you should remember it pretty clearly," McGavin said, his voice pleasant but relentless. "Thirteen, fourteen? You know what it's like to tell the cops something that you thought you'd never tell anyone, that you didn't even think could be put into words."

"I don't know what you're talking about, but I'd appreciate it if you'd shut up for a moment and let the woman think." Bobby snatched the form that Ardis had signed.

"I'll talk to her," Ardis said, pointing at Forché with her cigarette. "Just her. One-on-one, like he said."

Ruth had left for home by the time I got back to the house on Hunter's Point. The signs of her work, laptop and papers neatly arranged on the desk, somehow made the room seem emptier. Stretched out on the bed, I found my-self staring at the striations on the wall where the shotgun damage had been repaired. I reached down to make sure the Glock was in its place, tucked between the bed frame and the mattress.

McGavin had wasted no time contacting the press after bringing Ardis in. By the time a uniform was running me home in a cruiser, he was standing on the stairs in front of the station, at the center of a hungry knot of reporters. He was bathed in camera crew lights, the media gods anointing him with their Pentecostal fire as he spoke. Thinking of how much he liked the limelight, I pulled over the laptop, plugged the modem in, and brought up Ruth's Nexis account.

A full text search on his name brought up hundreds of newspaper stories. The first ones were from 1984 and 1985, when his investigation was in full swing. Another burst of articles came out when he published his best-seller, three years later, a mixture of reviews, interviews, and commentary. These were followed by spates of stories that clustered around high-profile cases of child abuse or abduction, where journalists had consulted him as an expert. There were also society page reports on fund-raising events for his foundation. But the stories dwindled in recent years. His public profile seemed to be steadily declining.

Until Bethany Lowell was abducted. After that, his name was back in the news.

I idly scrolled back through the articles, noticing one from the Chicago Sun-Times four years ago. I pulled it up, read the opening paragraphs, and something cold crawled down my spine. An interview with Mike McGavin, the national expert on exploited children, analyzing the brutal murder of little Sharla Peterson. The baby whose dismembered body had been found in Humbolt Park.

My case.

I didn't usually read the Sun-Times. I wasn't even reading the *Trib* back then, not for months. After a string of ugly cases, every one of them closed successfully, I caught a heater that had the mayor's office demanding updates twice a day. It was a bad time and my memories of it weren't very clear, but one thing that came back to me was the way the press kept a vigil outside Area 4 headquarters. Whenever I went through those glass doors they surged at me like a pack of dogs barking and snarling, demanding explanations. I didn't have any.

Apparently McGavin did. The violence of Sharla Peterson's murder had shocked and baffled the city, but he knew exactly what it was: a blood sacrifice made by someone who had dedicated his soul to evil. In his analysis, he brought together elements of satanic cult practices and abnormal psychology, and the profile he sketched out combined behavioral science and fundamentalist beliefs in a compelling portrait of a killer. The way he laid it out, it almost made sense. And that was what was causing a sick, twisting pain in my chest. Because nothing about that case had made sense to me.

I turned the computer off and shuffled to the kitchen. Put the kettle on, found a tea bag and a mug. Poured water in when it boiled and drank a few scalding gulps. As an afterthought I added a couple of inches of Bushmills from a bottle Flaherty had brought with him. I stood by the window but it was dark outside and all I saw was a reflection of my own face.

Hari called, all excited. "I hear a suspect is in custody."

"Where'd you hear that?"

"It's all over the news. I want to hear all the details. Have you had dinner? I could pick up some take-away for us."

"Let's go out. I'm sick of being stuck out here in the woods."

We ended up at a busy seafood joint on the edge of town. We found a table and placed an order. The waitress returned to set a pitcher of beer and two glasses on the table.

Hari chatted her up without effect. As she swept away, he said, too loudly, "Notice how her mouth looks just like a cat's arse?" Then he told me the news he'd heard, most of it suppositions based on McGavin's press conference; I pointed out where it departed from reality and fielded his questions, warning him to keep it down. Hari seemed in an almost manic state of hyped-up fatigue. We'd been attracting stares from the moment we arrived and I couldn't help wondering if any of those hostile glares was directed at me from someone who had been hidden in the shadows behind that blinding circle of light in the cooling tower.

The waitress returned to slap down our orders. The basket in front of me held limp french fries and a roll full of hard twists of deep-fried batter that Hari swore had clams inside. After a few bites I decided to stick to beer. As soon as Hari finished his dinner, I downed what was in my glass and suggested we hit the road.

"You haven't eaten a thing." He snagged some clams out of my basket.

"Let's just go."

"All right, but I have to use the bog first." He grabbed a handful of fries, then headed for the toilets at the back of the restaurant. I left a tip—a generous one to make up for the "cat's arse" remark—and went over to the counter to wait behind a couple that was settling up with the cashier. A pudgy toddler in a pink jacket was weaving around their legs, clinging to their trousers, chattering in some language of her own. She played peek-a-boo around her mother's shins and giggled when I pointed at her and winked. Her mother turned, smiling. The smile crumpled and she snatched her child up. "Tony? Let's get going, huh?" The man glanced from me to his wife, and concrete seemed to settle in his jaw as he put himself between me and his family before shepherding them toward the exit. Things had grown strangely quiet in the big dining room. The cashier took my money without looking at me. She jammed the ticket on a spike beside the cash register with such energy it tore in two.

Hari came up, oblivious to the bristling hostility in the place. "Paid already? Brilliant. Thanks, love," he called to the woman at the register, who fixed us with a look of pure hate. "Ugly slag," he added.

"Sorry," I said as we crossed the parking lot. "Wasn't a good idea, going out."

"Why do you say that? Just because they all act as if you're a deviant psychopath?" He barked a laugh and I could see his teeth glinting in a fierce grin. "Aren't you sensitive. They've given me that treatment for years."

CHAPTER 16

The phone shrilled. I fumbled for it, but heard a dial tone while the ringing kept on; it was one of the extra lines added when Flaherty and Forché moved in. I sat up in bed, rubbed my aching head, and noticed the time: five-thirty.

Hari had stopped at a liquor store after we left the restaurant. The whiskey only fueled his long-smoldering resentment against the benighted town he was stuck in, and he was on an extravagant rant when Flaherty and Forché joined us. Ardis was in custody, they said, but not for murder. She'd made a confession, full of lurid details and names of coconspirators, but over the next few hours as Forché dug deeper it all unraveled.

When confronted with the holes in her story, Ardis panicked, terrified of being alone and unprotected in that house of hers out in the woods. Forché came up with a solution: they took her home and Ardis showed them an unregistered Walther tucked in a bedside drawer. They were able to hold her on a weapons charge so everyone was happy, including the DA, who was finally convinced they couldn't make a good case against her but was already crafting his press release. Even if he stated clearly that the arrest was unrelated to the three murders, people would interpret it in light of McGavin's claims and it might release some of the pressure to make an arrest. It wasn't much to celebrate, but when Hari's bottle was empty Flaherty brought out his Bushmills. I couldn't remember if we'd finished it off or not. In fact, how I got to bed was a mystery to me.

Footsteps hurried down the stairs into the makeshift office in the living room and the ringing stopped. I heard Flaherty's voice, a sharp exclamation, then muttered questions. I located my jeans under the bed and limped out just as he was hanging up the phone. There was only a rumple of blankets to mark where Hari had slept. "What's going on?"

"Another statue went missing last night." Flaherty blinked at me stupidly for a moment, scratching his hairy chest, then headed for the stairs. I went into the kitchen and started coffee. When Flaherty and Forché came down, dressed for work, the coffee was ready.

"What do we know?" I asked.

"It's part of a fountain in the park behind the public library. A little bronze statue of Peter Pan." Flaherty screwed the top onto a thermos and turned to me. "We have two days to stop him. That's all—two days." I could see in his eyes, as he could probably see in mine, what would happen if we didn't.

After they left, I found some Tylenol in the bathroom and downed it with a cupped handful of water. *Two days*. And this time it would be even worse. I saw the body hanging in the woods, sexually invaded in every way, strangled, her skin stripped away, a little girl named Marcy turned into an unrecognizable piece of meat.

How could it be any worse?

Ruth came in at nine. She grimaced and waved a hand in front of her face. I had been going through the case files again. "Sorry. I'll open a window."

"Don't worry about it. I just came to pick up some

notes." She headed to the study. "I got hold of Julian Flyte last night," she called out. "We made an appointment to talk about his role in the child abuse case. We're meeting at a café up on the highway in forty minutes. Maybe some of this smog will have cleared out by the time I get back."

"I'm coming with you."

"Don't be silly. He won't open up to me if you're there. It's a different dynamic with three people. You should understand that, you've done enough interviews."

"Usually when I interview drug-dealing rapists they're cuffed to a chair. That's a dynamic I understand."

"Forget about it, Slovo. I don't need police protection to do an interview."

"What makes you think Flyte'll tell you anything anyway—you're the police chief's daughter."

"He doesn't know that. I still use my married name professionally. Why are you so jumpy, anyway?"

"Ruth, another statue disappeared last night. There's a possibility Flyte's involved in this."

"I already heard about the statue. It was on the radio this morning. All the more reason I should conduct this interview effectively. Nothing's going to happen to me in a public restaurant, Slovo. You're overreacting."

In the end she drove alone up to the highway a little early for the meeting and found a booth at the Harbor Grill. She ordered coffee and arranged a notepad in front of her, a pen, and a small tape recorder. It was after the breakfast rush, so it wasn't too hard for Bryn and me to find an empty booth next to hers. We ordered coffee and Bryn asked for a platter of eggs and sausages and hash browns. My stomach was too knotted up to handle food.

Before we left I had called Cobbett. He was in a meeting with the DA, but Bobby was available. I asked him if he could get me a copy of Julian Flyte's file from the child abuse case. "You're talking about McGavin's investigation? That's so long ago. I don't know if those files are still around." Bobby's responses were duller than usual. The long hours and stress were taking a toll.

"They must be. Cobbett had the one on Ardis Burke. I saw it on his desk. Might want to try his office—he may have pulled any that he thought might bear on the current case." He said he'd check and abruptly hung up.

"After all this, maybe the guy won't show," Bryn muttered. His fingers were drumming the table. He took another look at his watch, the fifth time in three minutes.

"He'll be fashionably late. After all, he was a dealer for the in crowd." I studied him, then added in an undertone, "Speaking of which, it's kind of early for drugs, ain't it?"

He pinched his nose, silently watched the waitress as she put his platter of food down. After she left he looked at me with an embarrassed grin. "Okay, Officer, I confess. I was chasing a bug all night. I set up a relational database a few months ago to collate case information and it crashed yesterday. The data was inaccessible until it was fixed. Coffee just wasn't cutting it." He shrugged.

"Better not let them see you at work messed up."

"I'm careful. And I don't do very often."

I watched him plow into the food, poured myself coffee from the plastic jug the waitress had left for us. "I used the shit when I worked Narcotics. The hours were brutal and you couldn't let your guard down. Got me in trouble at work, though, so I quit. You nail the bug?"

"About six this morning. Just a stupid little mistake in some code. Once you see it, it's so obvious, but I looked for it all afternoon, right through the night. I finally got home and was ready to crash when Ruth called."

"You okay?"

He grinned. "I feel great. I popped another black beauty soon as I got off the phone." The grin faded. "I want to be alert. I don't like this at all." I'd filled him in on the way up, his Ranger following Ruth's car to the restaurant on the highway. "People who go after kids like that..." He put his fork down, wiped his mouth with his hand. "Thirteen years old," he muttered to himself.

I remembered what he had told me about his sister running away at about that age. "What was your sister's name?"

He stirred a fork through the remains of his hash browns. "Eileen."

"She was older than you?"

"Two years younger." He drew a wavy track with the tines of his fork through the grease where his eggs had been. "She had a bad situation at home and I wasn't around to help. I didn't get along with my parents, so I stayed with friends most of the time. Nobody bothered to tell me she was gone for weeks."

A bad situation. At that age, just as girls were showing symptoms of being women, that usually meant sexual abuse. "Did anyone file a missing persons report with the police?"

"I thought about it, but I was afraid they would just send her home. I hope she found something better."

I risked a look at Ruth. She was reading a book, her hair falling around her face. She didn't look nervous. I drank two more cups of coffee. Every time I shifted to ease my hip, I felt the Glock digging into the small of my back.

"This must be him," Bryn muttered.

I glanced up. Skinny, with a wispy beard and hair cut short on the sides, moussed into bleached spikes on top. Clothes that looked worn but which were expensive gear, artfully aged. Three rings in one ear, two in another. A great smile as he asked a waitress a question. I caught all that in a momentary glance, then made myself turn away.

He walked past us, leaving a scent of tobacco in the air. I felt an overwhelming urge to light up, but Ruth had perversely chosen the no-smoking side of the café. I poured a fourth cup of coffee instead.

"Ruth Levin?"

"Oh, hi. You must be Julian Flyte. Thanks so much for agreeing to talk to me."

"No problem. I'm interested in this article you're working on."

She described it using a lot of big, important-sounding words. He asked a couple of questions, using the same vocabulary, but somehow turned it into a joke they shared. Finally, after a laugh, Ruth said, "Look, I have a confession to make." She lowered her voice to impart a confidence. "Forget the fancy critical theory, that's for my editor. I'm old-fashioned. I just want to know what happened."

"Oh, you want to know whether I actually got cornholed by those art teachers when I was five?" He didn't bother to lower his voice.

Ruth didn't speak for a moment. "I want to find out what happened in this town," she said evenly. "Was there child abuse on a large scale? Were there isolated instances that got turned into something else by people who were looking for a conspiracy where there wasn't any? If that happened, why did it happen here, at that point in time?"

Flyte didn't respond, but flagged the waitress and for a few minutes amiably contemplated the benefits of the various breakfast specials. Finally he decided on the Sunrise Skillet. The waitress paused by our table. "Can I get you anything else?" Code words for "time to go." It was approaching lunch now and the tables were getting full. She was tapping her pencil on her pad and when she looked down at me I realized my bruised face and splinted fingers were not especially welcome.

"How about a hamburger and some fries?" I said, buying time.

"And more coffee," Bryn murmured.

Ruth was saying, "So, are you willing to let me ask you some questions?"

"So you can get at the truth?" Flyte laughed. "You know the paradox of Schrödinger's cat?"

"I've heard of it."

"Of course you have, physics one-oh-one. The cat is in

a box with a vial of poison and a radioactive atom that has a fifty/fifty chance of emitting a gamma ray which will release the poison. You can't tell what's happened in that box, but the probability is equal that the cat is alive or dead. Two waveforms, two possibilities at once inside that box. You're about to lift the lid of that box, make the waveforms collapse. Is the cat alive or dead? Only, in this case, was the abuse real or a lie? Was he cornholed or not?"

"The problem with Schrödinger's cat," Ruth said without missing a beat, "is that the cat knows what happened long before I lift the lid. My lifting the lid doesn't collapse the waveform. It either happened or it didn't."

"And you call yourself a science writer."

"Excuse me?"

"That's what you do, right? When you're not slumming in a place like this, writing dreck for a weekly paper? I checked up on you."

My fingers were pressed against the mug, aching with tension. "Fair enough," Ruth said evenly. "You're wise to be cautious about who you talk to. I can give you my résumé if you like. And you can call the magazine and see if I'm for real."

"I know you're for real. As much as anything is. Slippery thing, reality. What makes you start this project now?"

"The magazine's editor approached me about it."

"Nothing like a juicy serial murder to boost circulation. Are you going to connect the murders of those three girls to the sex abuse case?"

"Do you think they're connected?"

I didn't hear an answer. After a pause Ruth went on. "I'm really not interested in anything but the events that happened here—or didn't—back in the eighties. Here and elsewhere. There were similar cases in different parts of the country and in hindsight it looks as if they were all, basically—" She hunted for a word.

"Bullshit," he supplied helpfully.

"That's one way to put it. Some critics call it a subversion myth, a social response when people feel their common values are threatened. Only from what I've found so far, there may be a grain of truth in the stories. It's how that core of truth got extended and reinterpreted that fascinates me. I'd like to hear your story."

"My story." An ironic sound to the words. "Is that thing on?"

"The tape recorder? No. Would you mind if I used it? It's easier if I don't have to rely on my notes."

"I really hate the way my voice sounds on tape."

"Me too. I'm always appalled when I hear myself."

"Why? You have a great voice. Sexy."

"Can we do the interview? It would help me out, but if you don't feel comfortable you don't have to do it."

"I have the right to remain silent?" Now there was another kind of irony in his tone: knowing and sharp. I glanced at Bryn. His jaw was clenched and his eyes were sharp with anxiety. The waitress came by carrying food for someone else, but paused to say indignantly to me, "No smoking in this section." I must have pulled out my cigarettes without thinking and had one hanging between my lips, a book of matches in my hand.

"Sorry," I muttered, putting it down, straining to hear Ruth's words.

"I can't make you talk to me, obviously. If you do, though, my editor will probably have the article vetted by the magazine's legal counsel. We won't publish anything you could sue us over."

The waitress cheerfully told Flyte his breakfast would be just a few minutes. He had the kind of charm that worked on waitresses. She didn't make any promises about my burger when she passed my way.

"I don't want to be taped," Flyte said at last.

"All right."

"What do you want to know?"

"I want to know what happened to you when you were five. And I want to know how that experience, whatever it was, has affected your life since."

"That's straightforward. You plan to talk to a lot of people?"

"I'd like to. But you're especially important because of your age at the time and because of the extensive coverage the press gave your case. Do you remember that, the reporters talking to you?"

"I remember being on television."

"What was it like?"

"Boring, mostly. Waiting around the set, people not knowing what to say to me, looking at me like I was some kind of little monster. They kept giving me snacks, sodas, coloring books and shit, but they didn't know what to say to me. Sometimes I'd sit around for hours while my father went looking for ass to kiss."

"Your father, J. B. Flyte?"

"He's famous now. But back then he had to hustle. At the tender age of five, I was his ticket to the big time."

"How do you feel about that?"

"I think it's funny. He preaches this feel-good line of motivational psychobabble but got his start taking me around as a traveling freak show. Hey, take a look at my seriously screwed-up kid!" He laughed. "He's such a monumental asshole. Can't believe people pay to listen to his garbage. I guess I shouldn't be surprised. People want to be told there's a reason behind the shit that happens."

"You resent the way he used your experience?"

"Resent it? He gets twenty thousand dollars just to run his bullshit at a corporate retreat. Why would I object to that?" His breakfast arrived. I could hear cutlery clinking. He said through a full mouth, "You suppose that's why people still listen to Mike McGavin? Because he has an explanation for bad shit? The devil makes us do it. Beats thinking it's just the way people are. God's design." He laughed. "You ever hear my dad speak?"

"No."

"Man, you should buy the tapes. You can get the whole series on video—ten hours that will change your life. Then you can sign up for the newsletter, get the E-mail update service, attend weekend retreats conveniently located at ten regional resorts. Learn how to deal with shame and guilt and all that bad stuff, how to feel wonderful about your miserable, fucked-up life. It's simple if you follow his advice."

"You sound angry." There was a pause; I wished I could see his expression. "How do you deal with it? Do you think about it a lot?"

"Aren't you doing this out of order? You forgot to ask what happened."

"All right. Let's talk about what happened."

"What do you think you'll see when you lift the lid of that box?" He didn't sound amused anymore. "Could be you'll find that I got signed up for that summer art program, because this was before my dad got famous and my parents couldn't afford anything better than a cheap day camp in the blue-collar town next door." His voice was deadpan, but it turned thin and cold as he went on. "And maybe you'll find out we started the day with some finger paints or messed around with clay, and after that Deirdre would get out the video camera and we'd all play one of our games. Like take off all of our clothes and let the grownups touch us and act all funny." His voice went softer and even more toneless. "Maybe after a couple of weeks of playing those games they'd take one of us to the little room in back and Angie would hold the camera while Deirdre and Steve did things to each other and things to me and sometimes it hurt but they always cuddled me after and told me how much they loved me and how special I was. Really special, but I shouldn't tell anyone else because they wouldn't let me go to the back room, I couldn't be special anymore." I heard him take a breath and go on in a lower tone, almost too soft now to be heard. "It could be that some nights when I undressed for bed I'd hide my underpants in the trash because I knew nobody should know and if my mom saw the stains I'd get in trouble. Maybe that's what you'll find when you lift that lid. You think?"

Then his words stopped altogether and I heard instead the clink of a fork on a plate. The sound of coffee being poured.

"You want some?" Flyte asked in a normal tone. Ruth didn't answer. "Maybe that's what you'll find. Maybe not." His tone had become cheerful. "Could be all that happened was the police asked me questions and I tried to answer them the way they wanted. Either way, I was eager to please. I was an easygoing kid. Still am."

"I don't know what to make of this," Ruth said softly.

"Make it whatever you want. I'd do some market research, figure out which version works best these days."

"But you were . . . I mean, the things you just . . ."

"I've had a lifetime of practice. You know Bud Rafferty, the indie film producer? He did that film about Jeffrey Dahmer, got a lot of attention at Sundance a couple of years ago? He wants to make one about Brimsport. With these murders the timing is perfect. So, I appreciate hearing about your project, but I've already promised Bud he gets my exclusive story. The only thing we have to figure out is whether I'm a victim of sex abuse or of a police investigation gone mad. Which do you think is more compelling?"

"Don't you know which one it was?"

"I don't give a shit. All I know is everyone loves a freak show. I mean, look how they're responding to these murders." He laughed. "Better than sex."

"I'm not sure what you mean by that."

"They love it, they can't wait for the next episode. And

now it's time for another kid to disappear. Two days and counting. People are going to go nuts with excitement."

"That's extremely cold-blooded."

"You're so pissed off." He was laughing so loudly people were turning to look. "You should see your face, it's really something."

"Are you making light of this situation because of the way the police treated you when you were charged with rape of a thirteen-year-old child?" Ruth kept her voice down but it had a tone I knew from my own experience. She'd lost control of the interview and was trying for a last-ditch score with a wild shot.

"She wanted it, I don't care what she said later. And you know something? It was really good. She was so fresh and I've had many, many years of experience. Too bad Angie wasn't there with her camera." He stood up. "Say, this was great. Your father wanted to ask me about this before, but my lawyer was with me so I couldn't wind him up. Lawyers have no idea how to have fun." I found I was out of my seat now, adrenaline making decisions for me as he leaned close over the table, putting his face up to Ruth's as if about to kiss her. "Good luck with your article," he whispered, his lips almost brushing her skin, making it sound obscene somehow. When he turned he grinned, looking me up and down. "Great look, Officer. I like the ratty shoes, nice touch." He peered around me to wave at Bryn. "Say hi to the boss."

CHAPTER 17

I feel so stupid," Ruth raged, driving back to the house on Hunter's Point. Bryn had left on his own from the restaurant, almost staggering with weariness now that his amphetamine rush was over.

"Why? You played him really well."

"I can't believe I paid for his breakfast. He manipulated me."

"You didn't get rattled, though, not until the end. And by then he wasn't going to give you anything anyway."

"He had me going with that story. I felt bad for him."

"And then he pulled the rug out from under you. Annoying, isn't it?" It didn't mean what he said didn't happen, though. Some of it had sounded rooted in reality. I hoped Bobby had found Flyte's file from the old investigation; it would be interesting to see if there was a social services report or a medical exam included. "You got one thing out of him: He's really angry with his father."

"Unless that was acting, too."

"It was real. And no wonder, it's pretty awful, using your kid like that."

"Do you think he could be responsible for these murders?" Ruth asked.

"In some ways he fits. He may be angry with the town,

wants to show them up. He's hostile to law enforcement. And the pranks, somehow I think that would be his style."

"There's the sexual interest in girls, too."

"Right. Though it's hard to say whether it's the same kind. I mean, some pedophiles think kids like sex, they're doing them a favor introducing them to it. Others get off on inflicting pain, humiliation, breaking the rules. They usually were sexually abused themselves, and they use kids to take revenge. I'm not sure which kind he is, but whoever is killing those children is the second kind."

"You've dealt with this before."

"Way too much."

As soon as we got back to the house the phone rang. Ruth reached for it and, after a brief exchange, covered the receiver with her hand. "It's somebody from the *Chicago Tribune*, Maura Doyle. You want to talk?"

It was Monday, I realized, feeling it like a fist in my chest. The day the CPD brass was having that meeting to decide my future. "Give it here. Maura? What's up?"

"Who's the lady?"

"A friend. What's going on?"

"Just out of the hospital and you're already fooling around? Fast worker, Slovo."

"Maura! What's happening out there?" There was something too cheerful about her voice. It filled me with dread.

"Okay, okay. Look, none of this is official yet, and the superintendent has to sign off on it tomorrow when he's back from some trip, but they're certain he will. They're going to suspend you."

"For how long?"

"Thirty days. Without pay. The main beef is the way you left town when asked to remain available, which showed, I quote, 'a serious lack of professional judgment.'"

"What else?" There had to be more, for thirty days.

"You had been uncooperative and obstructive in the investigation into the murder of a fellow officer." I heard papers rustling. "And, this was a little weird, some evidence had come to light that an unreported substance-abuse problem— they must be talking about what that sergeant of yours said— may have adversely affected your handling of a previous case which they're planning to reexamine."

"Which case?"

"I don't know. It doesn't say here in this draft report that I'm not supposed to have. How do you feel about this?"

"Like I've been fucked over."

"I can't use that as a quote, Slovo."

"You want a quote? Here: Tell 'em Robin Freeling was a good cop, the best, and they're wasting their time trying to nail me instead of moving this investigation forward. This whole thing about drugs, it's garbage. The people responsible for her death are still out there and they aren't even looking. Did you get that? The way they're handling this case, it's fucked, it's, it's... hell, you think of a big word for it, Maura, you know what I'm saying."

"Yeah, yeah. Let's just say 'dismissing potential leads prematurely, unwilling to examine alternative theories,' blah blah blah. Now, these other allegations—"

"I gotta talk to somebody about this." I disconnected and punched in another number.

Ruth asked me, "That meeting? You got suspended?"

"Thirty days." Then the voice came on the phone. "Zarelli."

"It's Slovo."

"Oh, hiya. Slovo, how you doing?" Another voice full of false heartiness. "Hey, that guy? The, uh, that Jewish guy? He came through for us."

"What are you talking about?"

"That old guy you told me about ID'd the rapist for us. Haven't made the collar yet, but we got a warrant out. Thanks for that tip."

"No problem. Donny, that meeting. They had the meeting, right? I got suspended."

"You heard already?" His voice flattened.

"What kind of case are they building against me?"

Zarelli sighed. "Man, I can't talk about that."

"Oh, too many people around? Can I call you tonight, at home?"

"No, that won't . . . I can't talk to you about it, okay?"

"What do you mean?"

"That kind of meeting is confidential. Slovo, you gotta understand—it would be totally inappropriate."

"What the—*inappropriate*?"

"It's, it's the principle of the thing, Slovo. If people went around blabbing everything that goes on in these sensitive meetings . . . Look, talk to your lawyer, you can appeal."

"Donny, I'm getting hung out to dry here. You talk about principles, these fucking principles of yours. What about justice?"

"I'm going to hang up now. I don't appreciate being yelled at."

"I don't appreciate being railroaded, Donny." It was getting hard to breathe, a red flush of anger coloring everything. "Whoever killed Robin is walking around out there. Don't you care?"

"I'm not going to tell you what was said in this meeting. I told you already, these things are confidential and I'm not—" His words were drowned out in the roar of noise and heat surging in my head, blinding me for a moment.

Then it cleared. I sat on the bed, looking at the phone that I must have slammed down, my head swimming. Ruth was sitting beside me. "Slovo?"

"What?"

"Who were you just talking to?"

"A guy." I rubbed a hand over my face. I felt hot, dizzy. "Leave me alone, okay, Ruth?"

She sat back as if I'd smacked her. "I'm trying to help."

"I can't, I can't—" I wasn't sure what it was I couldn't do, but it was choking me. I reached for the jacket I'd dropped on the floor, now hanging neatly over a chair, and that made me angry too, that she'd been bothered enough by the jacket on the floor that she had to pick it up. I pulled it on and grabbed my cigarettes, hating the way she was watching me, still and blank and as if I was doing it to her, somehow, when what I really wanted to do to her, to someone, anyone, was much, much worse. "You don't like the smell so I'm going to smoke these out on the fucking porch, all right?"

"I never said you couldn't smoke in here." Her voice was calm and cold. "Slovo—" She reached a hand out and I shook it off. And now her eyes were full of alarm and it took everything I had not to hit her in the face, smack, hard as I could.

It came on me this way sometimes, like the sudden rush of a strong drug hitting the bloodstream, a blinding, white-hot rage that tightened every muscle, sending jangling, random signals pulsing through my brain, scrambling everything up. It was something sleeping inside of me, something ugly and brutal that, when it awoke, was so big it crowded the rest of me out. It started happening in high school when I was trying to catch up so I could go to the academy but I was the dumbest kid there and every day was an exercise in humiliation. Sometimes I snapped and inflicted damage that surprised everyone, myself included. It happened on the job, too. Most of the time people didn't bother filing a complaint because they were used to cops roughing them up and getting away with it and I just walked away, feeling frightened and a little less human.

All I knew now was that I had to get out or I would hurt someone.

CHAPTER 18

After a while footsteps crossed the porch and I looked over to find Bobby standing there, his trousers dirty with dust and cobwebs, studying me warily. "What's going on?"

"I just talked to some people in Chicago. I'm going to lose my job." It was hard to talk, my jaw was so tight.

"What about your lawyer? Won't your union—"

"I'm in no mood for an interrogation, Bobby, okay?"

"Well... fine. Only those files you asked about? I found them in storage." He held an envelope up. His words made no sense to me, coming through a buzz of white noise. "Ah, forget it. I'll leave 'em inside for you."

I stared him off the porch and then sat in one of the wooden chairs that faced the water and pulled out a cigarette. It was chilly, a little breeze skirling off the water, making it hard to light the match. I sat and smoked, concentrating on the monotonous hiss of the waves washing through the rocks below. Ruth came out, hugging herself in a sweater. "What are you doing out here?"

I felt that coiled rage stir at the back of my head. "Nothing. Just... nothing." She started to pull a chair over. "Go away, Ruth. Please."

She went back inside. I stared at the line that marked

the horizon and focused on that big, empty sea in front of me. I'd fought off the anger, but it left me feeling wrung out and dazed, the way it always did.

Clicking sounds, nails on wood, and Chewie the collie came lolloping along the deck, coming up to lick at my hands, snuffle around my shoes, making loose thoughts rattle in my brain, chatter. It took all the energy I had to lift one hand and stroke the dog's head. He stuck his muzzle up to my face and licked my nose. Sylvester crouched down at my side, rubbing the collie's neck, burying both hands in his thick fur. "I was just checking some lumber stored under the porch," he said softly. "Heard you talking. You're in trouble?" He kept looking down at the dog, studying the furry head as he gently scratched his neck.

"I made a bad call. Depends on how you look at it."

"You can get all confused, trying to figure it out. There's different attitudes. It all depends on how you look at it."

"I guess. I don't know."

"I've been thinking about what you said." His voice was oddly quiet. "Different attitudes. People don't get that."

"They don't understand anything."

"I keep thinking about it. At night, especially, it keeps going around in my head."

A couple of gulls coasted, wings outspread, held in place in the wind. Something started to take shape in the meaningless jangle in my head: Huh? What is this? Something I had said made him want to come back and talk some more.

"You wonder if it shows." Sylvester's hands paused on the dog's neck until the collie turned and licked at his hand. "In your eyes or branded on your skin, because they all look at you so differently. All this hate." He shivered, tucked his hands into his armpits, and rested against the side of the chair, close and confiding. I looked at him and his eyes fixed on mine. They carried some urgent message. I needed to signal back, keep this connection alive.

"They look at me like that now." I needed to find the sympathetic vibration to tune to, harmonize with his own craziness. "I don't know what I'm going to do. I can't run from it anymore."

His eyes were wide and intense, but at the same time blank. "I ran, too, and started over. I got a different life for a while." There was something weirdly confiding in his voice. "A little life, just simple and clean. But it's happening again. The looks. They know, they all found out. Did you tell them?"

"No. I'm not one of them anymore, they don't trust me."

"Then how did you find out?"

"I just . . . I don't know, I felt it, I guess."

He smiled, a crooked, deformed kind of a smile. "I didn't hurt her, you know. I loved her."

"What's her name, Will? I don't even know her name."

"Sammy." He looked off at the sea, a big smile on his face now. "Samantha. I wonder if they changed it? I don't know where she is. I looked for a while. Once I got close, I called this number and it was her, I heard her voice, and I was going to go see her, but the police picked me up and . . . they twisted it all. To them it's all sick and dirty, but it wasn't like that. She loved me. Kids are so, they're just so . . ."

"You like kids a lot, don't you?"

"What do you mean?" He tensed.

"I just . . . I'm kind of afraid of them, tell you the truth. They look like they could get hurt so easy. They're so small, you know?"

He laughed, full of sudden confidence. "They're so fresh and truthful, so innocent, they know how to feel things without all that, all that complicated stuff women put into it. Kids aren't like that. They just want to be

happy, make you happy." I thought for a minute his eyes
were filling with tears, but he closed them and I wasn't
sure. "You just have to be around them, you'd understand."

"I've been around kids, but..." Think, think. How to
play this, how to keep him talking? "Oh man, I never said
this to anybody before, this is kind of..."

"It's okay. Hey, it's all right."

"Thing is, thing is if I have a kid with me? Like, God,
like my brother's kid, my niece... like she's sitting in my
lap? I get so scared."

"Why?"

"Scared maybe I'll frighten her or, or... you'll think I'm
crazy or something." I laughed uncertainly.

"No, it's okay."

"I'm afraid I'll... see, she's really small, sitting there in
my lap, and so trusting and she kind of rubs up against me
or slumps against my chest, like she trusts me completely,
and I get this crazy feeling that maybe I'll hurt her; they get
hurt so easy. I can't stand that feeling."

"Why would you hurt her?"

"What if I just got this urge?"

"You wouldn't... not to hurt her."

"I don't want to, but I could."

"No. I don't think you... I wouldn't hurt them."

"You never feel that way? I thought you might understand."

He delicately scratched the short hair on Chewie's
nose. "Depends on how you look at it. Like you said."

"But you don't feel that, that thing? That pull? See,
I'm not around kids much, I don't know if what I'm feeling,
like, whether it's normal, whether other people—"

"Normal? There are different attitudes. You said it
yourself. Remember?"

"Man, I don't know. My head's, my head's... it's real

strange. Like there's something inside of me, trying to get out, it's making me nuts."

"It feels like that sometimes."

"I keep thinking about cases I had, kids who get hurt like the one here, Marcy. People who do those things... See, maybe I could do that to a kid when my head's like this. Maybe I have done it."

"I had a dream about her."

"About Marcy?"

"It might have been Marcy. No, I think it was my daughter, in the dream. She was like...broken. A piece of her came off in my hand. I don't remember, a foot? Right there in my hand. I tried to put it back, but it wouldn't go. I have real strange dreams. I try not to sleep, lately. Sometimes I forget what time it is, where I am, I'm so tired."

"Did you know Marcy, Will?"

"She was the one who had her skin off."

My face suddenly felt so stiff and cold I had trouble speaking. "Will, you...you saw her like that?"

"She was hanging in my bathroom like that, no skin. Shiny and pink, wet. It was a horrible dream. Do you have bad dreams?"

"Sometimes. Did you take her skin off?"

"She was just hanging there. I don't remember how it started. I just remember how she looked."

"Will—"

A pair of squirrels chased each other up a tree beside the porch and Chewie darted forward, barking and leaping up. The noise and commotion seemed to jolt Sylvester, and he blinked, then looked at his watch. "Christ, it's late. I was supposed to be at the Morrisons' place for the plumber. Are you all right, Slovo? You're shivering."

"Can I come...can I come talk to you tonight, Will? I can't talk to other people like this. You understand, you know things."

He gave me a smile, his eyes strange. "We both know things."

After I heard his truck rattle away I lurched up, stiff and cold, and hobbled inside. Ruth looked up as I came into the study, and I said, "I need to call your father."

"Are you all right?"

"Yeah. What's his number?" She told me and I punched it in. He wasn't there; the dispatcher, a guy I didn't know, said he'd give him a message. I said it was urgent, very urgent, could they page him and tell him to call me right away? The dispatcher wasn't paying attention and I was getting angry, but then Ruth took the phone and persuaded him to make the contact. She hung up and looked at me.

"You're sure you're all right?" There was a chill to her voice, and I remembered.

"That thing, earlier. When I get angry like that it's best if I'm alone, Ruth, I have a real bad temper. Will Sylvester was out there. He's . . . have you talked to him lately?"

"He seems to be more shy than ever. I said hello yesterday, and he acted almost frightened."

"He's really . . . I think he's psychotic. You want to be careful around him."

"What makes you—?" she started to ask when the phone rang.

"This better be important." Cobbett's voice was edged with something brittle. "You realize we only have something like thirty *hours* before he takes another kid? If we lose another one—" He broke off abruptly.

Ruth stood up to go, but I put a hand out, stayed her. "I just talked to Sylvester. He's out of his mind, something's eating at him. And he knows what happened to Marcy's body." I told him what he'd said.

Cobbett didn't speak right away, but the breath he expelled sounded like a shaky prayer. "This is the break we've been looking for. Good work, Slovo. We'll bring him in right away."

"Hold it. He didn't give me anything that would be grounds for an arrest warrant."

"He knew about the body—"

"Neil's wife spread it around, Sylvester could say it was something he heard. And when he told me, he said it was just a dream. You pull him in now, he could walk and we couldn't stop him. Let me go to his place, see if there's any evidence there. I know you may have reservations, given the situation in Chicago, but I have a chance, here."

"It's the judge who might have reservations."

"We don't need a judge yet. Sylvester'll let me in without a warrant. And if I see anything, we can do it by the book. We'll be able to act before it's too late. Let me go to his place. He'll let me in, he trusts me. I can look around. And maybe he'll tell me more, give me details that weren't released."

"But watch it. If he gets carried away telling you about the crimes and he hasn't been warned—"

"I know. I'll be careful. You should touch base with Flaherty and with your prosecutor."

"I'll do that. When do you want to move?"

"Soon as possible. Tonight."

"What if it turns ugly? We have to have some kind of backup."

"What kind of equipment you got? I could wear a wire."

"Flaherty can come up with something. This is the first decent chance we've had to nail this son of a bitch. We can't afford to make any mistakes."

After I hung up I thought of something. "Hey, Ruth? That thing about me being suspended? Did you mention it to Bobby when he was here?"

"No, we didn't talk. He just dropped off some papers for you."

"It's not official until the superintendent signs off on it tomorrow. It would be best if we didn't mention it to anybody. Your father's taking a big risk, letting me deal this play. We don't need to make things more complicated for your dad."

"This seems like a convoluted way of asking me to lie to him." Her eyes were fixed on me, her eyebrows drawn together.

"Not lie exactly ... well, I guess it is, really."

She nodded.

CHAPTER 19

It was only half past seven when we drove down the narrow road that fringed the public land they called the School Forest, but the shadows between the trees that caught the car's headlights looked as if they could swallow things without a trace. Bobby was driving Ruth's car; we would trade places when we got to the narrow dirt track that led back through the trees to Sylvester's trailer and Bobby would hide in the backseat. A radio truck had found a place to set up not too far away on a fire lane. Screened by a bank of tangled junipers, it was invisible from the trailer but within range of the mike that was taped to my chest under my T-shirt. They would let Bobby know if things went wrong. They were also in touch with a gang of muscular toughs who were following us in an unmarked van, a state police tac team that would wait at the end of the track leading to the trailer, in case we needed backup.

"You're ready for this?" Bobby asked, pulling up to make the switch.

"I'm ready." I felt that extra current flowing in my bloodstream, that zinging, bright electric buzz that was better than the crank I used to pop to feel this good. The scent of pine needles and decaying wood was strong in the chill air as I walked around and got into the driver's seat. Bobby tried to find a comfortable way to conceal himself while we checked our communications. Then I pulled out and made the turn down the rutted lane through the woods, a little clumsy with my bad leg, having a hard time getting a feel for the gas pedal.

"Jesus," Bobby muttered from the backseat. "Where'd you learn to drive?"

"Fuck you, Munro. All right, there's the trailer. You got your strap handy?"

"If it's my gun you're talking about, yeah."

I parked next to Sylvester's truck, a spot well in the shadows but with a view of the trailer in case Bobby needed it. "Okay, this is it, I'm moving." I could feel the current sparking and crackling in my bloodstream as I climbed out of the car. It was an old trailer, rusted along the seams, set in a small clearing. The ground was barren, rocks cropping out through the scrubby grass. As I approached the porch, where a light over the door made a circle illuminating the ground around it, my foot crunched on something—a fragile sea urchin lying on the stony ground, pulverized into greenish dust by my foot. Sylvester opened the door and Chewie rushed down the steps, raced around me, darted over to the car, and put his front paws up on the back door, barked sharply, raced back. I hadn't thought about the dog, and hoped Bobby wasn't wetting his pants in the backseat about now.

"You came," Sylvester said. His hair was disordered, his eyes sunken, but he sounded calm, even sane. "You need a hand?"

I was nearly knocked over by the dog barreling past me up the stairs. "I got it, I think." I had to hoist my bad leg up one step at a time. I had taken nothing stronger than aspirin all afternoon, wanting a clear head. Will watched me make the first two risers, then came and helped. "There you go. Almost there," he murmured.

"Thanks," I said, making it into the trailer, noticing a smell that caught in my throat. I sat on a couch and looked around. The place was spotlessly clean and barren, the small living room featuring only the couch and one wooden folding chair, no books or papers or knickknacks. Certainly no stains, no spatters, no sign of murder or torture, everything scrubbed within an inch of its life. There was a counter between the living area and the kitchen, which seemed equally spartan. What was that smell?

"I'm glad you came," Sylvester said.

"I had to. I've been losing my mind lately, but you seem to understand what I'm going through."

"I think you'll feel better in here. I wired it up to block the signals."

"Signals?"

"You want some tea?"

"That would be good."

I limped to the kitchen where he was getting mugs out of a cupboard. There was a soup pot steaming on the stove, restaurant size. The smell was stronger here: astringent, vinegary, ammonia with a touch of something gamey. A block of wood, fashioned as a knife holder, sat beside the stove, five handles sticking out. "Nice set," I said.

"Careful. They're sharp," he warned. I had slid one out, then a second one. Where the blade was sunk into the wooden handle on the second one I looked at, there was a barely visible rim of dark residue stuck between the metal and the wood. It could be blood. It could be anything.

"What's that you're making, soup?"

"No. Why, are you hungry? I could fix you something."

"I just wondered. It smells...funny."

"Your head, is it better now?"

"Maybe, a little."

"I thought it would be, in here." He smiled at me mysteriously. "Do you want sugar in your tea?"

"Yeah, that would be fine. What's in that pot, there?"

"A mix of things. All natural, of course."

"What's it for?"

He looked confused. "It's just an idea I had. Why don't you sit down. I'll bring the tea in a moment."

"Nice place," I said after I returned to the couch. "In the woods like this."

"I like it. It's private."

"You must be an outdoorsman, hunting and fishing and all."

"No. I've never been into that."

The dog had been snuffling around my lap as if there might be crumbs there. Now he gave up and trotted out to the kitchen. "I had this crummy room, back in Chicago. I let it get pretty bad. Is it okay if I look around?"

"Why?"

"I just . . . it's a nice place, so simple and tidy."

"Sit still. The tea's ready." He came through from the kitchen with the mugs. "I cleaned it up this week. I had more stuff before, but it was interfering, it had to go. I even took up the carpet, hauled it out to the dump."

And any evidence would have gone with it. I sighed, thinking about combing a landfill for Sylvester's discarded belongings. I found myself picturing the truck, Forché and Flaherty piled in with the two techs, surrounded with equipment, looking at each other, wondering why I wasn't asking any questions, wondering what the hell was going on.

I tuned back in to that jangling noise that had plagued my head earlier, that music of failure and pointlessness, letting its incessant drone lead me to a crazier place. I put my mug down on the floor by my feet and hunched over, rubbing my palms together, letting him take the lead.

"What day is it?" Sylvester asked abruptly.

"I don't know. Tuesday? Monday?"

"Man, Slovo, you're almost as bad off as I am. I used to

be organized, but I'm getting all mixed up. I haven't slept in days."

"Because of the dreams?"

"They're really bad. I think somebody's putting something in my food. Drugs. I did some of that in college. Acid, meth, coke. You like that stuff at all?"

"I used to do a lot of speed."

"I could use some speed about now, keep me going. These dreams, they're scary. Like tripping, only I always knew it was the acid. With the dreams I don't know what's real."

"Like when Sammy's foot came off."

"I've been thinking about that." He finished off his tea, set the cup on the floor by his chair, and leaned forward to look at me intently. "I'm not sure, now, it was Sammy. I think it was another girl. You ever take PCP?"

"Naw, that stuff's scary."

"Maybe that's what they're putting in my food. Has your food tasted different lately?"

"I don't think anyone's doctoring my food, I think I'm going crazy all by myself."

"Because of what happens when your niece sits in your lap?"

"Because—because I shouldn't feel that way."

"What way? She makes you hard? You want to do it with her?" He sounded almost amused, like an older kid explaining the mysteries of sex.

"I busted people for that. We thought they were monsters. God, what's wrong with me?"

"Oh, man, Slovo. You have to be very, very careful with feelings like that."

"My own niece."

"Let me tell you something." He moved over to sit on the couch, close beside me. "They like it, if you do it right. My daughter—"

"Will, don't. You know my work—I'm a police officer."

"I know. Even though you aren't like them."

"I feel comfortable around you, Will. There's nobody else I can talk to about these, these feelings I have, but I am a cop." There was something new in his eyes, a cold blankness. "I'm sorry. I better go."

I started to rise but he pushed me back into my seat firmly. "I have the right to remain silent. I have the right to an attorney. If I can't afford one, the court will appoint one for me. You think I haven't dealt with cops before? I'm going to explain this to you once and for all: Sammy liked making me happy. I was careful, I didn't get carried away. Why can't you people understand that? I didn't hurt her."

He was staring at me with an intensity that teetered on the brink of anger. I had to decide whether to cut it off now or try to reestablish that connection and see where it led.

I took a breath. "But my niece, she's not a teenager or nothing. She's only six years old."

"That's the best, when they're so sweet and trusting." He relaxed visibly. "Tell her it's a special secret between you."

"I don't know, man. I had to keep secrets when I was a kid. I think that's why I'm crazy now. Why I'm so angry all the time."

"You had sex with an adult?"

"I got fucked by an adult." It came out in a low, strangled whisper.

"No, no. It doesn't have to be like that."

"He hurt me. Maybe that's what's going on. I sometimes think I'll hurt someone like I got hurt." I rubbed my hands together as if I wanted to rub the skin right off. "Do you ever feel like this?"

"What, like hurting someone?" He laughed. "After what they did? Taking her away from me? What do you expect?"

"I had a lot of cases . . . so many cases where kids were hurt. Once, a guy took his dog out for an early morning walk, and the mutt comes running up with an arm, this baby's arm in his mouth." I choked a little at that. "I had to go out there, all over the park, look for the parts. And I'm thinking, that's what could happen, that's where it could end up. I get so angry I can't always control myself. I could get to where I can't stop myself, when they're little, so easy to hurt. What if they don't want it anymore and I get mad and hurt them for it? I'm sick, Will, I'm going nuts, I hate this. Is that what it's like for you?"

"I've had dreams like that."

"The one you told me about, the one with her skin off?"

"Marcy." He sighed and slumped against the back of the couch. I saw he was aroused, his prick straining against his jeans. "She looked so innocent, sleeping there, and I wanted it so bad, I couldn't bear it anymore. So I took her out through the window and brought her home and had her, over and over. And then, I must have suffocated her and dressed her out the way they do animals because she's hanging upside down like that, her skin's off."

"Suffocated her?"

"No, wait." I heard him sigh, slightly, a ragged breath of a sound. His fingers tightened against his jeans. "I held my hands around her throat while I did it to her."

"What was it like? How did you do it, the sex?" The smell in the room was making me sick.

"Every way I could. You have to hear the details? Man, Slovo, you're as bad as I am." He laughed. "The man that had sex with you—it was a man?"

"Yeah."

"Did he give it to you in the ass?" He looked at me expectantly, my turn now.

"He—uh." I took a breath, tried to swallow without throwing up. "At first, he . . . Man, it's hot in here, can I open a window?"

"I covered the windows with plastic already for the winter. What's wrong?"

"I feel kind of sick. That smell..."

"I'll open the door." I had my head in my hands, thinking I was an idiot for letting it get to me like this when I was this close. But I felt so sick.

Chewie swished by, heading for the door, thinking there was an outing in it for him. He barked at the door and for a moment I was afraid Will would wonder who was out there, would go out and find Bobby in the car. But while Chewie still paced anxiously at the screen door, whimpering, Will came back and sat beside me. "Better?"

I nodded. "Thanks."

"So. Tell me what it was like." He looked at me expectantly.

"At first, he had me take him in my mouth."

"Oh, that... How was that?"

"I was scared, but it wasn't that bad. When he took me from behind it hurt. I didn't mind doing the mouth thing so much. Sometimes I think about how it would be if my niece, if she would... Did you ever do that with kids?"

"Oh, yeah, it's good that way. Sammy liked it that way."

"Marcy too?"

"Sure. I was so ready I did it every way I could with her. But I strangled her and after that I must have skinned her with one of my knives. You saw them. Good, sharp knives. I used them on the others, too."

"Others?"

"I remember one named Ashley. Lots of blood, that time." His eyes were closed, a smile on his face, hands tightening on his thighs.

I could smell the pine trees outside, the fresh breeze from the door, but the pot in the kitchen seemed to overpower everything. "Did you give it to her, too? Uh, sex?"

"I gave it to all of them."

"Bethany, too?"

"You can't expect me to know all their names, Slovo, jeez."

"You . . . you didn't hurt Sammy. Why did you hurt the other girls?"

"It must be those drugs they put in my food. That's how they found out about me." He sat up suddenly and leaned close. "Listen, this is important. Like, with your niece? You want to make sure you don't get too carried away, too rough, because once you hurt 'em, it's all over, that's when you start showing up on the screen."

"On the screen?"

"I think it has to do it with nerve impulses. They're electrical, right? I think maybe they're emitted on a different kind of frequency, and they pick it up on the airwaves, it shows up on the screen if you get carried away. I got carried away, see, from the drugs they gave me. It's part of their plan. They've been trying to get me for years." His face twisted. "Oh God. The *door,* the fucking door."

He shoved me away, his face full of panic and fury, gave me an open-palm slap, and then closed the door, leaned against it and shot the bolt home. "You want them to find me?" He came to stand in front of me, his hands clenched.

"I don't know what you mean. Why'd you hit me?"

"I have the place wired so they can't find me, but of course they can pick up the signals if the door is open." He went to the window and peered out. "I can't believe after every precaution, I let you do this to me."

"I didn't know anything about the signals."

"You're lying."

"No, I—honest, I never heard about signals. How'd you figure it out, anyway?"

"You're trying to get me to give it away now. Shit, they sent you here, didn't they?" He was pacing around the room now, peering out all the windows, checking out the darkness. The dog started to turn in hopping circles, following Sylvester and whimpering, breaking out with a bark every now and then.

"No. I couldn't find anybody to talk to until I met you. Will, you're my friend. Nobody else understands."

"Okay, okay, maybe they tracked your signal to home in on me, that makes sense. Only you *said*, you *said* to open the door. How do you explain that?" He stopped in front of me, glaring.

"Talking about that old stuff, it made me feel sick, I needed some air. See, it was different for me, I didn't know it could be good. Like for you and Sammy."

A smile twitched at his lips. "Yeah, it was good. We didn't send any signals then. It wasn't till my wife...my wife, she's the one who made me go through all of this shit. Oh, God, it hurts, all of this shit coming down. I'm getting this, this backwash. They're getting inside my head now."

"Will, I didn't want to bring you trouble. You want me to go?" I was standing now, edging my way toward the door. "Maybe I can lead them away from here."

"No." He shoved me back onto the couch, hard enough that my head hit the wall. "I have to check on things. Don't move, I'll...I'll kill you if I have to."

"Whatever you want. I'm not going anywhere."

He backed into the kitchen area, slid a knife out of the holder and set it on the counter, gave me a meaningful look and then turned to the stove. I wondered if they were picking up the thudding of my heart in the radio truck. I could feel the blood pounding somewhere behind my ears. Sylvester seemed to be adding things to the pot, every now and then turning to check on me, that knife within his reach. I smelled sage, more vinegar, something with an acrid scent. I thought about bolting for the door, but in the time it would take to work the lock, he'd be on me with that knife.

Then he came back and stared at me, the knife stuck in his belt, a thin, sharply pointed piece of steel. "Get up," he said brusquely. I climbed to my feet, trying to look mellow, cooperative. "I need something from you. But what?"

He sighed impatiently and started to search me, and I hunched my shoulders forward, hoping he wouldn't notice the bump of the mike taped to my chest under my T-shirt. Maybe he'd take that expensive piece of government equipment for his pot, throw the whole thing in, battery pack and all. Or maybe, seeing it, he'd just get mad and run that boning knife into my gut. One little punch and I'd have five inches of steel inside me. He yanked my flannel open, spitting buttons around the room. Chewie chased after one button, then another, yapping excitedly, thinking it was a new game. Sylvester groaned impatiently.

"Hey, what's the deal, here? I'll help if you tell me what you need."

"I need something for the pot, but it has to be natural."

"This shirt's cotton, I could tear some off for you."

"No, it's got chemicals in it." He grabbed a hank of my hair, considering it. "This would work, hair and nails. I have to find the scissors. Stay there, okay?"

"I won't go anywhere."

He studied me, his eyes narrowing. "You're going to open the door, let them in, aren't you? Man, I can't believe this. You betrayed me. I thought you were going to be my friend." He grabbed my hair and reached around with his other hand to hold the knife against the side of my neck, his elbow right over the mike. "I'll cut you if you do anything. Down the hall."

"Okay, okay. Hey, easy." He pushed me before him, Chewie getting tangled in our feet, eagerly pushing down the narrow hallway with us. Then Will reached down to open a door into a small bathroom and snapped on the light.

I took a breath and gagged on it. "There's a lot of blood in here, Will. Where'd all the blood come from?" My voice sounded loud, strange. He let go of my hair and stumbled a little, seeming staggered by the sight himself. I could smell it, thick and metallic, like rust. The sink was clotted with it, it was splashed on the mirror, against the wall, streaked on the floor. The dog squeezed past us, lapping at a pool of it, excited, and Will made a gasping, tearful sound as he pushed him out of the little room, closed the door against him. The collie whined and scratched along the bottom of the door, ecstatic with the scent that was making my stomach churn and heave.

"I forgot . . . I forgot about . . . I was going to clean this up. Hold still." He groped in a drawer, pulled out a pair of scissors and cut off a hank of my hair close to the scalp. Then he took my hands, one at a time, and carefully trimmed my thumbnails, catching the small slivers in his palm. "That might be enough. I'm going to leave you in here, all right? While I finish? You can clean up if you want. There's a sponge under the sink. Don't, please don't try to get out, they'll pick up the signal if you open the door, they'll be on us in no time. You might think they'll let you off because you helped them, but they hate people like us, they'll tear you apart."

I nodded. He looked at me for a long moment, his lips twisted, trying to hold tears back, then slipped out through the door, pushing Chewie away with his knee. I heard his steps retreating, and then said into my chest, "He's going to the kitchen, I'm in the bathroom. There's fresh blood all over the place. He's got a knife, a bunch of knives." I slid to the floor against the shower stall, onto my knees. "Try not to hurt the dog." And then the next thing they must have heard was the sound of my retching.

The door burst open, hinges ripping from the wall, and I heard barking and yelling and Will Sylvester's screams. I crouched over the toilet, puking up bile, sweat pouring down my face. The bathroom door banged open, and I could see a gun poised, lowered. "Don't come in here. I already messed the scene up too much," I warned, choking.

"Christ, are you hurt?" Bobby's voice.

"It's not my blood." I pushed myself up and out of the blood-spattered room, past Sylvester and his desperate, heartbroken keening. Out the door, stumbling on the stairs and staggering away from the trailer, from the screaming, until I was on the ground by Ruth's car, gulping clean, fresh air, feeling the solid earth under my palms, leaning back against a wheel and breathing deep breaths, trying to escape the stink of blood.

After a while Forché came down the steps, strode over the scrubby clearing, and crouched down. "We got him subdued. He's a real loony toon, isn't he?"

"He's crazy, all right."

"They're taking him to the Bangor Mental Health Institute for observation." We watched as three people, Cobbett one of them, helped a broken figure through the doorway, easing him down the stairs, soothing words from the cops as they proceeded to a squad car. They helped Sylvester into the backseat, the one cop leaning in to secure his cuffs to the U-bolt while Cobbett rested his head against his arm, folded on the open doorway. Then they took off down the dark track through the woods, the trees splashed red and blue as they passed.

"Did good in there." Forché rubbed her hands against her knees. "You okay?"

"That smell, that smell really got to me. What is it?"

"I don't know, all kinds of shit in that pot. Guy's a fucking loony toon."

I staggered to my feet, propped myself against the car. "Bastard stiffened up on me," I said, flexing the bum leg.

I lurched back over toward the trailer, Forché taking my arm to keep me from falling as I started to climb the front steps. "Slovo, hey. You don't have to go back in there, we got it under control."

The smell hit me again when I got inside, and I pitched forward, but Flaherty was there, helping Forché keep me upright. "I'm okay, I'm all right," I said, shaking them off, and Flaherty said a little crossly, "Keep your shirt on, Slovo, jeez."

The trailer seemed much smaller, crowded with large men who had Tactical Squad in bright letters on the backs of their jackets. One punched my arm and said, "Good job."

"What, that's the guy?" someone else asked.

I stood over the pot, looking down at the steaming broth. They'd turned off the flame, but the liquid still moved lazily, churning slowly. Small bones rose through the brown liquid, twisted in the current, sank back, small bones and twigs and my own hair and hanks of fur attached to scraps of pink skin. A delicate curved bone, a knuckle-shaped piece, a tiny vertebra, I watched each one rise lazily, revolve as it swam along the surface, sink back.

"Flaherty thinks it's a cat," Forché said at my side. "We'll know for sure when the techs are done with it."

"The blood?"

"That too, probably. No sign of anything human here."

"Nothing human here." That slowly turning liquid still had a powerful smell. The room seemed to shimmer with it.

Then I was sitting on the couch, my head between my knees. Someone's hand was on the back of my head, holding it down. "Easy." I didn't recognize the voice. "Take a deep breath."

"I'm all right." I finally felt the pressure leave my head and I sat up. "Kind of embarrassing." The tac officer sitting beside me wasn't paying much attention. He was chewing a toothpick and jiggling one foot impatiently. "It's that fucking smell."

"Yeah, I almost puked myself."

"I didn't realize he'd . . . man, those screams. What happened to the dog?"

"He's outside. He's okay. Real pretty animal. I wouldn't mind having a dog like that."

"Let's go, Slovo." Bobby bumped my shoulder with the

back of his hand. "We'll run Ruth's car back, then go down-town for statements. If you're up for it."

"I'm fine. I'm great. I want to change clothes, though."

"You'll have time to change."

He drove us back to Hunter's Point. Ruth was on the porch, waiting. "Slovo got him to confess. We nailed the bastard," Bobby called out triumphantly. They both looked at me, all smiles. I couldn't remember what they were so happy about.

"I have to take a shower," I said, the smell of blood all around me.

CHAPTER 20

I stared at flaking paint and a rust-colored halo where there had been a leak in the ceiling of the interview room. If you looked at it right, it was in the shape of the Virgin Mary. I could see the excited faithful crowding around, clamoring for a favor from the BVM, leaving flowers and candles and cast-off crutches on the dirty linoleum floor.

There was a clock on the wall protected by a metal grille, as if the authorities figured detainees would go ape shit about the time and attack the clock. It was just a little after nine. It felt past midnight.

Bobby wandered through, carrying a can of Coke and a bag of cheese curls, offering the bag around before he wandered out again. I asked for coffee, but my stomach already felt as if I'd poured some Drāno in it, and the stale coffee didn't help. Forché sat there with me, tracing a gash in the table with the side of her thumb, her eyes half-closed. She and Bobby were going to back up my solo riff with their accounts of the surveillance and the take-down. Flaherty was still at the trailer, overseeing the processing of the scene. Forché noticed me holding my stomach. "Slovo, you aren't supposed to take seven or eight aspirins at once. I told you."

"Never bothered me before."

"Give you an ulcer."

"Mm." I shifted in my chair, feeling uncomfortable. Forché watched me as I ducked down to check it out.

"What are you doing?"

"Thought maybe the legs were cut down."

"The chair legs?"

"Yeah. You cut a half-inch off the front legs? Sit your suspect down in it, they keep just barely sliding forward in the seat. They don't know what's going on. Drives 'em nuts."

"Gotta try that."

"Cheap but effective. And so far as I know it's even legal."

A guy in a suit popped his head in, and said, "Be right with you."

I pulled out my cigarettes, then noticed the This Is a Smoke-Free Building sign taped up on the wall. "Shit."

"You did a good job with Sylvester."

"I needed to get some details out of him, stuff that wasn't out there. Like the nature of the sexual assault on Marcy, that wasn't public information. I wish I could have got him to talk about the other victims more."

"We got time to do that." She stood up and studied the sign on the wall, reached up, tore it in half, and crumpled it up. "Give me one of your smokes, would you?"

"I didn't know you smoked."

"I'm lapsed. Sometimes I get my faith back." We both lit up. "Worked out good, the way you got him to talk. It was spooky, hearing you."

"Don't ever tell my brother I was talking about his kid that way."

She laughed. "I won't. I'd hate to be responsible for your violent death."

"My niece is a teenager now anyway, big kid, plays volleyball. She'd deck me if I looked at her funny."

Forché hooked a trash can over with her foot and flicked ashes into it. "That part about when you were a kid. . . . I know you had a pretty rough time." The smoke leaked out with her words, short wisps drifting up. "Leaving home and shit."

I felt hot suddenly and looked at the clock to see if it had moved lately. "It was all bullshit, Forché. I was just fucking with his head."

"Okay. It just sounded kind of . . ."

"The only thing I talked about that really happened was that murder, the kid in the park. That was real."

"Oh, the deal with the dog trotting up with the arm in his mouth? That's some story. Almost good enough for the list."

"What list?"

"Me and Flaherty, we started a list. That pervert jacking off on you, that went right up there. Someday we'll give you the whole list. Only we all got to get good and drunk first. Some of 'em aren't funny unless you're juiced."

We both looked up when the clock made a strange whirring sound, as if its hands were stuck and it was going to explode. We stared at it in suspense, hardly breathing. Then it stopped making that noise, the minute hand jerked forward, and we started laughing.

The man in the suit came back, followed by a woman. They paused, waiting for the joke to be explained. Forché told them it was nothing, we were just goofing. "Sabine, good to see you. Detective Slovo. We need to go over what happened tonight."

"Hey, *no problemo, mi amigo*." In spite of the late hour the knot in his tie was perfect, and his hair was holding its wave as if he'd just finished blow-drying it. And I hated it when people I didn't know acted like we were old friends.

"May I?" he asked politely, taking the back of a chair that I had my feet on.

I removed my feet, waved my hand generously. "*Mi casa es su casa*, man."

"I'm April Barnstaple, with the attorney general's office,

criminal division." The woman was young and her suit was snug, the skirt well up on her thighs and tight. I wondered what it was like to walk in something that pinched your legs together like that. The shoes too, they looked like a form of torture. Forché saw me duck my head down to look at them under the table and she elbowed me in the side.

"Been kind of a long day," Forché said to the suits.

Bobby Munro appeared at the door, looking like a sleepy kid searching for his teddy bear. "Oh, good, doughnuts," he said happily, pulling up a chair.

"We've just finished listening to the tape." The man put his briefcase on the table, unlatched it, and drew out a pad. "You have a creative approach to interrogation, Detective Slovo. Unfortunately, I doubt we'll be able to use any of it. If we're lucky, he'll cooperate with us, but the tape is a problem."

"I know it wasn't exactly—"

"Any defense attorney worth his salt would be all over your version of a warning," Barnstaple interrupted coolly. "His entire confession, if that's what it was, could be thrown out."

"Sylvester knew his rights. He knew I was a cop. He wanted to talk so bad he pushed me down on the couch when I tried to leave. I had to make a call."

"And the way you led him on—"

"There's no law against lying to a suspect. Cops do it all the time."

The man held his hands up. "Let's just go over it, shall we? We'll determine what we can salvage from this after we have all the facts."

I ate a doughnut, hoping to settle my stomach, as they took me through my attempts to befriend Sylvester. "By the way, that cop in Auburn will want in on this," I said.

"We've contacted her," the woman said, breaking off a tiny fragment of doughnut, leaning forward to avoid getting powdered sugar on her suit. "She's eager to do whatever she can to help nail him." She brushed her fingers off, looking around for napkins.

I flashed on Sylvester, his head tipped back, that awful sound coming out of his throat. I told them how I had developed a relationship with him out on the porch in the afternoon. The man in the suit took notes in tiny, neat handwriting. I sometimes lost track of what I was saying, trying to guess whether it would show up as a Roman numeral or a lettered subtopic. The woman held a notepad, but wasn't writing much, just watching me with narrowed eyes.

I got to when I was in the trailer, remembering the strange, heavy smell, and after a while I realized it had gone quiet in the room, I had stalled out. "You heard it," I said, shrugging. "You heard the tape."

"Why don't you tell us in your own words," the prosecutor said, studying his thumbnail with a frown.

"I had to get his confidence. He had to figure I was, you know, someone who would relate."

"So you led him to believe you were a pedophile." Barnstaple crossed her knees and pulled at her skirt. "Can we take it that was a bluff?" She looked over at me, her eyes wide and innocent.

"For fuck's sake," Forché muttered.

"For the record," Barnstaple added primly. "We just need to make it clear for the record when Detective Slovo was telling the truth and when he was fabricating."

"He had to get the guy to talk, he explained that," Forché said angrily.

"No, hey, that's all right," I said. "I don't mind clarifying it for the record. Fact is, lady, I am a pervert, it really gave me a buzz, watching a suspect get a hard-on while he told me how he sexually assaulted a little girl, then murdered her. Why do you think I joined the force?"

"Detective Slovo, please..." The other lawyer was holding his forehead now, looking weary.

I crumpled my cardboard coffee cup into a ball. "All those murdered kids I've had the opportunity to investigate over the years? You tell me, where else do you get such job satisfaction?"

Barnstaple looked up at the ceiling as if offering a little prayer to the stain there. "This is so unprofessional."

Bobby sat forward, the legs of his chair thumping loudly. "You don't get it. This nut case was picking out his next victim. He had a knife to Slovo's throat, could have killed him. You weren't there. It took four of us just to get the knife out of his hand."

Barnstaple was losing her cool. "I'm trying to get his statement. It would help if he would stop clowning around."

I was juggling the crumpled cup between my hands, trying to see how high it would go. The cup went cockeyed, heading for Bobby, who swatted it, making it spin into a corner.

"You're lucky he hasn't walked out already," Forché said angrily.

"Sabine, let's all take a deep breath," the guy in the suit said placatingly, and Forché glared at him.

"No cop needs to be treated like a criminal for doing his job."

"You're not exactly the expert on appropriate professional behavior," Barnstaple said astringently.

Forché opened her mouth and closed it, then turned to Bobby, who was staring hard at the last doughnut. "The bitch. Did you hear what she said?"

"I heard the bitch." He reached for the doughnut. "She thinks you're no role model, Sabine, that's the breaks."

"Hey, tell me, you guys." I pointed. "See those cracks in the paint up there? Doesn't that look kind of like the Blessed Virgin? We could have a miracle, here."

"I think we all need a breather," the man in the suit said, standing up and blowing air out of his cheeks. "Let's take five. April?" He motioned her outside with a jerk of his head. I watched her go out, trying to figure out how she worked her legs in that tight skirt. It looked tricky.

"You like that ass?" Bobby said.

"She's way too old for me."

"The bitch, bringing up that jacker I shot," Forché said. "So, I was on administrative duty for a while, I stopped him, anyway,"

"No more doughnuts," Bobby said sadly. He picked up the empty box, wiped powdered sugar from the corners with his finger, licked it.

"My stomach hurts." I rested my head on the table.

"I think I'll order up a pizza," Bobby announced.

"I need a drink," Forché said wistfully. "A lot of drinks."

"No anchovies," I mumbled. "I hate fucking anchovies."

CHAPTER 21

A little after eleven we wrapped up the preliminary statements, the older guy leading the questions, April Barnstaple giving me a death-ray look whenever I said something aimed her way. We demolished the pizza Bobby ordered and I pressed my fist hard against my stomach, which seemed to help, and after it was done we went out to celebrate the arrest at a bar where the air was dank and smoky, the tables sticky, and the clientele either noisily in the bag or comatose.

"I like this joint," Forché said, thumping a drum solo on the table to keep up with the grungy metal she'd just punched up on the jukebox. She had also punched up Flaherty on the pay phone by the toilets and he spread the word. Ruth, Bryn, Hari, and Irene the dispatcher joined us there. We all crowded around a corner booth, pulling up chairs and practically sitting on each other. The DA had put out a cautiously worded statement in time for the eleven o'clock news, and even though most of the customers looked like they usually avoided the police, there was a raucous burst of cheering from the bar as we arrived.

"You like this music?" Bobby asked, wincing at the grinding acoustics.

"What do you listen to, Garth Brooks?" Forché asked scornfully. He shrugged and she groaned her disbelief. "You touch that box and you're dead."

"This is a Garth-free building," I said.

I didn't want to think about Sylvester. I held the Jack Daniels up to the light, squinted at it, peered at Ruth's eyes, tried to line them up so I could make a comparison. "A match," I told her.

"What?"

"Never mind."

Ruth's eyes seemed extra big as she peered around the room, sipping at a beer and smiling at me whenever she caught me watching her. She looked small inside of her jacket, her sleeves swamping her hands, and something about that made me want to scrunch her to me, keep her warm and safe.

"So, you nailed him, eh, Slovo?" Hari said, eyes bright, mustache disheveled. "Isn't that how you Yanks say it, 'nailed'?"

"I wonder about that word. Sounds like there's going to be a crucifixion."

"There's a thought," Forché said.

"Aren't you going to give us a blow-by-blow replay? The thrilling end of a difficult case?" Hari persisted.

"This is a job-free building."

"Think how disappointed Mike McGavin must feel," Flaherty said. "His satanic conspiracy theory blown out of the water again."

"What about Neil?" Bobby twirled a longneck in front of him. "Thought we couldn't run the PD without him. He'll probably add it to his lawsuit: pain and suffering caused by our closing a case without him."

"That's not fair, Bobby," Irene said quietly. Bobby picked at the label on his longneck resentfully.

"Flaherty, something I been meaning to say to you," I

said, breaking the awkward silence. "I've dealt with feebs before. You're not like the ones I've worked with in Chicago. That's a compliment, by the way."

He took a sip of his Bushmill's, and said, deadpan, "It takes special qualities to get reassigned from the Boston field office to the Bangor Resident Agency."

Forché made a rude noise. "Special qualities? It was the penalty for violating..." She pointed helplessly at him, waggling a finger in front of his suit. "Violating the dress code." And she dissolved in snorts and howls, giving him a friendly shove on the shoulder, spilling half his drink, before announcing to the world she was going to the head. "Keep an eye on my purse," she told Flaherty.

"We'll guard it with our lives," I promised, peering into it. "What's this? A lipstick. Rosy Dawn. You wear this stuff? Keys, Lifesavers...whoa, looky here. This your throw-down, Forché?" I asked, fishing out an ugly little snub-nosed .32. A couple of guys at a nearby table looked up at her response. They looked like merchant marines, but even they seemed impressed by her vocabulary.

"You got a lurid imagination, Slovo," Flaherty said, disgusted.

"Well, she's got that big old forty-five on her hip, what's she need this piece of junk for? Close-up work?"

"Leave her purse alone." Flaherty grabbed it from me and set it between himself and Irene.

We talked about old cases, cold cases, lucky breaks, and mistakes made. For some reason nobody told the show-off stories you usually got out of cops when they were a little lit. I tried to get Flaherty to go through the list Forché had talked about, but he wouldn't play ball. "Some other time."

Irene got him talking about his old neighborhood, his aunt's diner in Southie, about the gang he had run with, doing reckless, stupid things. Bryn talked about boosting cars with friends in Red Hook, joyriding at 3:00 A.M. on the Long Island Expressway. Inspired, Hari related stories of urban blight in England, tales of mistaken cultural identities, narrow escapes from football hooligans who might have been charter members of the Aryan Brotherhood, encounters with policemen that, in his part of the world, were apparently called "filth."

I told some of my stories, funny ones, and Forché contributed tales from the dark side of rural Maine that had us almost on the floor, helpless with laughter, even though they all would have seemed grotesque and even cruel if we weren't drunk. At some point, well past one, I happened to look down at Ruth, resting against my shoulder. She turned her head and looked up at me. Something about the dark, noisy atmosphere, the slightly out-of-control edge to the place, was working on me, like some drug skirling around under my skin. I put my hand against the back of her head, pushed her face to mine, and kissed her hard, crossing some border and waiting to hear the sound of guns firing, someone yelling "Halt!" But she just laughed and said something about how much I was drinking. I felt her hand resting on my thigh, in the crease of my leg, and it felt like it belonged there.

Later on I made my way to the back of the bar to go to the toilet and found a guy swearing desperately at himself in the mirror, yanking paper towels from the dispenser to mop his bloody nose. He had the wasted look of an addict, and he turned around hopefully. "I think you're looking for someone else," I told him, and while I took a whizz at a urinal another wiry specimen slipped in and they started a muttered conversation, impatient to get the place to themselves and get down to business. I hadn't worked Narcotics for years, but it made me feel right at home.

Forché was standing at the jukebox, picking out another selection, and Flaherty was behind her, saying something in her ear. She laughed and he bent close, smelling her hair it looked like, and he put a broad hand on her waist. He pointed out something and she made the selection: Elvis Costello. She looked back at Flaherty and laughed, her eyes crinkling up. They stared at the lights on the jukebox and swayed a little together.

As I watched them a familiar voice at a nearby table gave me a strange jolt. "Equal-opportunity cunt, that's what she is." Someone laughed, repeated the remark in a dozy voice, adding extra syllables to the second word.

"Still goes out there to feed those damned cats, you believe it?" the voice went on. "Something wrong with this whole deal. People like that living here, her and her jig brat."

St. Sebastian.

"'At's right, Alvin. Teach that dyke a lesson, 'at's what we should do," his nearly incoherent pal mumbled.

"Could use some equal-opportunity pussy myself," someone muttered.

"Seriously, we should shake her up some." A couple of other voices chimed in, agreeing with him. "It's wrong, living like she does. Ain't moral."

Fucking St. Sebastian.

He turned to flag a waitress, and his eyes met mine. Then I knew for sure. His eyes went opaque with alarm. I kept my face blank and he turned back to his friends, a little smirk of relief breaking out.

I limped back to the table and leaned over Irene to snag the little .32 out of Forché's purse. Irene looked up at me, surprised, ready to laugh if it turned out to be a joke. I pushed my way back through the crowd, working out a way to hold the piece, hooking my good finger through the trigger guard, curving my palm to brace the grip, balancing it with my thumb. I got back to where the cluster of men were hunching over their beers, their table crowded with empty longnecks, picked out the one, *fucking St. Sebastian,* came up behind him and grabbed his hair, jerking his head back, bringing the barrel of the snub-nosed gun to rest against the slightly concave hollow of his right temple. His mouth gaped open, eyes staring up at me angry at first, then disbelieving, the other faces registering various responses from drunken incomprehension to alarm. Someone laughed abruptly, someone else said "Al? No, no, no, hold on, wait now."

I leaned into his face. "You guys fucked up. You missed my trigger finger, Al. How'd you forget that?" He gurgled something low in his throat and I thumped the nose of the gun against that curve of pale, sweating flesh.

"Shut up, Alvin. I'm drunk and I'm pissed off." He made a tight, high noise, looking up at me with his eyes wide. I leaned in close. "They're going to take my badge away. What do I have to lose, huh? I'm angry with you, Alvin, I'm angry at the whole fucking world, but Jesus God, it would make me feel a lot better to hold your brains in my hands." I thumbed the safety off.

He closed his eyes. "Please." It was a tight sound, like air going out of a tire. Elvis Costello was rocking in the background, but most of the conversations had stopped. I sensed a bartender moving close and Bobby said, behind me, "Slovo. Enough."

"Back off, Bobby."

"Give me the gun, okay? You don't want to do this."

"*Back off*. Or, see, I'll blow his fucking head off." Forché watched me, her eyes flat and blank. I gave her a little smile but she didn't smile back. I leaned my mouth down close to the gun, my lips practically on his skin, a private moment. "Who set it up?" I nudged the barrel in tighter. "Give me the name, give me the name."

He made that high whimper again, squeezing his eyes shut, water leaking out of the corners. I heard something liquid trickling, smelled urine along with the tangy reek of his flop-sweat. Even his nose had a bead of damp hanging on it, as if something in him was melting and oozing out everywhere it could.

"The name, Alvin." I stroked his skin with the gun. "Give it up, goddamn it, I'm losing it here." I pressed the barrel harder to prove it.

"Si—Si—Simons. Christ, don't kill me."

I let up on his hair and he started to shrug forward away from me, then I jammed the barrel under his jawline, leaning over the back of his chair to crowd him. "One more thing. If I hear that woman's been hurt, if anything happens to her or her little boy, I'm going to find every one of you and fuck you up." I looked around the table. "Fuck you up bad." After I gave each one of them a chance to see that little bit of craziness in my eyes I stepped back. Bobby took the gun and passed it over to Forché. Then he hauled me across the room and out the front door.

"Are you out of your mind?" Bobby didn't look so young and innocent anymore. He spread his open palm against my chest and pushed me back against the wall, held me pinned there. "You don't threaten people with guns like that. You're a cop, not a thug."

"So, I'm off duty."

"Fuck you, this is my turf and you're acting like a god-damn nutcase."

"Slovo?" Forché came to stand beside me, her face in shadow. I thought she might congratulate me. "Don't you *ever* touch my guns."

"Jeez, Sabine, that's the guy broke my fingers." I shoved Bobby's hand away. "Let's go back inside, it's cold out here."

Irene was there now, stepping outside with the others, her arms wrapped around her for warmth, her eyes big and worried. "Maybe we better call it a night, huh?"

"Yeah, we better," Bobby muttered, looking troubled.

Flaherty handed me my cane, saying to the others, "We'll take him home. See you guys tomorrow."

I looked around for Ruth, but she was talking to Bryn and Hari, and didn't look my way when I called out to her. Flaherty talked quietly to Forché about nothing much all the way back to the house on Hunter's Point. I leaned my head against the window and looked up at the stars, steady points of light between the treetops rushing by.

CHAPTER 22

It was dark when the phone rang, and alcohol still had its cobwebs strung through my head as I fumbled it to my ear. "Hello?" Nothing, for a moment. "Who is this?"

"I woke you up."

"That's okay." The windows were lighter than the room, a pewter predawn color.

"I haven't been able to sleep. I'm having a glass of wine to relax. Actually, several glasses of wine. You know something? You scare the shit out of me, Slovo."

"Ruth, I wasn't going to shoot him. I was just—"

She cut me off crossly. "I'm not talking about what happened in the bar."

I lay back on the bed. No. She was talking about earlier in the day, when I was angry, so angry I wanted to strike her because she was the only person within reach. When that dark thing inside of me showed itself to her. "Sometimes I scare myself," I got out after a while.

"He left me, you know," she said.

"Who?"

"My husband, the jerk. He met someone else, and I swore I'd let anything so stupid happen to me again. Promise me something?"

"Anything."

"Let's not get too serious, okay, Slovo?"

"Promise. Scout's honor."

"Hey. You said you weren't in Boy Scouts."

"You got me there."

We listened to each other's breathing for a minute, and then she said good night and hung up.

Two hours later I joined Flaherty and Forché for a hearty breakfast of coffee and aspirin, and they took off for the morning briefing where Flaherty would lay out the steps they would take to cement the case against Sylvester.

My lawyer called to tell me the suspension was official and said he'd file a grievance immediately. The news was going to be released to the press within the hour. He told me to refer all inquiries to his office. I didn't mention I'd already given a quote to Maura Doyle. He sounded depressed enough as it was.

I opened the thick envelope Bobby had dropped off yesterday and pulled out the contents, a photocopy of McGavin's file on Julian Flyte, the five-year-old witness to his imaginary chambers of horrors. I filled my mug and sat down to go over the medical and social services reports, study the grainy photographs, read through the interviews. When Cobbett called an hour later I asked for a copy of the tape made in Sylvester's trailer last night. He said he was sending a cruiser out to pick me up. He said we needed to talk. That didn't sound good.

When I got to his office he had me recap my encounter in the bar. "Simons, huh?" he said at last. "Figures."

"Who is he, anyway?"

"Sort of a fan club president. The Mike McGavin fan club."

"They're tight?"

"Not exactly. McGavin is weird and he was a lousy cop, but he isn't stupid. Simons is stupid. He hangs out in the café and holds forth to his band of merry morons on Christian living and family values. And he parrots every conspiracy theory McGavin comes up with. I can see where McGavin might make some offhand comment and Simons would take it on as a mission from God."

"So if McGavin wanted to administer his own kind of justice, all he had to do is wind up Simons."

"Like I said, McGavin isn't stupid. Simons will take the fall for this, if we're able to prosecute at all. We'll have to get one of his accomplices to talk without holding a gun to his head. I don't care how it's done in Chicago, that's not how we do it here."

"You've made that clear. So, what's our next step?"

"*Our* next step? You're out of this. I told you already, I don't tolerate cops throwing their weight around, pulling guns when they're half in the bag in some bar."

"I wasn't—" I started to protest, but realized what I was about to say wasn't true. "I wasn't going to hurt him, I just had to get his attention."

"Next time do it some other way. Because I'll bust you for it."

"I got it." I reached for my cane, thinking it was over.

"Hold on. There's something else. Got a call this morning from Chicago." He straightened some papers on his desk. "It's bad news. You're suspended without pay. Thirty days."

"I heard from my lawyer this morning."

"I get the feeling there's politics involved."

"My partner's father was on the job. A commander before he retired, still influential." I flashed on a moment in the hospital when two IAD detectives had been questioning me before I went in for another surgery. I was fading under a sedative as the orderlies rolled me out of my room and I saw Bill Freeling talking to them in the hall. He looked gaunt, grief and anger over his daughter's death consuming him like a cancer. I knew how he felt, but when he glanced over at me I could see he wanted me dead, too.

"Look—I'm not at all happy about what you did in that bar. But you did good work bringing Sylvester down."

"Somebody should warn Meg, the woman who lives at Northhaven. The guys in the bar last night were talking about jumping her at the cooling tower. She feeds the stray cats out there."

"Huh. I wonder...It was a woman who reported a body in the cooling tower. She thought you were dead."

"I would have been if she hadn't made that call. Make sure nothing happens to her, Cobbett. Her partner was already hurt bad, and she has that little boy to take care of. You have a copy of that tape for me?"

He found a cassette in the chaos on his desk and flipped it over to me. "What do you want to hear that for?"

"Just...I don't know, just wrapping things up."

"Your part in this is done. He confessed. Talked a blue streak all the way to Bangor. I told him to wait for a lawyer, but he couldn't shut up."

"He give you more details?"

"Only about his daughter. That and the way he sacrificed that cat, purifying the air, he said. Had this complicated theory. He's one confused, perverted son of a bitch. He'll fit right in there at that hospital. They'll get him all drugged up and let him bark at the moon all night long."

"You're worried he'll get off with some insanity thing?"

"That hospital's no picnic. Place is full of drooling loonies, it's noisy all the time, they give 'em these drugs, make em act like fucking zombies. I don't envy that son of a bitch, whatever he did."

"Cobbett, do you think?..."

"What?"

"Nothing."

"Let's see about getting you a ride home."

Back at the house on Hunter's Point, I went into the living room, found a machine among the equipment in the makeshift office area, and popped the tape in. I lay on the couch, looking up at the ceiling, listening to that scratchy, furtive bass line of surreptitiousness that you always get on a wire. When I got the sound of my barfing, I wound it back to the beginning, then listened to it all over again, hitting rewind from time to time, sometimes listening to the same exchange four or five times.

"What are you looking for?" Ruth asked. I didn't know how long she'd been there. She was sitting on the Oriental rug in front of the couch, her arms wrapped around herself.

"The truth."

"Is it there?"

"Not so's you'd notice. Sylvester was saying what he thought I wanted to hear. I was messing with his head just like McGavin messed with the people he interrogated."

"But Sylvester knew details that weren't public."

"He could have heard about the state of the body, it had been leaked. He didn't give details about the sexual assault; he only brought up oral sex after I prompted him. And he didn't tell me anything about the other two girls." *Tonight,* I thought. *It could happen again tonight.*

"He knew about Ashley," Ruth insisted. "He said 'lots of blood.'"

"But nothing specific about how she'd been mutilated. I may have busted the wrong guy. I have to talk to your dad, have to tell him—"

"This case has been so hard on him. He thought it was over at last." Tears glittered on her cheeks.

"Hey, Ruth." My mind was racing, thinking about how little time we had left, but now she was holding back sobs and it made my chest hurt. "Let me give him a call, anyway."

When I returned I sat on the floor beside Ruth. Her chin was trembling, her eyes magnified by tears. "They've found corroborating evidence at the trailer. The only thing your dad's worried about is whether they'll have to lock me up, the way I sounded on that tape."

She laughed, a broken little giggle. I wrapped her in my arms and held her. "I had no idea how bad it was," she whispered. "I didn't know that Marcy was... I can't even say what he did to her, it's so awful."

"Jeez, Ruth, you didn't have to hear all that."

She huddled into me, little sobs erupting like hiccups. "When I was little, when we still lived in New York, Dad never talked about the job because it upset my mother. Only sometimes we'd go to a picnic with other cops' families and they'd be standing over the cooler drinking beer and talking about their cases. Laughing."

"You have to, sometimes."

"I don't know how you can do that work."

"You catch bad guys. It feels good to bring 'em down."

"I heard you talking to Bobby on that tape before you went in. You like the excitement, the buzz."

I held her tight, thinking it over. I had to get it right, I didn't want to lie to her. "Ruth, the way I grew up, it could have gone either way with me. I could have been a criminal, I *was* a criminal, running drugs for Rainy. Only Tim helped me find something else I could do. Only time I didn't like my job?—aside from the paperwork, putting up with the boss, shit like that—was working all these homicides that were kids. I had a long string of them, one after the other. I got so tired, so mixed up. And in the end I wasn't even doing good work. There was one I couldn't close, couldn't get anywhere."

We sat there silently. I could hear her breathing, felt her breath on my skin as I thought about reporting to the scene that morning before dawn, the uniforms that had been securing it standing there wide-eyed, shaken, waiting for someone to come and take charge. The man whose dog had found the arm was sitting on a curb in shock, trembling uncontrollably, his face gray. Whenever the dog tried to nuzzle close and lick his hands, he'd push him away.

I marked the pieces as we found them with numbered

cards, watched the photographer and the forensic technicians do their work, going through the motions while feeling some sickness seeping into my bloodstream. I moved through the next months in a state of numbness, held meetings where I'd realize they were all looking at me, waiting for orders, and the silence would stretch as I tried to think of something to say, realizing I had no leads, no plan, no insights, nothing but an overwhelming sense of the complete pointlessness of everything. I finally had to walk away from it, file it away as a cold case, either that or lose my mind.

"She was nine, wasn't she?" Ruth asked.

"No, just a baby. Fourteen months old."

"God. I meant Ashley. The one that bled to death." She lay in my arms, trembling. I stroked her hair. "I was nine when we moved here," she said. "My mother used to talk about the sea. She hated the city, kept having to go to the hospital. I asked Dad what was wrong with her and he said doctors always used big words, but really what she had was the sad disease. That's what we always called it. And we thought she'd be better when we moved here, but it didn't turn out that way. They took her in an ambulance to the mental hospital in Bangor and after a while she died. Died of sadness. Actually, she got out and drowned herself, but no one told me. I found out later."

I held her, rubbed her back and murmured meaninglessly, "It's okay, Ruth. It's okay."

She pulled away, her cheeks still streaked with tears, and started to undress. We made love desperately, wordlessly, and lay entangled on the rug afterward, breathing hard, hearts pounding.

"That case you were talking about," Ruth murmured. "Fourteen months old? I don't understand any of this."

"Me either. Never solved that case. Never came close."

"And now this one. You think it isn't over?"

"No. He's still out there."

CHAPTER 23

It's right there, in the autopsy reports," I said. Ruth filled two mugs with coffee while I lit a cigarette. "Sylvester told me he killed those children because he lost control."

"That weird thing he kept saying about signals."

"Right, they picked up his signals because he got carried away. This killer has never been carried away. Like with Ashley, when he mutilated her, there was no slashing, no frenzy. Each cut was deliberate, considered. And the drugs in their systems, that's bothered me from the start."

"Why?"

"Those kids were loaded when they died, they must have been barely conscious. There's something cold, almost surgical about these killings. He isn't doing this for the thrill of watching his victims suffer. The pranks, the escalation of violence—he's motivated by watching the town react to what he does, not by the kill. Sylvester was trying to stay out of the public eye; the last thing he wanted—"

"What?" Ruth asked.

"When you interviewed Julian Flyte, he said some film director was interested in his story. You have your notes handy?"

We took our coffee back to the study and she flipped through her notebook. "Bud Rafferty," she said, booting up her laptop. "Let's see what we can find out." She hooked up the modem line, brought up the Internet, and started searching.

The phone rang and I picked it up. "Slovo? It's Pell. *Don't move, dickwad.*" The last words were roared so loudly that Ruth looked up, startled.

"What's going on, Tony?" Tony Pell was an agent with the Chicago field office of the DEA and a former CPD narcotics specialist. I first met him when I was a teenager, hanging out in Tim O'Mally's office after school. Tony had a reputation for keeping his dark side under control—barely.

"Read a story in the *Trib* this morning about your suspension. Got your number from the reporter, woman named Doyle. You two got something going?"

"Where'd you get that?"

"Her boss pulled her off your story when he found out you two were tight. She was leaving for an unplanned vacation, didn't seem real happy about it. Hang on—" An indignant whine in the background ended with a high-pitched squeal. Tony came back on. "Been talking to a pal of yours on something unrelated and he claims to know where your missing service weapon is. 'Course, he's a lying piece of shit, so— You want me to kick your head in, asshole? Quit fucking around, then, and tell Detective Slovo what you told me."

"Give me a chance, willya?" the familiar voice whined.

"Lemonhead?" I could picture the skinny, drug-addled man, a low-level dealer and occasional snitch. "What you got for me, buddy?"

"I help you out, you gonna tell this lunatic to quit busting my—*ow*! It was Lupe picked up your gun. Sheesh."

"Loopy?"

"Lupe Ruiz. Moved up from Texas, went to work for Gimp. She was hanging with your friend LaShayne the night you got shot. LaShayne went off to do some business and didn't come back. Lupe went looking for her and found her dead. Which she didn't like much, but she sure liked the gun she found nearby. See, this john had beat the shit out of her before Gimp took her over. I was teasing her about that three-four days ago? She opens this piece-of-shit red vinyl purse she carries, shows me the nine laying in there, and says next one who tries it gets to say *adios* to his *cojones*. So, last night she threatens to blow this john's balls off—turns out he's vice. All the other girls know this freak, he roughs 'em up all a time."

"Schemansky? Burt Schemansky?"

"The girls just call him Dickhead. When he took the gun off Lupe, he near broke her arm and all."

"That would be Schemansky. Let me talk to Tony."

"Tell him to cut me loose, would ya? He's busting my—" Over the crackling cell phone I heard scuffling, a thump.

"Any good?" Tony came back on the line, breathing hard.

"Sounds like my gun's over at Homan Square."

"In the evidence room?"

"With Dickhead Schemansky's name on the tag. Can you get it over to your lab?"

"That's CPD. I'm a fed, now, remember? How'm I supposed to—?"

"I need that gun, Tony."

"*Hey!* Who said you could go, asswipe?" Tony sighed. "Look, I hear what you're saying, Slovo. I'll see what I can do."

Ruth looked up from her computer as I put the phone down. "They found your gun? That's great. Isn't it?"

"Yeah, if Tony can get it out of the CPD evidence room and over to the DEA's lab for testing before someone loses it accidentally on purpose."

"Could that happen?"

"Twenty kilos of cocaine went missing from that evidence room last year. It wouldn't be hard for an insider. And there are plenty of people would like to see this suspension made permanent. I hope Tony can pull this off. Say, you find anything on Rafferty?"

"Nothing about a film project like what Flyte described, but I have a phone number." I reached for it but she said, "Nope. This one's mine." She got on the phone and talked her way through to an assistant to an assistant to someone who worked closely with Bud Rafferty, who was, of course, unavailable. Meanwhile, I had picked up the file on Julian Flyte that Bobby had brought by and flicked through the contents again to refresh my memory, stopping at a picture of a button-nosed kid with a heartbreakingly sweet smile, something anxious in his eyes.

Ruth introduced herself as a reporter working on a piece for *The New York Times*, throwing around some editors' names to give her lie credibility. "I'm trying to track down an intriguing rumor. Someone mentioned Mr. Rafferty was looking at a treatment for a film on a big sex abuse case that happened in Maine years ago." I heard a muttering at the other end. "Well, I was surprised to find there are two projects that are so similar in the works right now. Sorry? You didn't? Well—this is kind of awkward. I thought you must have heard already. My sources say Oliver Stone has a script on the Brimsport sex ring investigation he's very excited about. Have you—really? That would be *terrific*."

She shot me a wide-eyed look. "I'm going to talk to the big guy," she mouthed.

I beckoned her over to sit on the bed beside me and she tilted the phone so I could listen in. "Mr. Rafferty. Thanks for taking the time."

"You're with the *Times*?" I could hear him clearly, a nasal, whiney voice. "Stone's got something in the works, huh?"

"Oliver's looking at a treatment, I heard. It's fascinating you're working on a similar project. Are you seeing this as a documentary or a dramatization?"

"Oh, please, these categories. If you knew my work you'd realize all my films are part of a larger project to explore the interstices between image and reality. Who told you about Stone?"

"Sorry, Mr. Rafferty. I can't reveal my sources. Your focus will be on how what happened was...manipulated? Falsified?"

"No—haven't you seen my films? I'm exploring a situation where two realities coexist. It's up to the viewer to decide what happened."

"I hear you have someone on board who was actually involved in the investigation."

"Right, we're working very closely with the authority on this case. You may remember his book, a real blockbuster few years back? Mike McGavin."

CHAPTER 24

Ruth and I stared at each other, but she recovered before I did. "Fascinating. But I thought I'd heard something about one of the children—"

"Julian Flyte. Yeah, interesting kid. Mike put us together. Julian was involved back when he was, like, three years old. We got film from back then that we can use."

I gripped Ruth's knee, biting my lip so I wouldn't speak out loud. "Are you saying you have film of the abuse?" she asked.

"No, no, video of this little kid talking about it to talk show hosts, talking to reporters. Look, if you write this story I hope you get this straight. Evidence is not what I'm after. I'm not trying to paint a simple picture here, okay?"

"Right, you're working in those, uh, those interstices. How exactly did McGavin get involved in your project?"

"I met him at a party after my Dahmer picture was released. He suggested I might find the Brimsport investigation an interesting subject. To be honest, it didn't grab me. But then a few months later one of my assistants caught a story in the paper. Maybe you don't know this, but that town's back in the news; kids have been kidnapped and sexually assaulted and even murdered."

"I'd heard, yes."

"It started me thinking. The contrast of the current crimes and the past with its unresolved allegations, still raw in people's experience, there seemed to be a lot of potential there for exploring my themes. So I contacted Mike a couple months ago and we started talking. Matter of fact, they made an arrest last night, but Mike tells me they got the wrong guy. Rich, huh? I *love* this story."

"Really? Does he know who—"

"Honestly, I don't want to know, that's not what I'm trying to do here. He's sending me an audiotape of the interrogation, tells me it's a prime example of police coercive tactics which will help illustrate the way these mistakes happen."

"A tape? How—?"

"He's well connected. Deeply involved in this investigation, even though the brass out there seems to be totally incompetent. Only you have to understand, this isn't some cheesy true-crime thing, I'm practicing serious culture criticism. It's an exploration of how we approach the transgressive tendencies in society and how children objectify our greatest fears and desires. My theme here is the ways we all use the rehearsal of violence in the media to satisfy some dark urge in our souls. Real social critique."

"Sounds fascinating. Um—" Ruth looked at me, wondering where to take it. "I'm kind of surprised you got McGavin on board. From what I've read, he's pretty opinionated about what happened. I wouldn't think he'd appreciate the, uh, ambiguities."

"The guy's devoted his life to the welfare of kids. He's happy to have the opportunity to reach a wide audience with his message. Hell, he must believe in my project. He just plowed a hundred grand into it."

"You mean he's financing it?"

"His foundation is making a contribution. And think about it: we hit the festivals, take some major awards, it'll get commercially distributed, and then there's cable. We're talking a very wide audience. Off the record, Mike casts his bread on these waters, it'll come back and then some. Look, what angle are you taking with this article? I can give you some back story that your readers will be interested in...."

It was hard to get Rafferty off the phone, but Ruth simulated an incoming call from her editor and hung up. I shook my head in wonderment. "You lie like a pro. You should have gone into law enforcement."

"It comes in handy in my field, too. Can you believe McGavin's part of this?"

"I wonder how he plans to get a copy of that tape without Forester there to feed him stuff? Say, let me check in with Clayton and see if he got anywhere with Flyte's phone records."

"Phone records? Isn't that illegal?"

"What's your point?" I punched in Clayton's number, waited through his message, and told him to pick up. I filled him in on the latest developments. "We just confirmed that Rafferty's working with Flyte on a film. But get this: he's using McGavin's money. His foundation contributed a hundred large."

"No shit? I came across something.... Hang on—" I heard a clunk and a keyboard clicking away in the background. "I was fooling around and found what I thought was a connection between your subject and McGavin, but it turned out to be J.B. Flyte, the wealthy papa. Let's see here...okay, J.B. has been a regular donor to the Innocents Foundation over the years, Mike McGavin's charity. An annual gift, usually five to ten thousand. But what's interesting is his giving has gone way up recently."

"How recently?"

"Those dates you gave me? That recently. A gift of twenty thousand dollars in January this year. Another gift of, let's see, twenty-five thousand in June. And just last week he really went all out: fifty thousand. Of course, J.B. can afford it. Guy's worth something like twenty million."

"But the timing."

"Right. Smells like a payoff."

"This is great, Clay. Thanks."

"This is it, right? No more free favors?"

"Not until I need another one."

I told Ruth about J.B.'s timely philanthropy, and she frowned. "That's fishy. Flyte's father makes payments to McGavin, who publicly advocates a theory that the crimes are being committed by the sexual deviants he tried to stop years ago."

"Which leads the investigation toward Ardis and away from a guy who looks pretty good, has a record as a sexual deviant, who lawyered up soon as the police started asking questions. Meanwhile, McGavin's using the money to buy back his career as an expert." I stood up and limped across the carpet, too restless to sit still.

"By supporting the movie deal that will publicize his work. So let me get this straight: you think Julian Flyte might be the killer but Mike McGavin doesn't realize that and is taking payoffs from his father to protect Julian?"

"No, that's not it." Something was blooming in my head, taking shape almost too fast for me to see its outlines. "How about this: Years ago McGavin used little Julian to give his crazy investigation credibility. And in turn his father, J.B., used his kid's notoriety to jump-start his career. Now, years after the investigation McGavin's lost his place in the spotlight. The kid's messed up in the head, sexually confused, violent, getting in all kinds of trouble. But J.B., he's doing great, he's got the fame and fortune McGavin craves." Ruth was frowning at me as I paced, but my thoughts kept jumping ahead of my words. "McGavin sees a way of getting back in the limelight when he meets Rafferty, but his movie idea gets the cold shoulder. Until a kid is murdered and it suddenly seems like there's a movie worth making there, if he can get the cash together. McGavin goes to J.B. and says, That kid of yours, the police have their suspicions. We know how screwed up he is, it ain't his fault, I can protect him. But my foundation does important work, we need your support. J.B. gives money each time he thinks his son is at risk, and McGavin gets Ardis to confess."

"Only her confession fell apart."

"So now they have Sylvester. And when his confession falls apart McGavin will just put the blame on someone else. He has the town all riled up, they'll find a scapegoat. Meanwhile, he funds this film which will dramatize how he crusaded for justice and got the shaft for it. And he'll make Julian look like an innocent victim of a system gone sour." I turned to face her and stumbled a little, wrenching my hip painfully. "McGavin's pulling the strings. And what I think will happen? Once he has what he wants, which is everyone's attention, this'll be the final touch. He'll plant the evidence, he'll coerce a confession. He'll solve the case. I've seen him at work, he's so good it's scary."

"You said he ran a lousy investigation."

"But he puts on a hell of a good show. And that's what this is; his show. The way these murders were set up, it's not about some lunatic killing children to get a sexual thrill, it's about every sick thought that McGavin conjured up out of this town when they thought satanic forces were at work here. The killer makes those fantasies real. And McGavin's encouraging him all the way."

"High marks for creativity, Slovo, but there's no evidence to support any of this."

"*Nobody's looked!* Ruth, it fits. McGavin has inside information, he's obsessed about vindicating his investigation all those years ago. He wants to control public opinion, be the star. He sets it up, gets someone else to do it so he doesn't get his hands dirty—the same as when he primed those guys to nearly kill me—and then he uses the increased violence to ratchet up the public's fear so he can feed off it. It has McGavin's signature all over it."

"Oh, jeez, Slovo. I admit it's suggestive that McGavin is receiving contributions from J.B. Flyte right after each murder, and this movie deal is a little weird. But it's a leap from there to claiming McGavin is causing Flyte to kill children. You realize how crazy this sounds? Maybe J.B. donates the money because he wants the movie made, too. Maybe his mixed-up son wants to be famous and he's indulging him while making a tax-deductible charitable gift. You're not being rational. Quit pacing a minute." She took my hand and pulled me down to sit beside her on the bed. "You're still angry about what they did to you in the cooling tower. You went into a high-pressure situation last night and nearly got your throat cut. You just found out that the gun that might clear your name is sitting in an evidence room in Chicago but you can't get at it. And you're worried that the man you helped bring down for these terrible crimes isn't the right guy." She smoothed my hair back with one hand. "You need to take a deep breath."

"But Ruth—"

"You're anxious and upset and you're jumping to conclusions much too fast."

I closed my eyes, felt the tingle across my scalp as she moved her fingers lightly through my hair. I still held one of her hands in mine, rubbed my thumb across her knuckles. "Ruth—"

"Hush. Relax." I felt myself slipping into a trance when the phone rang and Ruth reached for it. "Hello? Who? I think you have..." She looked over at me, holding the phone to her chest. "Your wife wants to speak to you." She had an expectant look in her face, waiting to share the joke.

"My wife?" Ruth was holding the phone out to me, barely holding in a grin. "Shit, I don't believe this. What does she want?"

It wasn't the punch line she expected, and her face

went blank. "Wait, Ruth, it's not—goddamn it." I sat up and fumbled for the phone as she dropped it, rose, and started out of the study, a dangerous tension in her stance. "Ruth? Wait."

"I'll let you take this call in private," she said distantly.

"It's not what you think. This marriage, it's not . . . let me explain." But Ruth had left. I finally picked up the phone. "Jeannie? What are you trying to do to me?"

"I'm doing this to you? You're so selfish, Kostya, you always were."

"Jesus Christ." I hadn't heard her voice for a long time, but its pitch was instantly familiar, the everlasting, reverberating echo of one of those moments in your life that makes you wonder later: How did that happen? One of those mistakes that you wear like a scar the rest of your life.

"So who's the girl that answered your phone?"

"She's important to me. Thanks for fucking it all up. Jesus, Jeannie, I got enough problems."

"Your attitude, you take the cake. Last I checked we were still married."

"Married? I haven't seen you since you showed up at my grandmother's funeral uninvited. I haven't talked to you for even longer. Why are you doing this?"

"This is great. This is typical." Her voice went into a different mode, a harsh, desperate whine. "What am I supposed to do for money, huh? How am I gonna pay the bills? I heard on the radio—the radio, not like you'd call and tell me, you jerk—they gave you thirty days without pay, you might get fired and lose your pension. What are we supposed to do?"

I realized I hadn't thought about her; it never crossed my mind. "Maybe you could, like, get a job. That's how most people pay the bills."

"You know how much I'd have to spend on day care? What kind of job am I going to get that would pay enough?"

"How about Leon watches the kids while you work?

He's good with kids." Hell, Leon was a kid himself. He had been living in a basement apartment in the house I bought when we got married and, after I left, he moved upstairs. I liked Leon.

"He'd let them eat candy all day, watch TV. I can't believe you're so irresponsible. What am I saying, you always was that way." •

"Jeannie, one thing: listen, okay? We ain't been married for years, I don't care what the paperwork says. I got medical bills piling up. I'm gonna lose my job. You can't expect me to keep supporting you. Is Leon there?"

"I know you don't go to church, you never had any faith in anything, but the way I was brought up, marriage is a holy sacrament."

"You threw me out, Jeannie, remember that? Eleven years ago."

"You deserved it."

"I know I did. Put Leon on."

Something in my voice must have told her I was at my limit, because after a pause Leon picked up the phone. "Hey, Kostya. What's happening, man?"

"You probably heard I got problems with my job."

"Yeah, Jeannie heard it on the radio. That really sucks."

"I think I'm going to get fired. You understand what I'm saying, Leon? No paycheck, no disability money."

"Bummer."

"So you guys are going to be on your own from now on. And here's the deal. I have big medical bills piling up. I owe all kinds of money. If I can't make the payments they could take the house."

"What house? You got a house?"

"Your house. The one I bought, Leon." I reined my temper in. Getting impatient never helped. When he got nervous you couldn't get anything sensible out of him.

"Oh, yeah."

"So you're going to have to persuade Jeannie to get divorced from me."

"Oh, jeez. You heard what she said. It's like a-a-a sacrament to her."

"Yeah, I heard it, but it's the right thing to do. Just take her to that guy up the street, isn't there a law office still on the corner by the drugstore? Fraley and Plum?"

"That's the sign on the window. I never been in there."

"They're lawyers. Tell her to go there, file for divorce."

"Whoa, I don't know, man. This is kind of complicated."

"What's complicated? You guys can keep the house, all the stuff in it. You're more her husband than me. What you do is tell her that she needs to get a divorce or they might take the house to pay off my bills. You got that?"

"So, wait now, could we, like, get married then?"

"Yeah, you could, Leon."

"The kids would like that. Get all dressed up and shit."

"Leon, get the divorce first, then you can work on the wedding thing. Okay?"

CHAPTER 25

I found her in the living room, looking out at the sea. "Let me explain, Ruth."

"I didn't know you were married." She gave me a weird, brittle smile.

"I'm not. Well, technically I guess I am. We've been separated for over ten years."

"Do you have other secrets you'd like to share at this point? Children?"

"Well, technically speaking . . ."

"*Technically?* Do you have kids or not?"

"They're not my kids, but on paper . . . Look, let me explain, please?"

"The thing I liked best about you, Slovo, was that you seemed so honest. Now I find out you never bothered to tell me you're married, for God's sake, that you have kids."

"I haven't spoken to that women in years. We were together for a few months and then she threw me out. She wouldn't file for a divorce, and I felt bad about the whole thing so I've been giving her a piece of my salary, that's all that we have in common. And the house I bought, she lives in it but the deed is still in my name, I been paying off the mortgage for her. She doesn't have a job."

"Ten years and you didn't get a divorce?"

"I never got around to the paperwork." She glared at me, speechless with fury. "Look, Ruth, I always felt like it was my fault. She'll divorce me now, though. That's what she called about, she heard how I'd been suspended without pay, she was mad about the money. No reason to keep up the whole stupid thing anymore."

"What about the children?"

"That was—" I stopped to sort it out in my own head. "Three years ago I wanted to get it over with, I even talked to a lawyer, but then I found out she was in the process of adopting three kids. They needed a home, their mother was an addict that died and they didn't have anybody that wanted them, not all three of them. She convinced the agency we were married, still living together. I don't know how she pulled it off but my name is on those papers."

"I'm finding this all a little hard to believe. It's not normal, letting someone use your name in an adoption."

"It didn't matter to me, married or not, but to her it was a big deal. And I had plenty of money, more than I needed. What did I have in my life? The job, that's all. There wasn't anybody I cared about, there was nobody to get divorced for. What does it matter to you, anyway? What we're doing is just sex, a few laughs. Nothing serious, right?" She gave me a wounded look, but I was swinging a little blind by now.

She folded her arms across her chest. "I don't sleep with married guys, even if they're just too lazy to get a divorce. I'm not like that. Why were you so dishonest?"

"Dishonest? I told you stuff I haven't told anyone else. You know things about me nobody else does. I signed some shit in front of a judge and lived with this woman for a few months, bought a house and all this junk to put in it, and then she asked me to leave and I did. A mistake. What do I know about families?"

I reached out for her, but she backed away, her eyes filled with tears. "Don't. I can't trust you." The phone started to ring.

"Ruth—"

"That's probably for you. I need to get some air." She pushed past me, grabbed her purse and jacket from the study, and hurried through the kitchen. By the time I got there her car was backing up, turning, heading a little too fast down the curving drive through the trees. I slammed the door shut, leaned my head against it for a moment, then reached for the shrilling phone extension hanging on the kitchen wall just to make it stop. After a minute I remembered to talk. "Slovo."

"Congratulations, Detective."

"Who is this?"

"I understand you're the hero of the hour, the one who finally cracked the case."

"McGavin."

"Will Sylvester a pedophile, that came as a total surprise to me, I must admit. I was unaware of his criminal background."

"He didn't have one, he was never indicted."

"If he had been I would have known about it. You must be feeling pretty good. Entrapping the perp into a confession. Closing the case."

"McGavin—" I rubbed my head, feeling weary beyond bearing. "What do you want from me?"

"I wanted to congratulate you. Only it's too bad you don't have lab results back on those pubic hairs found in Marcy's mouth. They'll come too late for the next child who's going to be abducted."

"Oh, yeah? You know something the authorities don't?"

"Quite a lot, I would imagine."

"Withholding information from the police? That's some kind of crime, isn't it? Speaking of which, your fan club president just got fingered for beating me up."

"Fan club? Oh, you were making a joke. I sincerely hope the people responsible for that assault are brought to justice. Why wouldn't I?"

"Because they might implicate your ass, McGavin. This information you have, are you planning to share any of it?"

"Should I? I thought you wouldn't want it, given you have a suspect locked up. Might dampen the celebrations."

I could feel it coming, like you feel an oncoming train through the rails before you can hear or see it. "I need to talk to you."

"What do you have in mind, a private meeting?" He sounded so cool, so in charge, I wanted to bang the phone against the table until it shattered.

"What do you think, I'll bring the fucking palace guard?" It was rushing closer, I could feel its hot breath, cinder and smoke, the world vibrating with its weight as it bore down. "Just you and me. Private."

"You know my house on Atlantic?"

"I don't have transportation, your fan club torched my car."

"I wish you would stop calling them my fan club. I can send someone to pick you up, but not today. I'm about to leave for a local radio station, and then I'm heading up to Bangor to do an interview. Won't be back until late."

"We'll do it *late*, then. We have to talk." It was there, now, full bore, roaring through my head, a pulsing engine pulling a full freightload of anger. "You think you're so cool, in every reporter's Rolodex, their kiddy sex expert. Got something perverted going on, some really exciting story? Call McGavin. He's good on camera, dresses right, good hair, I bet they all love you, don't they? These *kids*, these little girls . . . you ever think about what it must have been like for them? The pain, the fear, the . . . the confusion?"

"I think about it. I think about it all the time."

"What's going on in their heads while this, this horror is happening to them? Are they thinking, Why don't they come? Isn't anybody looking for me? Do they think, What did I do wrong? Why are they punishing me? They're just kids, they didn't deserve this. It's got to stop."

"You got a confession. Sylvester said what you wanted

to hear. I remember you criticizing how I conducted inter-rogations. But who do you think is more likely to tell the truth, an innocent child or a half-mad pedophile?"

"When are we going have this talk?"

"Not tonight. Tomorrow, let's see ... Hmm, I'm pretty booked—"

"Clear your fucking social calendar, would you? Tomorrow morning. Early."

"All right, calm down. I'll cancel something. Let's make it ten o'clock. The man that will pick you up is named Frank. He drives a white pickup."

"I'll be ready."

I went into the study and picked up my Glock. It was bulkier and heavier than Forché's .32. As I racked the slide, I heard knocking, then the door opening. "Slovo?" Hari came to the study and stopped at the door, startled to see the gun. "What on earth?"

"Just practicing."

"I ran into Ruth on the road, almost literally." He was staring at my Glock. "I nearly went into the ditch and she had to pull over until she calmed down. She's quite upset. That gun's making me nervous."

"It won't go off unless I pull the trigger."

"I'd feel much better if you put that away. Why are you fooling about with a gun, anyway? They've identified the vig-ilantes and locked up the fellow that killed those children."

"Sylvester didn't do it, Hari." I took the bullet from the chamber, ejected the magazine, thumbed the bullet back in, and slapped it home.

"You're raving, mate. You have a knack for making things complicated. Listen, you've been under a lot of stress lately. You look exhausted. Have you been able to sleep?"

"Sleep? You did those autopsies. You know what's at stake. Another child might be abducted soon and you're worried whether I'm getting enough sleep?"

"I'm your physician, you git. I'm supposed to worry

about these things even if you won't." We heard the kitchen door bang open as Flaherty and Forché arrived. Hari went out. I slipped the gun into my jacket pocket, then hung the jacket on the back of a chair.

The three of them were muttering together, but they fell silent as I entered the kitchen. "Sorry to hear you and Ruth had a misunderstanding," Flaherty said, embarrassed.

"The dumb shit's married," Forché protested. "That's not a misunderstanding, that's motive for homicide." She laughed. "Wait'll Cobbett hears about this."

I pulled a chair out and sat down at the kitchen table, feeling sick with the realization. If I went to him with my theory about Flyte and McGavin he'd throw me out of his office. Whether that was before or after he ripped my head off was the only question.

Flaherty pulled a cheap jug of white wine out of a grocery bag and cracked it open. "I was married for twenty years. What a disaster." He poured us each a glass, then started to make dinner.

"Cobbett told me you found corroborating evidence at the trailer," I said.

"Pictures of the victims in his bedroom." Forché drank some wine, making a face as if it tasted sour.

"He took photos?"

"Cut them out of the papers, it looked like. Had a whole collection in a box under his bed, along with some kiddy porn."

"We sent a lot of stuff to the lab, including those knives," Flaherty added. "We're checking the properties Sylvester looks after, too, he could have committed the crimes in one of those empty houses. The doctors won't let us interview him until his meds are stabilized. It's all going to take a while."

"What if we don't have that kind of time? What if it isn't him? There could be an abduction tonight. I think we should be—"

"I thought Cobbett already explained this to you, Slovo." Flaherty put his knife down, wiped his hands on a towel. "You performed a valuable service, getting him to talk like you did, even if it was unorthodox. But what happened after, the little incident in the bar? We already have some explaining to do, letting you get mixed up in this case. But when you get shitfaced and start holding loaded guns to people's heads in public places—you're not part of this investigation anymore, understand? Even without the suspension, you'd be off the case."

"Fine. That's how you want it."

"That's how it is." He gave me the stare for a moment, then turned back to his cooking, his knife making a busy rattle against the cutting board.

I was on my own, then. Until I partnered up with Robin, that's how I did most of my work. How I lived my life—on my own. I'd just have to get used to it again.

Hari scooped up some of the buttery, garlicky shrimp and rice. "This is fantastic, Flaherty." It smelled good, but I lost my appetite after the first bite.

"Hey, we had some good clean fun today," Forché announced. "We picked up Simons. Him and me had a long heart-to-heart."

"Did he finger McGavin?" I asked.

"Didn't say anything about McGavin."

"Did you even ask?"

Forché looked at me. Her eyes were black, smooth and opaque like pieces of basalt polished by the sea. "I don't like the way you said that."

"Fuck you, Forché." I pushed my plate away.

"What's your problem, Slovo? Oh, that's right, your squeeze dumped you. That don't mean I'm gonna put up with shit from you."

"Hey, Sabine," Flaherty muttered. "Easy."

"Acts like I don't know how to conduct an interview. He's questioning my professionalism."

"Look, Slovo." Hunched over his plate of shrimp, fork clutched in his hand like a shovel, Flaherty looked straight at me. "I was there, okay? She operated on his head for hours, open-brain surgery Forché-style. You couldn't have

done it better. Nobody could. So lay off and eat your goddamn dinner. You're supposed to get some of it on your fork
and into your mouth, not just stir it around in circles."

"He's questioning your cooking," Forché said.

"No, I'm not." Hari was giving me a considering look. I
picked up my fork, pulled the plate back and ate just to
keep him from giving me a hard time.

After dinner I tried to call Ruth. Cobbett's home number
rang seven times before I disconnected. When Hari was
getting ready to leave I grabbed his arm. "Look, can you do
me a favor?"

"What do you have in mind?" He looked at me warily.

"Can you run me over to Cobbett's house?"

"I don't want to get in the middle of this."

"I need to talk to her, I need to explain—" I broke off,
unsure that anything I said would make a difference. "She
won't answer the phone."

"I suppose we can try."

It was a dark night and the streetlights seemed to have
their light sucked up by the surrounding gloom. Dead
leaves scuttled across the road in front of us like crabs.
Hari pulled up in front of a small bungalow. The windows
were a deeper shade of dark than the night outside.
"Nobody home," Hari said.

I got out anyway and limped up the front walk. Her car
wasn't parked in the gravel driveway to the side of the
house. I pushed past shrubbery to peer through a window
but there was nothing to see.

"Sorry, mate," Hari muttered as we pulled away from
the curb. "Let's go to my flat. It's a right tip, but I do have a
decent bottle of whiskey."

"There's somewhere else we need to go."

"I don't think—"

"Loan me your car, then. It's important."

"Which way?" he asked, rolling his eyes.

I directed him to the harbor and then onto the coastal road. We wound around coves and over rocky headlands as I explained what we knew of Julian Flyte's background, how Ruth had interviewed him yesterday, the way he'd reacted, his involvement in the film project with McGavin.

"So, what exactly does this have to do with finding Ruth?"

"Maybe she tried to talk to him again. Maybe he got spooked and went after her. I don't know, I just have a bad feeling."

"Flaherty said—"

"Fuck Flaherty. Just drive, will you?"

It was only twelve miles from Brimsport, but Tally's Harbor belonged to another world, a postcard coastal village with Victorian sea captains' mansions, new condos clinging to the shore like barnacles, pricy bed and breakfasts. The prosperity that had long ago abandoned Brimsport had blossomed here. We reached a tiny commercial center, a cluster of expensive clothing stores, art galleries, gift shops, and restaurants. I signaled Hari to pull into a gas station. I borrowed a phone book to find the address and located it on the map, then got back in the car and gave Hari directions.

We parked on the street in front of the Victorian that, according to the phone book, was the home of Laura Flyte, Julian's mother. The porch light was on and a front window was lit with a small lamp, like a candle in the night.

"Now what?" Hari demanded.

"We knock on the door. Wait in the car if you want."

He sighed nervously, but when I got out he followed, combing fingers through his hair and twisting his moustache into neat points.

We climbed the steps to the porch where a wooden swing hung and a mat said Welcome, but before I could knock the door opened. A woman with tired eyes and graying hair pulled back into a loose braid looked at us through the screen door, rubbing her arms crossed in front of her. I showed her my tin. "Mrs. Flyte?"

"What happened?" She spoke with a kind of certainty, her chin rigid.

"I was just wondering if I could talk to your son Julian. Is he here?"

The rigidity leaked out of her face. "No, he's not here. I don't know where he is." And after a moment she said dully, "You'd better come in."

She sat on the edge of a chair and we took the couch across from her. It was a pleasant place, with one wall lined with bookshelves, a fireplace, a handsome rug on the floor, but it didn't look like the kind of money I'd expected. The furniture was nicked and scratched and the upholstery on the couch was worn through on the arms. There were personal touches—African carvings on one shelf, a basket full of dried flowers, papers and books strewn across a small desk—but none seemed to reflect the personality of the young man we'd talked to, nor that of the high-powered motivational speaker she'd married.

"I'm Detective Slovo, this is Dr. Chakravarty."

"Why are you looking for my son?" She kept her tired eyes on me.

"I just want to talk to him. You haven't seen him recently?"

"Not since yesterday."

"Is that unusual?"

"How do you define 'usual'?" I let the silence grow between us. She looked at her hands for a while, twisting them together, before looking up at Hari. "I'm a clinical psychologist. I've been in practice for more than twenty years, helping people deal with their problems. And I can't do a damned thing for my own son." Tears started down her cheeks; she brushed them away impatiently. "Sorry. I'm worried about him."

"Any reason in particular?" Hari's voice was gentle.

"He's been in trouble once or twice."

"Do you think he's in trouble now?" I asked. She shrugged, her lips tight. "Has he mentioned a woman named Ruth Levin to you? Said anything about a reporter doing an article on the Brimsport sex abuse case?"

She frowned suspiciously, then shook her head.

"Do you have any idea where he might have gone?"

"I checked with his father, who lives in Boston. He hasn't heard from him." She sighed again, a catch in her throat. "I'm just so worried," she whispered.

"Mrs. Flyte," Hari said, and she looked up. "You say Julian has been in trouble. It's not my place to ask, really, but...he was called as a witness in that sex abuse case when he was very small. I've worked quite often with adults who were abused as children, it leads to any number of problems later in life."

"He was such a sweet little boy. Now he's...so confused, so angry."

"Was he sexually abused, then?"

"Oh, yes." The whispered admission was dipped in acid. Her mouth was so tight it drove lines into the skin above her lip. "But not by those art teachers."

"By whom?"

"His father." The words fell like rocks into the quiet room. After a moment she looked up at me and shook her head slightly. "Not like you think. It happened after that police chief had turned our lives upside down, after the reporters had discovered Julian. My former husband exploited him by making him tell that story over and over, making him believe that those things had happened to him, using the headlines to further his career. You don't know what damage that did. Twice during high school he made suicide attempts. And the trouble he's been in since, it's more of the same, it's patently self-destructive behavior."

"A few years ago he was accused of being involved with an underage girl," Hari said gently, choosing his words carefully.

"What he did . . . I know it's hard to understand, but he's so confused about his sexuality. It was wrong, she was far too young, but I truly don't think he would hurt anyone intentionally. No one but himself."

"Has he seemed distraught in the past weeks?" I asked. "Or agitated, excited about something?" That seemed to strike a nerve. Her eyes filled as she twisted her hands together. I leaned forward, touched her knee. "Is it like him to stay out all night without telling you?" She didn't answer, but I could see the fear there. "Look, maybe we should get some paperwork filed on this, get a search rolling. Can we take a look at his room?"

"There's nothing to see." But she led us up two flights of stairs to a finished attic. It was a large, airy space, full of strange angles and low windows tucked under the eaves. It was aggressively barren, just a mattress on the wooden floor in the center of the room, covered with a sleeping bag. "He wasn't very happy living here," she murmured, almost to herself as I looked in a closet. I went through the clothes quickly, then checked through a chest of drawers. I found an empty film canister hidden among his socks and, after running a finger along the sides, found yellowish flecks on my fingertip. I tasted them, then tucked the canister back among the socks. There was nothing else, other than a disposable lighter with most of the fluid gone.

"Do you see anything missing from the room, Mrs. Flyte?"

"No. But he doesn't have anything, really, just his clothes and his car. A Porsche Boxster. His father gave it to him two years ago. He left his clothes, but his car's gone."

"Can you describe what he was wearing?"

"No, I left for work before he was up."

"When exactly did you last see him?"

"Yesterday morning. Well, I didn't see him but I called up to him to say I was leaving for work. I heard him say good-bye." She blinked back tears, her mouth twisting with the effort. Hari made signals to me with his bushy eyebrows that it was time to leave.

I beckoned him over, and muttered to him, "Go downstairs with her; ask if he's been using drugs recently." I followed them slowly down the steps, one at a time, giving them plenty of time for a chat. At the bottom of the stairs I said I would file a missing persons report that evening. She nodded, not looking at me.

Once we were on the sidewalk I asked Hari what she said. "Did you actually think she'd grass to the filth?" He strode away from me and settled into the car, seething like a thundercloud.

I climbed in on the other side. "Sometimes it's like you speak another language, Hari."

"She declined to betray her son to the police," he translated, and glared at me.

"He smokes ice. I found an empty canister with traces."

"So, you've decided to do a drugs investigation. Brilliant." He jammed the car into gear and pulled out. "And we've deceived that poor woman that we're going to go looking for her miserable son."

"We'll look for him." He shot me an irritated look. "I don't mean you, the cops."

"'We' is the wrong word!" he roared, furious. "You've been suspended, remember? And before that you were on a medical leave. You should be attending to your health, you git. You could hardly manage those stairs."

"I know I'm not on the job anymore, Hari. It's just taking a while to get used to it."

"You're a daft bugger, Slovo, you've no sense at all."

I wasn't paying attention. I was composing a missing persons report in my head. One for Ruth.

At Hunter's Point, I went into the study and tried Cobbett's number again, but no one answered.

"Have you been taking your antibiotics?" Hari asked when I came back out into the kitchen, picking up one of the many amber bottles on the table.

"I forgot today. Maybe for a couple of days. I still can't get hold of Ruth. I'm worried about her."

"Hari tells us you insisted on talking to Julian Flyte's mother," Flaherty said. He didn't look happy about it.

"Yeah. He's been missing since yesterday. I told her we'd report it."

"The only medication you seem to take regularly is the painkiller." Hari started fussily opening bottles.

"So, my leg gets sore."

"Because you won't give it a chance to heal. You berk, it's bloody important to take the antibiotics and the NSAID and—"

"Give me the pills, but spare me the lecture, okay?" Hari dumped four pills in my hand and gave me a glass of water. I choked them down.

"I suppose you'd better fill us in," Flaherty said wearily.

First I gave him particulars needed to get a missing persons report on file. He phoned the dispatcher and relayed it. Then I laid it all out for them. They listened and asked good questions, but saw nothing particularly sinister in J.B. Flyte giving McGavin money to help produce a film about his son.

"But the guy raped a child. His own mother says he's sexually screwed up. And you should have heard him talking with Ruth. He's full of anger. We gotta find him." I was feeling desperate and tired.

"There's a BOLO out as we speak," Flaherty said. "That doesn't mean I buy a word of your theory."

"Take another look at those autopsy reports. The pattern's there. Will Sylvester just doesn't fit."

"When Sylvester was questioned the first time, after Cobbett learned of his past, he was calm, in control. You can't say he doesn't fit based on what he said during a psychotic episode."

"Oh, yeah? We based the bust on what he said. You called it a confession."

"And thank you very much. It's a start. Now we're doing the legwork to build a real case." He added, more gently, "I know you care about this investigation, but you're not part of it anymore. You gotta let go."

"But that statue was taken nearly two days ago. We're out of time." I felt so tired I had to fight off an urge to lay my head down on the table and close my eyes.

"We got a ton of people on the streets tonight," Forché said. "Nothing's going to happen."

"Hell, we even have Mike McGavin on our side," Flaherty said. "He's been speaking on the radio and TV to make everyone aware of the danger. The children are all tucked up snug in their beds, while visions of serial killers dance through their heads. Relax, will you?" And for some reason as he said that he looked at Hari and frowned. Hari shrugged.

"The killer created this situation," I insisted. "He knew people would go nuts when the statue was taken. That's his plan; he'll take it into account. My guess, he's already got a victim selected and it's someone vulnerable, someone he knows he can get to. Some kids don't have anyone looking out for them. You think it's just luck he chose children whose parents weren't there when he came after them? Okay, the first one, she was on the phone for a few minutes, could have happened to anyone. But Ashley's parents..." It was strangely hard to talk, as if my tongue was swelling inside my mouth.

"Slovo, just take it easy. We got it under control."

"He picked their child because he knew they weren't paying attention." Things were shutting down, cell by cell, neural synapses hanging up the Gone Fishing sign and curling up in the dark for a little nap. "And then there's . . . there's that last one, wasser name, she was all alone, didn't have a chance. Fuck this. What did you give me, Hari?"

"A sedative," Flaherty answered for him, taking me under the arms. "Beddie-byes, Slovo. Get his legs?"

"You need rest." Hari speaking this time. He was sitting on the edge of the bed where they'd laid me, peering down at me as I fought my eyes open, trying to surface.

"Bastard."

"That's Dr. Bastard to you, mate. You keep forgetting you're recovering from a nearly fatal gunshot wound. You can't keep burning your candle at both ends. That's better. Go to sleep."

I kept a few of those synapses stoked with the embers of whatever indignation I could scrape together until I felt him rise from the bed, heard his footsteps leave the room. And then I got up, no longer sure why I had to, only knowing it was very important, but before I could take more than two steps toward the door the floor caught me by surprise and that was that.

CHAPTER 27

The next morning I smelled coffee before I was even awake. Then I remembered.

Flaherty and Forché were talking as I limped down the hall to the kitchen, Flaherty relaying something to someone on his cell phone, but he saw me, mumbled "Later," and pocketed the phone. "No word on Julian Flyte," he said as he put on his jacket.

I poured myself some coffee.

"While you were sleeping no kids were abducted, no murders committed," Forché added. "The universe rolled along without your help, imagine that."

I looked at her and drank my coffee. She finished hers in a gulp and slammed her empty mug crossly in the sink.

Flaherty checked his shoulder rig, patted his pockets, getting ready to leave, his eyes looking anywhere but at me. "Ruth told Cobbett about...the situation between you. He's not pleased. Better stay out of his way for now."

They went out. Forché pulled the door shut behind her, then threw it open again. She glared at me, one hand cocked on her hip. "Your doctor said you needed rest. It seemed like the right thing to do, okay? You got a problem with that?"

"It's not Sylvester. We got it wrong, Sabine. It's not over yet."

"I know." The door slammed behind her so hard the windows shook.

At a quarter of ten I was smoking a cigarette beside my burnt-out car. A brisk wind pulled leaves off the trees, making a sinister whisper through the pines, whipping the water so that waves were curling and topped with foam. I watched the white pickup truck come toward me through the trees.

The driver was a grizzled man who might have been sixty, weathered from years of work outdoors. "Slovo? McGavin said you needed a ride."

I ground out the butt and pulled myself up into the truck. I slipped my hand into my jacket pocket to grasp the butt of the Glock, just in case. He didn't look dangerous, but he was wiry and the knobby hand resting on the gearshift was big, his knuckles thick with scar tissue. I wasn't taking any chances. He drove into town without another word and dropped me off in front of a white clapboard saltbox.

It wasn't a big house, but it was old and well-kept and on a prosperous street that whispered "money" in hushed, tasteful tones. McGavin had a large, sloping lot with old trees and a view of the water that must have tripled the value of the property. Across the street a skinny old man raking leaves darted glances at me. I rang the bell.

McGavin came to the door and raised a palm at the man with the rake. "Come in. I just put coffee on. My office is down there, first door on the right. Can you handle the stairs?"

"No problem."

"Make yourself at home. I'll bring coffee when it's ready."

It was dim in the downstairs hallway, lit only by one dusty window set high in the wall, and it smelled of earth and antiquity. I checked out the room to the left, a utilitarian space housing a furnace, water heater, washer, and dryer, before I opened the door on the right. It was dark as a cave. A strange, churchlike smell hung in the air like incense. I groped for the switch.

A crowd of faces jumped suddenly into view, the walls covered with photographs pinned so close together they sometimes overlapped. I stared at the hundreds of faces that stared back.

Children's faces, some with gapped teeth and ribbons in their hair, a baby posed on a rug at a studio, gazing solemnly out at the world. School portraits, some of them, others eight-by-tens, pinned to the wall with drawing pins. Fuzzy pictures cut from newspapers. Amateur snapshots, slightly out of focus, and those grainy pictures that look out at breakfast tables everywhere off of milk cartons. Have You Seen This Child?

Smiles, grins, cowlicks, braces, crooked glasses perched on button noses. And in between, in no apparent pattern, photos from scenes of crime, crumpled bodies tossed against broken earth, a tiny foot extended from a culvert pipe, hands tied together with wire showing through dead leaves, close-ups of bruised flesh, ligatures, broken teeth, sightless eyes staring at nothing. Before and After.

I circled the room, bumping into furniture, eyes staring at me, grins and dimples amid the scenes of carnage. I saw a familiar face and peered closer. Bethany Lowell, looking up from a slice of birthday cake, pointed hat askew, the elastic band holding it on making a slash of shadow under her chin. Pinned next to it I saw the photo I'd pored over from the files, the light from the flash reflected against the shining folds of the black plastic garbage bag that framed her pale corpse like a strange seed pod holding something cancerous. I followed along the wall. Across the room, Ashley Underhill's smile beckoned me in triplicate from her first, second, and third grade school portraits, each one slightly more mature, more assured, lined up over the crime-scene photos of her mutilated body. Going, going, gone.

More destruction among the smiling faces. In the center of the third wall there was a class picture, rows of smiling kids with the smallest ones in front, tall gawky ones in back, a fat girl at the end of one row, her smile carrying some desperation in it. She stood at a slight distance from the other kids, as if they knew she was marked. Overlapping the class picture there was an eight-by-ten of the obscene bundle of flayed flesh that had once been Marcy Knox.

McGavin came in with mugs of coffee and eased the door shut behind him.

"Where'd you get this?" I asked him, leaning my shoulder against the wall and tapping the picture of Marcy with the barrel of my gun that for some reason I was now holding in both hands.

"It came anonymously, slipped under my door in a plain envelope. Someone believes I should know what's going on."

"What is this place, some fucking trophy room?" My voice was jagged, breaking.

"A shrine, Slovo. Show some respect for the dead." He set the coffee down, and fixed his eyes on mine. "This is a shrine to the missing and the dead, the ones that mustn't be forgotten. I know every one of their names. Put the gun away, Slovo."

I lowered the gun, slipped it into my pocket, but kept my palm against the grip. "Where did they all come from?"

"Parents send them to me. Parents and cops. I'm glad you called, I've been wanting to talk to you. Sit down. Have some coffee."

I went over to the chair and sat, tried to pick up the coffee but put it down when it splashed, hot, over my shaking hands. "Why?"

"Why do people hurt children? I have never understood that."

"Why do you sit here and look at them? You get off on it?"

"Slovo. I told you, show some respect."

I focused on the rug on the floor. It was a braided rug, rust and red and brown, colors of blood running in concentric rings around each other.

"They're the witnesses," he said. "Like that verse in the New Testament, a cloud of witnesses. I want you to look at these. They came today." He held out some photos, inserting them into my field of vision as I stared down at the floor.

"Oh, God, no."

"Yours?"

After a minute I nodded dumbly, unable to speak.

The one on top was a little boy that had been found rolled in a blanket in a landfill. His body had been lying in a footlocker in a basement for a couple of weeks before being dumped, and the smell came back to me looking at the picture, the smell and the sound of gulls making their hungry noises all around us as we stood there looking down at what was left of Michael O'Connor, aged eight. The next one was the curled-up figure of a three-year-old girl, her hair tied up in tiny braids all over her head, bright with ribbons tied to the end of each one, her little shirt pulled up to show a mass of bubbling blisters where she had been scalded by her mother's boyfriend, jealous of the attention the child had been getting. "Shirley Malouf," I said out loud, my voice strange. I looked at the next one, a girl, eleven years old and starting to get a faint down of pubic hair, a hint of breasts, a strangely beautiful face in the picture looking off to one side with her hair spread around her in a cloud, but she had been opened in a long cut from her pubis to her sternum and her organs were swarming out. "Lauren Alvarez," I whispered.

And then there were a lot of pictures, ones from the park, the pieces each shot separately, some unidentifiable and others bizarrely obvious, the joint of a knee, a foot. That little arm, laid out by the photographer on a piece of tarp, a dimpled elbow, tiny fingers curled up, like a piece of marble broken from an angel marking a grave. I stared down at my hands after McGavin reached over and took the pictures out of them.

"You worked those cases. You had convictions on all but one. What happened with Sharla? How did you handle the secret all those years?"

"What?" I felt his eyes boring into me.

"They're reopening the case. They're going to find out."

I took a breath, sat up. "This room is something, McGavin. Bud Rafferty seen it yet? Make a great scene for his movie."

"How do you know about that?" He may have been surprised, but he hid it well.

"Going to make you famous again. Is that why you're financing it?"

"It's a worthy project."

"And you can afford it, what with J.B. Flyte paying you to protect his son. Only you're not protecting him, you're making that fucked-up kid perform for you all over again. Don't you feel some responsibility for making him what he is?"

"I rescued him."

"You invented him, and he's a disaster. A sweet little boy, his mother said, until you got your hands on him. How many kids did you mess up with that investigation?"

"I rescued him, but it was too late." His voice was soft. "That sweet little boy was sodomized repeatedly by vicious adults. There's nothing in him that escaped the damage they did when they used him for sex. An experience like that takes root inside, spreading corruption and decay like a cancer." He was so close I could feel his breath against my cheek. "It all goes back to the past. There's no escaping it, even if you try. Look at Bobby Munro—he pretends nothing ever happened to him. I hear you've been looking at some of my case files. Have you seen his?"

"I don't know what you're talking about."

"Ah, well. I shouldn't be surprised. Bobby may think he can destroy the record, but he'll always live with those memories. Like you. I know how you grew up, I know what you've been through." His voice was calm and hypnotic, sinuous empathy snaking around me, drawing me toward him. "Living on the streets, hungry and dirty and all alone, selling your body for something to eat and a little kindness—"

I shook my head to clear it. "You don't know anything about me."

"It isn't something you can just push away into the dark recesses, something you can put behind you as if it never happened. That damaged child inside, he needs to speak." I felt his fingers on the back of my neck. "Tell me what happened to Sharla."

I knocked his hand away. "I don't *know.* Some sick fuck abducted her and cut her to pieces and we never found out who it was. And you can't connect me to the murders here either, I have alibis for every one of them."

"A bar receipt, a friend's word, your name on a passenger list? You know how to make things look right, it wouldn't be hard to arrange."

"They were corroborated."

"Not thoroughly. A few phone calls. You even had the drugs with you. Cobbett found them, right there in your car, and never made the connection."

"The Percocet? It was for my leg."

"It contains oxycodone, same as what was given to those girls." His voice had softened, deepened, it surrounded me like smoke. "You came to Brimsport because you knew there were others here like you. Tell me who else is involved. You'll feel better if you share this burden."

"This is all bullshit, McGavin. I didn't kill those kids and you know it. You're not going to get away with this. I'm not the only one who knows about J.B.'s payoffs."

I thought I caught a contraction of irritation around his eyes but when he spoke he sounded puzzled. "He's the father of an abused child. Naturally when another child is hurt he wants to help. He knows firsthand how badly scarred his son is. How a child abused the way you were can turn violent as an adult. They've already uncovered your drug problem, Slovo. Now they'll know your other secrets. They'll have it in your own words."

He reached for a small tape recorder on the desk, switched it on. I heard a voice that didn't sound like me, but I knew it was because I'd already played it back over and over, my voice tinny on the wire, sounding crazy. *"I'm so angry all the time."* A pause. *"I can't stop myself when they're little, so easy to hurt."* A moment of hissing silence. *"They don't want it anymore and I get mad and hurt them for it. I'm sick—"* He switched it off.

"Son of a bitch."

"You've as good as confessed."

"That's out of context."

"I'd be happy to put it in context for them. I've had some long conversations with your dead partner's father. He believes she died because she began to suspect what really happened to Sharla Peterson, that case you never closed. You knew your partner was onto you, so when your conflict with a dealer led to an exchange of fire one night you used that opportunity to solve the problem. You killed her in cold blood."

"No. He can't think that. He knows me, he—"

"He hates you. And with that tape he won't be the only one who thinks it."

"You set me up. You're trying to destroy me."

"I promised her father I would put a stop to this. And I think deep inside you want it to stop too." He learned forward. "Slovo, for God's sake, I don't want another child to die. Let's end it before it's too late. Tell me how you killed those children." He put his hands on my shoulders. His eyes looked like hard chips of ice glinting with a strange excitement. "Tell me now so it won't happen again."

"Don't you touch me." Without thinking, I had my hand on the butt of my Glock, drawn halfway out of my pocket.

He lifted his hands as if dispensing a blessing and sat back. "Easy. I'm only trying to help. Why don't you give me the gun."

I looked at the palm he stretched out toward me and for a moment my hand wanted to obey his command. "Slovo, listen to me. The things you've buried won't stay hidden. It's tearing you up inside, but I can help. You can prevent the next tragedy if you talk to me."

I stood and felt for the door behind me. "Don't follow me out." I fumbled the door open and backed through it, those cold blue eyes of his fixed on me as he flipped a cell phone open and started punching buttons.

Outside, I lurched down the hill. Leaves spiraled down, skirtled across the pavement with the sound of dry fingers grasping at the ground. There was a bitter edge to the wind. I stopped at the bottom of the hill and tried to clear my head.

A cruiser drew up with a squeal of tires and a uniformed cop got out on the far side of the car, aiming his weapon at me across the roof. "Stop right there! Hands on your head," a bulky guy barked, jumping out of the car, extending his .38 in both hands across the hood.

I laced my fingers on top of my head. "What's the problem?"

An officer wearing a Kevlar vest put on so hastily over his uniform shirt its Velcro straps were crooked, came out from behind the car to hold a weapon on me while his partner holstered his .38, approached and patted me down. He pulled the Glock out of my coat pocket. "Caller was right. Hey, buddy, you got a permit for this?"

"Check my wallet."

I felt it slide out of my back pocket. "Konstantin— wait, you're the guy that brought in Sylvester." He showed his partner my shield.

"Aw, jeez." The one covering me lowered his arms stiffly. "We got a nine-eleven reporting a man walking around with a gun." He laughed but his eyes stayed cautious, uncertain. He holstered his .38, peeled the straps of his vest open, shaking his head as he returned to the cruiser, the vest flapping around him.

"Can you give me a ride downtown? I need to talk to Cobbett."

"Sure. You don't mind riding in back?"

CHAPTER 28

I don't understand you." Cobbett leaned forward across his desk.

"I think Flyte could be the actor and McGavin is protecting him by setting up other people to take the fall. I'm next on his list."

"This is all bullshit. You have no evidence. And Sylvester confessed."

"I made Sylvester say that stuff, Cobbett. Time's run out. We're going to lose another kid." He was staring at me oddly.

"I don't know where she is," he said at last. "Do you?"

"Who?"

"Ruth. I don't know where she is." He repeated it slowly, as if I were a dense child.

"Oh, God. Flaherty said she—I thought she was at your place. Where is she?"

He slammed a fist on the desk. "Goddamn it. She was crying when she called last night." His voice was hoarse. "I could hardly understand what she was saying."

"Ah, Jesus."

"I explained to you, I told you, I *said* she just got out of a bad marriage, I didn't want her hurt. Slovo, I want to kick your fucking brains out."

"I'm sorry."

"Fuck sorry." A little saliva flew out of his mouth and he wiped it with his fist.

"Where would she go?"

"I don't know. I tried some of her friends in New York. If she shows up there, they'll call."

"What else did she say?"

"Not much. She said she wasn't sure why she had been acting like she did lately, but she wasn't sleeping with some married guy, she drew the line. She told me she was sorry. Sorry?" He looked at me, fury and bewilderment in his eyes.

Bobby pushed the door open. "Boss? Need you out here."

Cobbett looked as if a layer of skin had been ripped off his face. "Ruth?"

"Something else." I heard a tense murmur of voices. Forché passed by, her arm wrapped around a woman, speaking to her in a soothing voice.

"I'll have someone run you home," Cobbett said, back under icy control as he rose.

I watched ten minutes tick by on the wall clock. No one came to give me a ride. I finally limped out into the empty hallway.

The squad room was dead silent. About twenty officers stood in front of the interview room with the mirrored window. I couldn't see whoever was in there, but the voices came floating across the room on the system. "He wouldn't leave the house. Travis is a good boy." A woman's voice, gummy and slurred.

"Candice. Candice?" Forché's voice, using the same low and gentle tone she had when talking to Ardis Burke. "We found the back door open. Was it open like that when you went to bed?"

"No, I swear. Only the lock's busted. Been like that for months. Damned landlord never fixes nothing. S'not my fault."

"Drunken slut," one of the watchers growled low in his throat.

"Let's talk about when you got home. It was around three, you say? Was the back door closed then?"

"'Course it was. I even checked it, I think."

Flaherty's voice: "You think you checked or you actually checked?"

"Don't talk to me like that. It's my baby he took." She started to weep, an ugly, jerking burble of snot and tears and indignation. "You guys don't do anything right. You better find my little boy." Her voice kept rising until it was a bellow of outrage.

"Let's take a break." Flaherty again, sounding old and tired.

The men in front of the window stirred, started to move away. Bobby turned and saw me.

"Another one," I said, and all he could do was nod.

Cobbett came out of the interview room and blinked at me. "That ride. I forgot."

"It's not important." Someone called his name and he turned away, moving as if all his muscles ached.

"A boy this time," I said to Bobby. "When did it happen?"

"Hard to say. His mother came home from the bar at around three A.M., she thinks. She woke up an hour ago and realized he was gone. Could have been almost any time last night, though."

Another cop came up, clutching an empty coffee mug. "Candi Dowan went out to the bar last night, like she always does, leaving the kid all by himself. Didn't even bother to check on him when she came home. Maybe the poor little bastard just went looking for something to eat. There wasn't nothing in that kitchen but dirt and roaches." He glared around. "You suppose anyone made coffee?" He stalked off.

"Any leads?" I asked.

Bobby shrugged. "They got people still processing the house."

The pumped-up cop didn't get far in his quest for caffeine. He came back immediately to slap a sheet of paper into my hands. "Hot off the press. That's the kid: Travis Dowan, five years old. Brown hair, brown eyes, weight twenty-seven pounds, height thirty-five inches. Scar on the back of his left hand from a burn off a kerosene heater, kind of mother she is. You need a license to have a dog, doesn't it just piss you off?"

Missing printed in big letters over the grainy picture, a reproduction of a cheap studio photo, the boy's smile so big it could hardly fit that little pointy-chinned face.

"We're taking these around town?" Bobby asked.

"Yeah. They already started a canvass of the neighborhood." The other cop snatched the sheet back and stared at it, his mouth tight. "My wife's been trying to get pregnant for three years. Wouldn't believe what we've been through, and women like that—" The sheet of paper was trembling in his hand. He handed it back. "Ah, fuck. I gotta get some coffee before I kill somebody."

Flaherty had Forché move the interview into a smaller, more intimate room in the hopes her low-keyed, sympathetic approach might coax something useful out of the mother. Flaherty then took charge of organizing the restless, antsy cops. I sat in a corner and watched the chaos take shape under Flaherty's direction.

The Crimes Against Children coordinators at the FBI's Boston field office had been informed and would be sending a resource team. Additional personnel were on their way from the Orono barracks of the Maine State Police, other neighboring jurisdictions had been notified, technical resources were being marshaled. Flaherty divided up the police to canvass different sectors of the town. They were dispersed, armed with flyers. Then he came over to my corner. "What the hell are you doing here? I told you—"

"For Christ's sake, Flaherty, isn't there something I can do?"

Bryn came into the squad room wheeling a dolly laden with boxes. "Know anything about computers?" Bryn asked me, sizing up our standoff with a quick glance.

"Not a lot."

"Can you use a screwdriver?

"That I can handle."

"Give me a hand setting these up."

Flaherty was called away to take a phone call. Bryn explained he was adding a bank of computers for the increased personnel. Four new computers ordered for different town offices had arrived in the last week; Bryn hadn't had time to set them up, so he requisitioned them for the duration. In addition to those, he had targeted six more computers to borrow, including a new and powerful machine that sat on the mayor's desk for status but was hardly ever used. Though the mayor was tied up in a meeting and unavailable, Bryn was sure he would want to do the right thing and donate it to the cause.

"You show initiative," I told him.

"Thank you."

"Initiative like that will get you fired."

"I don't care. Let's make room." We shifted some furniture to make space along one wall and Bryn went off. He returned with a couple of city workers who carried in folding tables borrowed from the community center.

"Have you seen Ruth lately?" I asked him.

"Not since Monday night when we all went to that bar."

"We had a fight yesterday. She got pretty upset."

A civilian employee came to the door with a stack of copies of the flyer. "Where do these go?" she asked no one in particular. A cop took them from her.

"Sorry to hear that," Bryn said, embarrassed.

I started unpacking CPUs while Bryn went off with the dolly for more. We were both afflicted with an excess of nervous energy and got into a fast synched-up rhythm, me hooking up keyboards and monitors while he loped around me, turning things on, troubleshooting problems, stringing Ethernet cable. An hour into it, on my back under a table and screwing in network lines that Bryn fed me from above, I raised myself on an elbow and swore.

"You okay?" Bryn asked.

"This dumb hip." I mopped my forehead with my T-shirt. "Where are you getting all the energy, Bryn?"

He squatted down. "You want some?" His eyes were bright and mischievous.

"No! I don't use that shit anymore. Hand me a T-connector."

As we worked, we caught scraps of news, reports coming in from the canvass, plans to publicize an anonymous tip line, offer a reward. We got the ten machines assembled and running and I began installing software as Bryn worked on a computer that kept dropping off the network.

"Why do you think he took a boy this time?" Bryn frowned at the monitor and jabbed at the keyboard. We'd been making a race of it, letting our adrenaline burn off in the physical act of slinging hardware around, but that initial buzz was off and something darker was leaning over our shoulders now.

"I don't know. Shock value, maybe. Girls are three times more likely to be victims of sexual abuse than boys, but people tend to get more upset about male victims."

"Does this make it likely there's more than one person at work?"

"Mike McGavin's satanic underground?"

"I just mean, well, you'd think one person would have a sexual preference and stick with it."

"It's not about sex. It's about violence. It's about increasing the violence with each victim." My eyes flickered between the three nearest monitors that showed their progress in extracting software files, my hand poised to bang the return key as soon as the "next" button appeared. I flashed on the face on the flyer that was being distributed across town and felt something twist in my chest. *How could it be any worse?*

"I've heard rumors Marcy's body was field dressed." Bryn glanced at me. "Like hunters do. That's not true, is it?"

"Afraid so. Don't spread it around, though. That's never been publicly confirmed." A dialog box said "next" and I hit return, repeating it on the other machines as soon as they caught up.

"Jesus," he whispered. "I've seen skinned deer hanging in people's yards here, right in town." He stared at his monitor for a moment, then something that flashed up on it made him unleash a stream of curses and he banged a fist on the table before diving under it to turn off the CPU, pull the chassis off and yank out the network card.

He was still working on it as I finished installing the last of the software. I went to the staff room to feed some quarters into the vending machine for something cold. Flaherty nodded to me as he came in to draw some sludge from a forty-cup coffeepot borrowed from a church. Someone at the church had provided sandwiches, too. There were a few triangles left on the tray, the bread dried up and starting to curl. I was going to ask Flaherty if there was any progress, but the sag of his shoulders and the bruised-looking bags of flesh under his eyes told me there wasn't. He took his mug and left without a word.

I limped down the hall to a back door and went out into the cold air. Frustration shot through me, as hard a jolt as if I'd just put my hand on a strand of electric fence. I wanted to be out in the streets, hitting the squats and the dives, rousting drug dealers to find out where they last saw Julian Flyte. I wanted, badly, to have one of those conversations that involved slamming people into walls.

I smoked a cigarette, drank the Coke, and then went in to find someone who would give me something to do.

CHAPTER 29

Phones.

The Innocents Foundation announced a generous reward for information leading to arrest and conviction and enough people were taking their chances that they needed extra bodies to man the tip line. I took down the particulars of hints, rumors, obvious fabrications. I jotted down things that had nothing to do with the investigation but would have to be followed up—a neighbor that took naked showers with his ten-year-old stepdaughter, a pair of ninth-grade boys who allegedly rounded up stray cats at the city dump and set them on fire. At least a quarter of the calls were people asking how exactly this reward thing worked, interested in cashing in but not at present actually aware of any particulars.

In the eleven years since I'd made detective, with the exception of a relatively desk-free undercover stint in Narcotics, I'd probably spent five years of my professional life on telephones. I hated the damned things. But today I would stay on until my ears bled if there was a chance it would do any good.

Before I lost any blood, Forché came to take me back to Hunter's Point. Bryn Greenwood needed help setting up yet more computers out at the house. As personnel from the state and the Boston field office arrived, all available room in the Municipal Building had been absorbed, taking over the mayor's office, the city planner's suite, the public works and finance departments. They were out of space. That vast living room with the fireplace and fancy rugs would make a fine annex.

"Isn't it a little remote from the action?" I asked her as we shot away from the station. It was dark now, but there were plenty of people in the streets. It wouldn't surprise me if half of them were reporters trying to get local color from the other half. Several vans parked near the station had satellite dishes on their roofs and television station call letters on the side.

"There's a theory that could be a tactical advantage. People are getting pretty worked up. There may be a need for a backup command post if people start letting off steam and it gets out of hand."

"You buy into that?"

"Could happen. The media attention ain't exactly having a calming effect." She took the right at the harbor without slowing down, the unmarked Crown Vic rising on two wheels. "I have another theory, though. The FO in Boston sent up a bigwig to take over the management of the case. He wants to humiliate the guy he's replacing."

"That stinks. How's Flaherty taking it?"

"He doesn't give a rat's ass about the politics. He just feels shitty about the kid."

"What about Cobbett?"

"He's not doing so hot." She downshifted for the next turn, but was still traveling fast enough the centrifugal force slammed my shoulder into the door. "I'm concerned about his health, tell you the truth. He looks strong as an ox, but he's been on the verge of exhaustion since Marcy was abducted, and now with Ruth—"

"Is there any news?"

"No."

"I'm really worried about her."

"So's her dad. He's going to end up in the hospital if he

ain't careful. I even tried to call Chakravarty, see if he could maybe give him something—"

"Slip him a mickey like you did me? That was low, Sabine."

She pulled up along the side of the drive. The gravel area in front of the garage was a crowded parking lot. "A decent night's sleep didn't do you any harm. It's not like you could have prevented the kidnapping."

"We should have prevented it. We let this happen, Sabine. If I hadn't gone after the wrong guy—"

She gave me a drill-sergeant glare and poked my chest with one finger. "Focus on finding that kid. That's all that counts right now."

Inside I helped Bryn turn a pile of hardware scrounged from the DA's office into a bank of eight networked computers while a telephone company employee added phones. Bryn was growing clumsy as he came off his drug-fueled energy. He'd been working flat out for over twelve hours and was beginning to crash. He lifted an arm to push his hair back from his forehead. "You hear from Ruth yet?"

"No."

"I'm sure she's okay. After that creep of a husband left her, she took her phone off the hook, wouldn't let anyone in her apartment for days. She just needed some time to herself." He pounded some commands on a keyboard. "Goddamn it! Is this piece of shit hooked up to the network?"

I checked the connections. "Looks like it."

He rebooted and flung himself back in the chair, staring at the screen. "All this effort and we're getting nowhere. It seems so damned pointless."

"You just do what you can and hope something breaks," I said, but felt a twisting sense that he was right—none of this was doing any good. All the knocking on doors, the phone tips, the gathering of data was accomplishing nothing except giving the killer the satisfaction of watching us chase our tails.

Flaherty pinned a large street map of Brimsport and environs to the wall, then briefed his retinue of six state cops and two SAs from the Bangor Resident Agency on the state of the search.

"What's our focus?" someone asked when he was done.

Flaherty described the group's task of collating information as it was gathered, looking for patterns or connections, keeping an eye out for gaps in the search, and providing feedback to team leaders. Any questions?

"Any progress on locating Julian Flyte?" I asked.

"His car was found." Flaherty jabbed at the map. "Parked in this alley. No sign of him as yet."

"Are we talking to dealers? He might have tried to score some ice."

"It's one of several angles being pursued. Anything else?"

"Did we get anything useful from the mother?" someone asked.

Forché took that one. "Nada. We've been talking to some of the men in her life, but I'm not optimistic."

One of the feds asked a technical question about how data was being entered into the database. It was all suddenly too much for me, this complex machine clanging and grinding and getting nowhere. I went to the kitchen, poured myself some coffee, and drank it, staring out at the darkness. The trees were stirring in the wind, shadows shifting behind my own reflection.

Like this case. Too many layers, too many reflective surfaces, while in the darkness underneath, the killer made his moves unseen.

I closed my eyes and emptied my mind. Start with the facts: a boy abducted by someone who'd planned ahead and knew he was neglected. Three girls, kidnapped and raped and murdered by someone with insider's knowledge and some deep-seated pain that had calcified in his soul so when he committed his violence it was done coldly, without passion. Someone who moved through that darkness invisibly, presenting a different face to those who were closest to him. Surfaces and shadows.

A fragment of memory flitted past as I thought it through, and for just a moment that shadow took on a familiar shape.

A rapping at the door interrupted my trance. I set my mug down, went over to open it, and was confused to find Maura Doyle grinning up at me. "Hiya, Slovo."

"Maura? How'd you get here?"

"Rented a car at the Bangor airport. Mind if I come in?" She pushed past me into the kitchen. "Bill Freeling complained about my story on your suspension and my editor made me take a week off. So I decided to do a piece on the murders out here. Show him, the son of a bitch. This is going to be a hell of a story. I couldn't believe it, driving through Brimsport. There's a riot on the main street. The place is swarming with cops."

"There's been another abduction. A little boy this time." I had to close my eyes suddenly.

"Hey, Slovo. Easy. Maybe you should sit down."

"No, I'm...it's been a long day."

"I was sort of hoping you'd come out with me, fill me in, but I don't know..." She peered up at me through her bangs.

"I'll go with you. Let me get my jacket."

She followed me curiously down the hallway, peered into the busy living room filled with cops. "Who's this?" Flaherty frowned at us suspiciously.

"A friend from Chicago. We're going out."

"Things are ugly out there," another cop said. "Better take the coast road over to Tally's Harbor. You don't want to go anywhere near Brimsport right now."

"We'll be real careful," Maura said, giving him her most innocent look. He turned away, duty done, but Flaherty watched me with narrowed eyes until a ringing phone distracted him.

CHAPTER 30

Outside, the waves were crashing against the rocky shore. The wind was cold off the water and whipped the trees into a dark frenzy. Maura kept up a steady stream of chatter as we headed for town, firing questions about the missing child, wondering out loud what might be happening, enjoying the hell out of it all.

"The last one he took, Maura? Seven years old. She was raped and sodomized. They found pubic hair in her mouth."

She drove in silence for the next six blocks.

As we approached the Municipal Building we were caught up in a confusion of vehicles and people milling around the street, hurrying from side to side, a simmering mob on the verge of boiling over into full-scale riot. I caught a glimpse of Neil Forester hunched in a peacoat on the sidewalk, his collar turned up and a watch cap pulled down on his head, watching the scene, a little smile tugging at his face.

There were four sound trucks with satellite dishes, cables snaking along the pavement. Bright floodlights focused on the steps of the police station, where a podium had been set up. Wind was whipping up the street from the harbor, snatching at trash and rolling cans noisily along the sidewalk.

Maura nosed her rental car as far as she could up the street. She put the car in park and turned to burrow into a case in the backseat, emerging with a camera with a long lens and a big flash attachment. I took it from her, saying, "I don't like the look of this crowd. This'll make you a target."

She opened her mouth to argue when we heard the sound of glass breaking and a roar of approval. Someone had thrown a brick at a sound truck, shattering a back window. I detached the flash and set it and the camera under the seat. By the time I straightened up, she was already out of the car, pad and pen in hand. "Maura? Hey!" She just started to wade into the mayhem, elbowing between taller men to work her way to the front of the crowd. I got my cane untangled from the seat and followed, trying to keep track of her short figure in the mob.

Two men came to the podium, the bright floodlights painting giant shadows behind them. The sound system shrieked and popped before words came through intermittently, the wind snatching them away. "... effort is being made to find Travis Dowan ... assistance from the Federal Bureau of Investigation ..." The local official stepped aside and a tall, lean man stepped up to the mike.

"... one of the largest search efforts in the history of ..." I caught sight of Maura, at barely five feet a figure easily lost in the crowd, and was pushing through to reach her side when someone grabbed my arm.

"Look who's here. You got some nerve, you pervert."

"... every confidence we will find the child before ..." The wind snatched the words and shredded them.

"Where's little Travis?" A woman was screaming at me, her face a twisted mask of rage and hate. Spittle flew out of her mouth, a little string of it swinging from her chin. Someone grabbed my shoulder and swung me around, the faces yelling at me a blur of eyes and wide mouths and teeth. The woman started scrabbling at my clothes as if trying to tear through them. "Satanist. Pervert."

Two cops in riot gear pushed forward. They took my arms and hustled me along, less gently than the mob. Their faces weren't visible behind their helmets, and their padding and shoulder radios made them look like extras in a cyborg film. They handed me off to a uniform who took me through a side door of the station, where cops with logos on their jackets from surrounding jurisdictions were milling around the hallways. Not sure what to do with me, the uniform pointed to a chair in the hallway and told me to wait there, but as soon as he left I clipped my shield to the waistband of my jeans and limped down the hall to see what was going on.

The interview room with the miraculous stain on the ceiling was being used to process arrests, a half dozen guys waiting their turns, most with black eyes or bloodied noses. The squad room was now a command center, the desks taken over by federal agents working the phones, tracking the course of the search, relaying information to Flaherty's outpost. I kept on going to the break room, which was crowded with cops catching a cup of coffee before going back out, comparing scratches and bruises, speculating on tactics to deal with the mood outside. A television was tuned to the Bangor station that was broadcasting live from the steps outside. The FBI official was ending his speech when something exploded against the podium. The camera focused on the glittering remains of a bottle hurled from the crowd, then swung around to a stuttering and shaken reporter, whose commentary I couldn't make out over the noise in the room.

I heard Maura's voice in the hall. I went out to find her stanching a nosebleed with a handkerchief. The cop with her wanted to take her to a first-aid station, but she wouldn't cooperate. He shot a look at me as if to indicate she was my problem now, and retreated. She handed me my cane and mumbled around the handkerchief, "Thought you might need that thing. I found it on the street."

"Thanks. You okay?"

"Some asshole caught my nose with his elbow." She took the wad of cloth away from her nose and checked it. "I think it's done bleeding." I led her into the break room, dropped some coins into the machine and handed her a drink.

The room had quieted down to a resentful murmur, faces drawn to the television where Mike McGavin was fielding a reporter's questions with his usual aplomb, urging calm, asking citizens who might know something to come forward, then putting out a message directed to those responsible, pleading for the life of the child, his compelling eyes turned directly to the camera. He came across as being more in control than the bigwig from the FBI.

The room fell silent as a picture of the missing child filled the screen: eyes squinted almost shut with the intensity of his grin, hair trimmed so short you could see the bumpy shape of his skull beneath the skin, an oversized T-shirt hanging loose around his fragile neck.

Then, as the reporter recapped the case, Bethany Lowell took his place, grinning under her birthday hat. A school portrait of Ashley Underhill with a brilliant smile. A snapshot of Marcy Knox, a chubby blur with black curls holding up a kitten. I went out in the hall and leaned my head against the cold tile, fighting off an urge to howl or punch the wall or break something. Maura peered up at me, puzzled and curious, but before she could say anything Bobby came hurrying around the corner, almost colliding with me. He eyed Maura suspiciously.

I introduced her. "Maura Doyle. A friend from home." *Don't say it, Maura,* I thought, *don't say it*—

"I'm with the *Chicago Tribune.* Listen, could I—?"

"A reporter? What did you bring her in here for?"

"We got attacked on the street. The cops brought us in."

"You guys got any leads?" Maura asked, and Bobby's face grew dangerously red.

There was a commotion as the tall man that had been speaking to the crowd came up the hallway, surrounded by an entourage. "Who is this?"

"Name's Slovo." I noticed one of his followers had a photocopied picture of Julian Flyte in one hand. "Have you located him yet?" I asked, pointing. The guy hugged it to himself guiltily, as if he'd accidentally revealed a state secret.

The tall man looked me up and down. "Would you see that this fuck gets escorted out of here, Munro? I don't want you anywhere near this investigation, you got it? You've done enough damage already." He put a palm to my chest to push me aside and, having had enough abuse for one night, I pushed back with both hands. Three men the size of linebackers rushed to his defense. Maura must have decided to make her exit during the scuffle. She wasn't in the hall when it was over, had no doubt slipped back outside to soak up more local color. "That son of a bitch," I sputtered after the entourage had passed.

Bobby ran a hand through his hair. "He's in charge, now. The town's in a meltdown. We have almost as many people tied up with crowd control as we have on the house to house. The mayor's even talking about the National Guard. It's a mess." He looked pale under the fluorescent lights, and his eyes were shadowed with exhaustion. One of the bulbs overhead was humming like a demented mosquito.

"How's Cobbett handling it?"

"I don't know. Ruth went back to New York or something, and he's ape shit. I never seen him so upset."

"I'm worried something's happened to her, Bobby. We should pull in McGavin, he knows more than—"

"You just don't *get it*, do you? You see that crowd out

there? The town would go up in flames if we went for McGavin."

"Maybe you're just scared of him, Bobby."

"Scared? I'm not—"

"What happened when you were interviewed back in 1984?"

The buzzing light fixture was flickering, making shadows leap. "What are you talking about?"

"There was a file on you. What happened to it?"

"Who says there was a file?"

"McGavin told me."

"He's full of bullshit. You know that." As he stared at me, the back door banged open suddenly and a couple of cops escorted a third one in, blood streaming down his face and soaking his shirt. It snapped Bobby into a trained response and he went to help. Ten minutes later he came back and muttered he'd get someone to run me home as soon as a car was free. In the jumping fluorescent light his face was so pale it looked as if the blood under his skin had been flushed out and replaced by ice.

Nearly an hour crept by before I got a ride back to my house from a cop who didn't say a word, just frowned in absent concentration as if he had a toothache. His crackling radio described scuffles on the main street, a car set on fire, reports of looting down by the harbor. He dropped me by the kitchen door and then sped back down the drive, returning to the fray. Rain spat down now, and rags of clouds raced along the sky.

Inside the house the weather wasn't much calmer. In the command station set up in the living room the cops were moving a little too fast, their gestures jerky, their voices overloud. People on phones, on computers, in huddles, shuffling papers, swearing. The smell of stewed coffee was starting to permeate the place. One guy was taking notes, a phone crooked in his neck. "When was this? Okay. Was he alone?" He covered the phone and turned to say to someone studying the map pinned to the wall, "We got a visual half an hour ago. Corner of Walnut and Calais."

"There's a squat near there." The cop tapped the map. "Shooting gallery on the first floor, lot of drugs changing hands." Some understanding flashed between them.

"You got a line on Flyte?" I asked. One of the cops started to answer me, but the other one intercepted with a warning shake of the head. They turned their backs to me and continued their conversation in lower tones.

Meanwhile Flaherty was on another line. "Right. Right, I got it," he was saying calmly into the phone, but after he hung it up he kicked a trash can over and kept kicking it until it hit the wall, fury knotting up his face. He turned and saw me, frozen in embarrassment.

"Say, Flaherty, you haven't heard anything on Ruth, have you?"

He bent to scoop up the trash. "Ruth? No." He straightened up and massaged the back of his neck. "Thanks for getting that equipment set up. Greenwood went home to catch some sleep. Which you might—"

"I'm real worried about her."

"She's just pissed off at you. Hey, Slovo, get some rest, huh? You don't look so good."

"Rest? Now? You out of your mind?"

"What I mean is you gotta stay out of this. Way out of this. Boss's orders." He put a hand on my shoulder and turned me around, started walking me toward the hallway. I shrugged his hand off. His eyes were sunk deep in those baggy pouches of skin and desperation edged his voice. "Don't look at me like that. It's bad enough as it is. Christ, I shouldn't have let this happen."

"Let what happen?"

"What do you think?" He pushed a shaking hand

through his hair. "I should have nailed the bastard by now. Where the hell is the kid?"

I went out into the kitchen and started a fresh pot of coffee.

Forché came in carrying a stack of pizza boxes. As the cops poured into the kitchen to take their share, she filled a mug with coffee. "How's the new career, Forché?" one of them called out. "Her new specialty—counseling sluts."

Forché stepped in his path. "You got something to say to me?"

"Ease up, Forché. Can't you take a joke?"

"Let's keep our priorities straight. You're talking about a mother whose kid is missing. Save it for the bastard that took the child, okay?" She poked his chest for emphasis.

"Is the lecture over? Okay with you, Sabine, if I eat now?"

She studied him coldly, then turned and left the room. I slipped my jacket on, picked up my cane, and followed her onto the porch.

She was leaning on the railing over the water, watching the waves smash against the rocks. I shook out two cigarettes and we lit up. The rain had let up and stars littered the sky between rags of cloud.

"How's the mother holding up?" I asked.

"Hard to read that woman." She studied the glowing tip of her cigarette. "Can't take care of herself, much less a child. She's a juicehead, blows guys in the parking lot of the bar for her next drink. Doesn't know how to handle it, her kid disappearing. Crying one minute, then asks if she's going to be on TV. Keeps looking around like she can't remember where she put her drink down. Follows what you're saying for four, five minutes before she starts to drift. Poor bitch."

"She have any idea what might have happened?"

"A life like that, it doesn't pay to have ideas. She's getting that thing with her hands already." She demonstrated an alcoholic palsy. "I got Hari down to look at her. He knows her from the clinic. She took the boy there for checkups sometimes." She tapped ash off her cigarette. "So who's this reporter from Chicago?"

"Maura Doyle. She's an old friend."

"I like her attitude. She's out front, interviewing McGavin? He thinks she's eating out of his hand, like reporters do, but she starts asking hard questions. Made him look like a fool. You're good friends?"

"Nothing serious. Not like Ruth. I wish I knew where she was."

"Ah, you worry too much. She's probably staying with a friend until she gets over being sore at you. It'll pass." She tossed her butt out into the darkness. It made a tiny explosion of sparks as it hit the rocks below. "Weird, living in this fancy house while we track a fucked-up killer. I had money to own a place like this, I'd quit the job and move away from here. Somewhere warm where they have, like, orange groves and shit. Palm trees. And I'd have a bunch of dogs." Forché pushed herself up from the railing. "Always wanted dogs. Come on, let's go back in."

I shook my head. "Got some thinking to do."

"Thinking won't bring her back."

"I know."

She studied me, then shook her head and went inside.

M

y heart was beating like an overwound clock as I turned to stare up the hill. Bryn's castle was just a couple hundred yards from where I stood. Ruth was close to Bryn. If she needed help, she would trust him to lie on her behalf, keep her whereabouts secret as long as she wanted privacy. She was there with him, suddenly I was sure of it.

And that frightened me. Because earlier this evening, when I had glimpsed that familiar shadow moving through the darkness, something Bryn had said came back to me and I realized I'd caught him in a lie. And starting from that lie, it all began to match up.

Bryn had access to information, possibly more than anyone realized, running the cops' computer network. Being so close to the murder investigations, he would know what evidence would be collected at a crime scene and how to avoid leaving it. He was in a position to feed selected information to McGavin to fan the flames of hysteria and rage. I didn't know what deep-seated hurt might be driving him to murder, or why he'd chosen this town to act out his revenge, but he'd deliberately sought out Ruth's acquaintance and wormed his way in.

He said he'd never been to Maine before taking his current job six months ago. But he'd mentioned seeing deer hung in people's yards here in Brimsport. If that were true, he had to have been here before. The hunting season ran from the end of October through November. Maybe he'd been here last fall, scouting for his first victim. Maybe he had a connection with Brimsport that went back even further. A number of children had been taken from their parents during McGavin's investigation and placed in foster care; maybe he was one of them, unrecognized on his return because he'd grown up and changed his name.

I looked back at the windows facing the porch, catching a glimpse of the cops working inside. There would be no point in my trying out this line of reasoning on them. There wasn't anything solid there, just guesswork and gut feeling. And as Flaherty had made all too clear, I was off the case.

But with that new certainty that Ruth had gone to Bryn after our argument, I couldn't afford to let it go. The Glock was still in my jacket pocket. I checked the load, then left the porch and started up the hill.

It took longer to reach the top of the hill than I expected. The ground was uneven moss-covered rocks that held together just enough soil for trees to take root. At the top of the rise the trees thinned and the house, with its towers and crenellations, hunkered on a rocky cliff over the ocean. I stepped onto a flagged terrace, looked over a knee-high stone wall and saw the sea break in hissing whorls among rocks far below.

I sidled up to the nearest of the French doors facing the terrace. Music throbbed loudly behind the glass, Fugazi turned up high. A gloomy, high-ceilinged room, shabby furniture, threadbare Oriental rugs. In one corner the blue flame of a computer screen flickered, Bryn hunched over the monitor.

I backed away from the French doors and walked over

to a shambling carriage house with a cockeyed cupola.
Bryn's Ranger was drawn up in front. I put a shoulder to
one of the big wooden doors and slid it open just enough to
reach in an arm and run a penlight around the space inside.
There was a fluttering as pigeons sleeping in the rafters
protested the disturbance. Ruth's car was parked inside,
splattered with their droppings. I squeezed through the gap
and took a look around, finding nothing but broken-down
equipment laced with dusty cobwebs. There were tracks on
the dusty floor. Two distinct sets of shoes. One pair was the
right size to be Ruth's. Those moved in one direction, out of
the car and toward the door.

I stepped back outside and studied the house. There
was a cellar door on the side of the building, down a short
flight of steps. The door, designed in a more trusting age,
had a four-pane window. Hoping that music was still blast-
ing upstairs, I found a rock and cracked the lower right
pane, pulled the wedges of glass out, reached an arm
through, and opened the dead bolt.

The music was still playing, loudly enough that it
seemed to vibrate in the ceiling overhead. I had expected to
be in a musty, disused basement, but it was an old-fashioned
kitchen with a stone-flagged floor, deep sinks, a long wooden
table in the center of the room, an old gas stove on legs. A
modern refrigerator, though, and a coffeemaker, the warmer's
red light glowing in the shadowy room—all I was able to see
before a ceiling light came on and Bryn came trotting down
the stairs, coffee mug in hand.

"Slovo? What are you doing here?" He looked pale
under the bare bulb.

"I need to talk to Ruth."

"I told you, I don't know where—"

"She's here. I know she is."

He sighed and set his mug down. "Ah, man. She
doesn't want to talk to you. You have no idea how badly you
hurt her."

I looked away, burning with shame, and caught sight of a painting on the wall behind me, a flayed side of beef, dripping and red, taut muscles and tendons stretched across the splayed shape. A weird panic tightened my shoulders.

Turning back, I caught Bryn's eyes twitching away from the stairs. "You shouldn't have come," he whispered, his eyes big and intense, trying to hold mine.

I looked over to where he had glanced and saw there was a door in the angle under the stairs. It was let into the paneling without a handle or molding so the only sign it was there was the barely visible outline of its shape and a keyhole. My cane pulled out of my hand and I turned to see Bryn twist back and swing it at me with all his weight thrown into it. I put out a hand without thinking to block the blow, screamed as it glanced off my fingers, snapping them again along the healing fractures. The cane connected with my hip, knocking me to the floor, making the room flood with darkness that crackled and exploded.

He raised the cane again and again. I lay on the cold floor, aware that he was saying something, loud and angry, but I couldn't process the words. After a while, the waves of pain ebbed and I said without meaning to, "Ah, man. It hurts."

"Shh. Let me think. I have to fit this into the plan." He crouched down and stroked my head absently. There was something too bright, too wired in his eyes. I wondered how long he'd gone without sleep.

"Okay," he said finally. He rose and went over to the wall and inserted a key into the lock. He pushed it open, and I could see two shapes in the faint light that spilled through, a small one hunched into a ball, the other crumpled on the ground. A bewildered cry came from the small shape, but it stopped as Bryn made a gesture of warning. "In here with the others," he said. "Move it."

I pushed myself forward, dragging my right leg along. Pain flared around the periphery of my vision like licking flames. He grabbed my jacket collar and dragged me the rest of the way, then stepped out, pulled the door shut, and locked it.

"Travis?" I asked the darkness after a moment.

Nothing. I could hear breathing, though, high and thick and panting with fear.

I tried to get my bearings. The room was cold and dry and a fine claylike dust covered the floor. I started to pull my way across the space, and reached out to where I thought the small, hunched shape had been, but there was a scuttling sound and my hand encountered nothing but dust. "It's okay, Travis. I'm not going to hurt you. I'm a police officer." Something in me suddenly wanted to laugh, but I fought it down, knowing it would only frighten him.

"Travis, a lot of people are looking for you," I went on, turning course and heading for the long shape that might be Ruth lying on the ground, dragging my right leg behind me and trying to shut out how it felt. "They're going to find us, okay? So hang in there, Travis."

As I reached out I felt cold flesh with my palm and heard a low-pitched moan. "Ruth? Oh, jeez, love, it's me." I tried to hug her toward me, but she started to thrash convulsively and I backed off. "Okay. It's okay," I said blankly, knowing it wasn't.

Her skin felt so cold. I took off my jacket and carefully laid it over her. A weight dragged the jacket down in one corner, and I remembered the Glock. This time I did laugh, cutting it off and biting my lip, trying to get a grip. I had a penlight, too, if it was still in my pocket. I found it, snapped it on.

"Hey, look, I got a light here. Are you okay, Travis? That guy hurt you?"

"I'm okay." The piping voice came from the dark, sounding reasonable and calm and completely out of place. "That lady don't talk, though."

"I think she's hurt, Travis." Ruth had her arms wrapped up over her face. Her clothes were filthy and torn, her hands abraded and oozing pus. I gently took her wrist, and got a quick look at her misshapen face, eyes swollen shut and lips crusted with blood, before she pulled away and covered her face again, rolling into a fetal ball, chanting "No" in a whisper over and over. I covered as much of her as I could with the jacket, then took off my flannel shirt and tucked that around her too.

I scanned the room with the light. There was a shape in one corner, legs crossed and arms akimbo, dark and as stiff and shrunken as a centuries-old mummy. I almost dropped the penlight with shock and then realized it was the Peter Pan statue that had been taken from the park fountain, stored here until it would make its public appearance again. Its eyes, small holes drilled into the metal, stared back at me over a vacant bronze smile. As I continued to scan the room I caught Travis in the beam for a minute, a little guy in an oversized Celtics jersey with a nearly shaved head, screwing up his face in the sudden brightness. He grunted in protest, and I moved the beam on, deciding where I thought the door probably was based on the line of shelves and the angle of the stairs above.

I switched the penlight off. "Okay, Travis? Here's the deal. I got a gun here. When the door opens again, I want you to cover your ears, okay? Gonna be loud."

"You really are a policeman. I thought you were fooling."

"No, I really am. You okay with this? You know what to do?"

"Cover my ears." His voice had that strident pride that little kids have when they know the right answer.

"Good boy."

"I want to go home." He sounded suddenly tired and querulous.

"We're going to get you home."

It wasn't going to be easy, not with those newly broken fingers, but I racked a hollow-point into the chamber and imagined a target rushing toward me at the range, visualized putting holes through the center of the outlined figure.

My fingers were already swelling, crowding my grip. I took some deep breaths, slow and easy.

The sound of the key, the bright angle of light when the door opened. Then a shape moving into the light. Uncertain for a fraction of a second, I heard his voice, strangely cheerful. "Okay, Slovo."

I squeezed the trigger. The recoil was much stronger than I expected, my hands too weak to handle the kickback, and I fell back, crying out with the pain. The shot whanged off the brick, and I heard myself cursing, screaming with fury, as I tried to get off another one, knowing it was no good.

"A gun? You asshole, you could have killed me." He wrested it out of my grip, and pressed it up under my chin. I felt the barrel nudge my jaw as he squeezed the trigger two, three times, but nothing happened.

"It won't work, I stovepiped the son of a bitch."

He tucked the Glock into his jeans and pulled me up by the collar. "Get up. I don't have time to waste."

"I can't, not with this leg."

He let me go and prodded me with his foot until I crawled out of the wine cellar. He locked it, then took me under the shoulders and dragged me up the steps and into the room overlooking the ocean.

Consciousness flickered in and out as he propped me up against the couch. A big moon had risen, spilling its light across the floor and over my legs. The right one was twisted from the hip at an odd angle. It was hard to get enough air into my lungs. "Slovo?" I felt his palms tapping my cheeks. "Come on, focus." Something forced between my teeth, his hand on my chin. "Swallow."

I choked, got it down. "Ruth. She needs a doctor."

"It's not my fault. She made me almost lose control. See, she was like a *sister* to me, but she—she came onto me like some slut. I couldn't put up with that. I'm not going to do that to my sister, am I? They said I did, but I wouldn't do that."

"Who said that, McGavin?"

"Not just McGavin. The whole town." He patted my leg, his fingers quivering with crank. "Hold on, I want to get this on tape."

He stood up and went over to the computer flickering in the corner, returning with a digital camcorder. He pulled a small table over and pointed it at me, checking through the viewfinder and adjusting it until he had it the way he wanted. "I've been documenting everything, every step of the way. I want the whole world to know."

"Know what?"

"What happened here. What kind of town this is." He came around to sit on the floor next to me, and spoke to the camera. "This is Konstantin Slovo. A detective, believe it or not. Want to start the interrogation?" Bryn laughed.

I blinked stupidly at the camera. "Bryn, what are we doing? I don't understand." I could feel the speed beginning its rush, the tingling on my scalp.

"I told you, I'm making a record. Ask me some questions." He sighed impatiently. "Okay, I'll just start, then. I was born here, in Brimsport. When I was little we didn't have money, but I had a real family, a mom and dad and a little sister. My father was on disability after an accident. He was always talking about politics, society. How things should be. He even wrote pamphlets, begged the storekeepers to put them out on their counters." He laughed suddenly. "It was embarrassing. I used to think, Jesus, this is fucking terrible, my parents are so weird. Why aren't they like other people? But I didn't know then."

"Know what?" The speed felt strange this time, like things crawling under my skin.

"What other people are like. What they want to do to you. You know what I'm talking about. Ruth told me you were abused and neglected, ended up on the streets."

"She told you that?"

"She tells me everything."

"She needs a doctor."

"Shut up about the doctor. Everything went bad the day the cops picked me up at school and took me to this room with a big mirror and tape recorders. They turned everything I said into something dirty. Like, me and my sister would jump in the bed with our parents to wake them up in the morning, and we'd start tickling and giggling and wrestling. Just playing. Only when I told them I thought, man, we did something wrong."

"Bryn? My leg hurts bad."

"You're not checking out on me, are you?" I felt him pat my cheeks. "Come on. Open your eyes. I need you for a while. It won't take long. Maybe fresh air will help."

He rose and crossed the room to pull the French doors open, and the sound of waves and wind rushed in. I sucked the cold, salty air into my lungs. I had to do something. Push him over the cliff or bite him in the throat or hit him over the head with something.

Kill him. I had to kill him.

CHAPTER 32

Bryn went over to study the computer monitor, then sat beside me again. "We used to drive by this house when I was a kid. It looked like a castle and nobody even lived here. Made my dad talk about the rich and the poor, but I just wanted to have it. And now I do. Ha, you motherfuckers. Slovo? How you doing?"

"Let the others go. Keep me as a hostage. Hold the gun to my head, they won't know it's jammed."

"That won't work."

"I can help you with the negotiations. I know how they think."

"They're looking for Julian Flyte now. We got some time to play with." He straightened me up, pushed my hair out of my eyes. "What happened, they arrested my parents and my sister got sent away because they said we had sexual relations, which was total bullshit. I never saw her again. I have no idea what happened to her. I dream about her, though. They're always bad dreams." He stared at the moonlight spilling across the floor, then roused himself. "A woman who said she was a relative came and took me. She wasn't exactly motivated by family feeling, as it turned out. She was an addict. She'd trade my ass for a fix."

"Aw, jeez, Bryn. That's awful."

"It wasn't that bad. Some of them were kind of nice, actually. But then she sold me to a guy who made porn, the greedy bitch. And this is funny." His laugh sounded lonely and lost in the big room, echoing off the high ceiling. "All that stuff those lunatics were making up in Brimsport? It was like they wrote the script for us. The orgies, the satanic rituals, we made movies of it, but it was all fake as shit. We just did it like that because we knew it turned them on." He looked over at me to share the joke, and frowned. "I can give you some Tylox. You wouldn't feel any pain."

"No. More crank?"

"Sure." He took two white crosses from his pocket, put them in my open mouth. "*Dominus vobiscum, corpus Christi,* all that jazz."

I swallowed them, hoping they might give me the edge I needed to go after him. "So you were in the movies?"

"A child star. I found some of that old shit on the Internet a couple months ago. A ten-second .mpeg file, this buff guy doing me from behind. Can't believe that shit's still around. We had an .ftp site on a server in Europe. It's how I learned about computers. Which turned out to be a good thing. This whacked-out couple borrowed me for a weekend when I was fourteen and got carried away." He lifted his shirt and twisted to show the camera. Across his back and ribs there were pockmarks and long, puckered fingers of scar tissue. "That's what they did to me. Made me so ugly nobody wanted me after that. The only reason they didn't throw me out on the streets was because I knew so much about computers. You got burned when you were a kid, right?"

"What?"

"I saw those scars on your back. What you told Sylvester about how you got abused, that was true, wasn't it?"

"I don't want to talk about that."

He patted my leg absently. "Okay. I'm just making the

point, we have a lot in common. Only difference, unlike you I'm doing something about it. A couple of years later, the FBI had a sting and raided the place. I cooperated, taught the feds how it all worked, the way we encrypted the files, how we handled the traffic so it couldn't be traced. They nailed everyone connected to that porn operation, and set me up in witness protection, but I still had to make Brimsport pay. I created a set of documents, a new identity nobody knew about. One day I walked out and became Bryn Greenwood. I struck up a friendship with Ruth and took it from there."

"But I don't get why you killed those children. Why didn't you go after McGavin? He's the one who locked up your parents and sent away your sister."

"Those kids I took, they didn't have a future. The first one? Bethany? I drove past that house five days in a row and she was always outside with nobody but her doll to keep her company. I don't care what her mother told the cops, that kid was neglected. Once I took the tech support job here, I used the Child and Family Services database to select the others. Those kids had been dealt a lousy hand. At least this way their lives had a purpose. Also, I gave them Tylox, so they didn't feel a thing. I took good care of those kids."

"You . . . you had sex with them, though."

He gave me a feral grin. "And you know something? It was great. The first one, Bethany? I screwed her just to drive them nuts, but God, it was such a rush. I had no idea. It feels so good to be the big one for a change."

He lowered his voice and leaned close. "But the best part—you ever watch someone die?" His face was so close to mine I couldn't focus, only saw the light glittering in his eyes. "It's so cool. You look at them when it's going out, that spark or whatever, you watch their eyes when it happens? It's amazing, being there at that moment."

I knew what he meant. That night trying to get Robin to the hospital, I felt the moment she died. It was a threshold; you could feel the draft against your skin, empty and dank.

"You sure you don't want some Tylox?" he asked, studying my face. "Make you feel better." He brushed my hair back with trembling fingers.

"What are you going to do with this tape?"

"It all goes up on the Web. I filmed it every step of the way, from Bethany on. I'll send out some messages to the right places. Enough people will download it that even after they pull the plug on my server, copies will survive. Just like that old .mpeg of me, they'll run these films over and over." He rose and started to pace back and forth, too excited to stand still. "People won't be able to forget what happened here. I've made sure of that. It's almost finished. Just one more to go. Little Travis." I watched him cross the room, pivot, cross it again, his fingers plucking nervously at the seams of his jeans. "I have plans for him. This'll be incredible, even better than Marcy. It's going to drive them insane."

I caught him as he crossed in front of me, lunging out, wrapping my arms around his legs and bringing him down hard. We rolled kicking across the floor while I sank my teeth into his cheek, tasting blood. A chair fell over, and we crashed against a low table as he shrieked in outrage. I reached for the camera, grasped it with my left hand, and bashed it over his head once, twice, a third time, hard as I could. He finally knocked it out of my hand, kicked it out of reach, and backed away from me, screaming in outrage. I was sucking deep breaths into my lungs, fighting to stay conscious, when he discovered my gun still hooked into the back of his pants and pulled it out. Even though it was jammed, the weapon seemed to give him new courage. He pulled me up by the collar, and backhanded it across my forehead.

Rage was making me strong. I pulled myself up on a

chair and launched myself at him, snarling like an animal. We went spinning out through the open doors, onto the flagged terrace, out under the moonlight and into the wind. I got my hands around his throat and dug my thumbs hard against his larynx, but he kept banging that gun on my head, on the side of my face. We were right on the edge now, the hungry waves hissing far below.

Reaching up to squeeze my broken fingers in his left hand, his eyes bright with excitement, Bryn backed me to the low stone wall. I lost my grip on his throat and grabbed for his collar. We teetered there together, bent over the low stone wall, and I could see the fear in his eyes, but the cloth of his shirt ripped loose and he caught himself as I fell.

I was stunned for a moment. The angle was wrong, the shape of darkness that was Bryn looking down at me, stars around his head, all upside down. My head was tipped back against a rock that was slick with strands of seaweed, and I felt my hair stir as water receded through the rocks, then swirled back around my face.

His shape disappeared from the edge and I looked up at the stars, far more stars than I had ever seen before, a deep cosmos sparkling with sprays and strands of twinkling lights, drawing me into their depth, increasing in number as I stared at them. He came back with a Maglite, shining it down at me, taking all those stars away. "It's your leg."

I moved my hand down to where it was angled in some impossible way. Something jagged poked through a tear in the denim. I could feel blood pulsing through my fingers, sluicing out faster than the water swirling around me. It was hot, but I was growing cold.

"If it's the femoral artery, you won't last long. If it's not, well, the tide's coming in. It won't be long either way."

He hung there, making the flashlight beam skitter over the water as it slipped in silver streams through the rocks. Then his dark shape went rigid with tension before he left, taking the light with him.

Faintly, very faintly, I heard voices. Someone droning, patient and polite, then Forché, louder, demanding. "Cut yourself shaving, Greenwood?"

A laugh, words growing closer, then Forché's voice right above me, peculiarly close, confidential. "A trail. See? I don't like this, Tom. Keep him occupied while I check this out." A flashlight beam started to probe the rocks near me, then Flaherty called out, urgent and strangled: "Sabine, gun, *gun*!"

And a shot. It might have gone through me because the night rushed down, stars and all.

The street glowed, glazed with last night's rain. The tires of passing cars hissed against the asphalt, red taillights spilling bands of reflected color on the shining pavement. The rattle of security gates sliding up. Engines idling, news nattering on a car radio, an ambulance siren in the distance. Morning music.

I decided to sit outside in the air that smelled clean and fresh from the rain. The waiter that never talks nodded at me. He had on two-tone wingtips, brown-and-white and about fifty years behind the times.

"Look at that footwear. Sharp." He smiled but didn't say anything. He never did. I spent a lot of time trying to come up with questions he would have to answer, comments that would spark a riposte, but I hadn't trapped him into speech yet. He brought me some coffee and a couple of doughnuts without having to be asked.

Antoine, the owner, refuses to acknowledge that his restaurant is in one of the roughest neighborhoods in Boston and has delusions of grandeur, now and then indulging in some showy addition to his joint like bowers of plastic grape leaves stapled over the booths. Lately plastic chairs and tables to set out on the sidewalk, trying to recapture his childhood memories of cafés in Port au Prince.

Antoine's mother even brought potted geraniums to set by the doorstep, give the place an air. They quickly picked up a nice collection of cigarette butts and other trash; this morning there was even a wilted condom.

I watched kids saunter up the street to school as I drank my coffee. After the majority of the short traffic had passed, the boy came weaving up the sidewalk, hands behind his back, angling over to my table. He had a funny way of walking, dragging one foot, not because he had to but because it fit his image, his own kind of cool.

"Hey, Shorty, how you doing?"

He wrinkled his face up. "Don't call me Shorty, Dewayne's the name, why can't you never remember that?"

"Okay, Dewayne, you wanna go to that rack there on the corner, get me a *Globe*?"

"What you wanna read that junk for? I got things to do."

"Go get me a paper, Shorty, and you can keep the change."

"Keep the change? Oh, boy, I'm gonna be wealthy." He produced a paper from behind his back, snapped the dollar bill out of my hand, one easy, practiced move. We did this most mornings. "Gonna whup Bill Gates's ass, I be so rich. A whole dollar. You one cheap ass, man."

"Hey, Shorty, 'fore you go, one thing."

"Don't call me Shorty, I said."

"Well, you are short."

"You're a cripple, you want me to call you Crip?"

"That's Mr. Crip to you, buddy, and I'm a six-foot-tall cripple, so there. Hang on. One thing."

"I'm *going* to school." His shoulders slumped, burdened with good intentions.

"Makes a change. I'm glad you're going to school now, but it's something else."

"Oh, man. You always bugging me."

"Your sister, she don't look so good."

"She has a cold." He folded the bill, put it in his pocket, took it out again and smoothed it between his fingers.

"She's back on the stuff, and you know it. That guy she's hanging with, what is it, Louis? He's bad news, Shorty. He ever ask you to do him a favor, don't do it, okay?"

"I can take care of myself."

"You take care of yourself by staying out of his way. I find out you're working for Louis, I'm going to bust your head."

"With what, your crutch, Mr. Crip?"

"With a brick. You're a smart kid, don't mess up like your sister. Hey, I hear you like those computers."

"Yeah, I can do that. Only at school, they don't got good ones, they got this old Macintosh shit. I'm gonna save me up for some decent hardware."

"I hear you're good."

"Who you hear from?"

"Just around. On the street." Actually, I heard it from Dewayne himself, showing off, quoting some random lines from a *PC World* he'd just been reading at the drugstore. It sounded good to his friends, even though it was just hardware specs strung together with lies, but at least it was something he was interested in. "Here's some venture capital." I pulled ten bucks out and held it up.

"What's that?"

"Venture capital. Means I invest in your project, see, and when it's going, you pay me back. With vig. I'll spot you ten bucks a week toward your computer business so long as you keep away from Louis. You hang with Louis, I ain't investing in you no more."

"A'ight. Only you make it twenty, I can get going sooner, get your money back to you twice as fast."

"Good thinking, only I gotta pay the rent this week. You coming by this way tomorrow?"

"I always do. Gotta get going, man. I miss the bell, they give me detention."

"I'll have a contract drawn up. This here's an advance. Earnest money."

He took the ten and folded it three times, tucked it in his pocket, his lower lip pushed out. "A'ight. We sign the papers on it tomorrow." All serious. And he sloped off, his backpack swinging from side to side on his shoulder.

The waiter came out to refill my cup and I didn't see the other man approach until he was sliding into the chair opposite mine. "Coffee for me, too," he said cheerfully to the waiter, who nodded and left.

"Hari, how's it going?"

"Hullo, mate. Been a while, eh?" He slumped back in the cheap plastic chair, leaning on an elbow and twisting his moustache into points as he studied me. I unfolded the paper and looked at the front page. Drank some coffee. We sat like that for a while and he finally erupted, "Aren't you going to ask me how I tracked you down?"

"I would guess that Flaherty told you I have breakfast here."

"How—? But he only just—" Hari sputtered.

I shrugged modestly. "Standard detective work." Not mine, though. A Boston cop named Faron had been keeping an eye on me, friendly and joking but suspicious as hell, wondering what a guy like me was doing in his old neighborhood. He decided to do some digging.

He found out I didn't have any outstanding warrants and I wasn't working undercover for the DEA, his two favorite theories. But he learned I had worked on the Brimsport case with an old acquaintance, a Boston detective that had joined the feds and made such an impression he'd gotten himself banished to a remote corner of Maine. A week ago, Faron picked me up in his unmarked car, drove me to some docks overlooking Boston Harbor and, as planes from Logan roared over us, made me explain why I had disappeared for the past few months. He'd talked to Tom Flaherty, who was very interested in knowing where I had my morning coffee.

So I was expecting this. Only not Hari.

"As it happens," Hari said, "I was signed up for a symposium at Mass General today so I could enlighten the backwaters of Darkest Maine with the latest medical research. Dunno why, they'll all think it's newfangled nonsense and they'll insist on leeches. But Flaherty told Cobbett he knew where you were and since I was going to be in Boston anyway—" He reached into his inside jacket pocket and pulled out an envelope. "I volunteered to deliver it personally."

I took the envelope from him, set it on the table in front of me. My name, typed on the front, the return address embossed with the logo of the Brimsport Police Department. "Thanks."

"Aren't you going to open it?"

"Later." I had an idea of what was inside.

"Let's do it now, shall we?" He reached for it, but was neatly intercepted when the returning waiter leaned in with his coffee.

I folded the envelope and put it in my pocket, out of reach. "How are things in Brimsport?"

"Predictably provincial and dull." He tore open a sugar packet and tipped it into his coffee. "I'm rather enjoying dull, for a change. Travis Dowan was in the ER the other day. Playing the fool at kindergarten, swallowed his lunch money. Three quarters and odd change." He shook his head at the memory. "The staff were a bit shocked, didn't understand why I was so happy to deal with a crisis so utterly mundane."

"How's he doing?"

"When he isn't imitating a piggy bank, amazingly well. Tough little bugger. He's still in foster care, but I think there's a chance he'll be reunited with his mother. She went through detox and has been sticking with the program. Born again, as well. She can be quite tiresome about her personal relationship with Jesus Christ."

"Has to be better than the personal relationship she had with alcohol."

"True." He stirred the coffee, watched the swirl subside. "How are you doing?"

"With which, Jesus Christ or alcohol?" He obliged with a weary smile but his eyes were insisting on an answer. "The leg's not a problem. I can get around." I nodded to the crutch propped beside me. It was the serious kind that hooks around your arm, gives you a firm handle to grip. Not as debonair as the cane, but it worked a lot better.

"I didn't mean that."

"I'm fine, Hari. I just needed time to think things through." He kept studying me. I took a doughnut and pushed the plate his way, but he ignored it.

"The way things went that night—been difficult for a lot of people. Flaherty tells me Sabine Forché is still on leave. He's worried, thinks she's lost her nerve."

"She just needed a break." I heard the whole story finally when Bobby and Irene visited me one Saturday at the Boston rehab place where I spent a few weeks learning how to walk with a leg that wouldn't cooperate. Soon after I headed through the woods to Bryn's place, Julian Flyte was found unconscious in a squat, having spent the past twenty-four hours mainlining meth and working on a quart of Everclear. There was no sign of the missing child. Forché stepped out on the porch to fill me in on the developments and found I was gone. Something about it bothered her enough to bully Flaherty into going with her to Greenwood's place. Bryn came to the door to say he hadn't seen me. He was shirtless and holding a towel to the side of his face, claiming a migraine. She pushed past him inside and into the room where the furniture was knocked over and blood trickled across the floor, following it to the edge of the terrace over the water.

But it was Flaherty who screamed out a warning as Bryn lifted my gun, Flaherty who saw Forché freeze up while Bryn raised the weapon and started to pull the trigger. So it was Flaherty who put a round in his chest and two more in his head when he raised the gun again and they didn't discover until it was over that it was jammed, wouldn't fire. A popular form of suicide, these days, but not easy to take.

I got a postcard from Sabine a few months earlier, just before I left the hospital. A picture of an orange grove. Remembering the conversation we'd had on the porch that night, I had an idea. "Tell Flaherty to get a dog."

"Not much of a substitute."

"No, I mean, she likes dogs. If she hears he has a dog..."

"Ah, subterfuge. I'll pass it along." He sipped at his coffee. We sat there for a while, the traffic going by, a young mother pushing twins in a stroller, a couple of fat old ladies in hats waddling down the sidewalk on their way to the market. "Ruth is much better," he said suddenly, as if I'd asked a question. "She's living in New York now, sharing an apartment with some college friends, taking some classes."

"That surgery turned out?"

"She looks fine. You can hardly tell, a tiny scar on her jaw is all. And she's not so...she's going to be fine. Cobbett tells me she's seeing someone."

I took the other doughnut, and broke it in two. "Good. She needs to get on with her life."

"I mean a therapist, you prat. It was hard for her, given she and Bryn were such close friends."

I looked down at doughnut I'd absentmindedly reduced to a pile of crumbs, and pushed the plate away. "I liked Bryn too. We had a lot in common. That's one reason why...one of the things I had to think through."

"You're not like him at all, unless you have a violent, psychotic side I've never noticed."

"Hari, I left Chicago because I was so full of anger it

scared me. I was angry about my partner getting shot, me getting blamed. About losing my job. And stuff in my past, things I never really came to terms with. He had bad stuff in his past, too, and anger took over his life. I could have gone down that path myself."

"Have you ever thought of seeing someone to talk it through? A professional?"

"Not my style, Hari. I'm working it out on my own."

"Have you been in touch with people at home?"

"Like who?"

"Your brother, for instance?"

"Well, I . . . it's complicated, Hari."

"Families can be that way. At least your name was finally cleared on that shooting."

While I was still in the hospital, I got the word that my Beretta was tested and found not to match the bullets that killed Robin. With me out of the picture, someone had the bright idea of checking out Bill Freeling's enemies. A hard case he'd sent down a dozen years earlier had recently been paroled. The parolee got together with some of his buddies and set up the ambush using my snitch. By the time I was at the rehab clinic, I was fully vindicated, though it didn't seem much of a victory. And I doubt it made Freeling's life any easier, knowing who had killed his daughter.

I left the rehab clinic on impulse one day, realizing it reminded me too much of that group home with all the rules. I took the T to Roxbury, looked at ads on a grocery store bulletin board and found a room to rent in a house full of Dominicans who were friendly enough but left me my privacy. I read the *Boston Globe* every morning with coffee at Antoine's, slept a lot, drank too much cheap Canadian whiskey. When winter ended and it got warmer I cut back on the whiskey and started taking walks, exploring more of the neighborhood each day, feeling my leg get stronger as the walks lengthened. At night I lay on the bed, listening through the thin walls to a mélange of voices and music from any number of radios, working my way through those memories, buried for so long, that had come swarming out of the shadows.

Sometimes, drifting off, I thought I could hear the waves washing around the rocks, pebbles shifting with the undertow, that vast movement of the sea that sounded like the whole world breathing. There was something I liked about the way those waves moved in and out, endlessly, without meaning, just moving back and forth forever. A kind of peace.

I realized Hari was still looking at me thoughtfully. "I'm doing okay, Hari. I like this neighborhood, these people. I feel at home here. Only lately I've been thinking it may be time to move on."

"Where to?"

"I'm not sure."

"Don't move before you've read that letter."

"So you know what it says. Did you steam it open?"

"Me?" The picture of outraged innocence. "The bloody flap wouldn't come unstuck. I think they used special police glue."

The waiter that never talks came back with more coffee. I enjoyed watching Hari try to chat him up, with no more success than I'd had. When the coffee cups were empty again I caught Hari glancing at his watch. "Time you went to that symposium." I put some bills on the table, hooked on the crutch. "I'll walk you to your car."

When we got to where it was parked, he shook my hand a little awkwardly, as if he had something he wanted to say, but couldn't remember what it was, climbed in, then rolled down his window to tell me irritably to keep in touch for a change before he drove off.

I walked on up the street and, on an impulse, went into the laundromat where there was a pay phone. I sorted out the change in my pocket, shoved some in and punched in a number. I found myself short of breath, waiting through the rings. When a machine whirred on I had a hard time thinking of what to say. "Uh, Steve? It's Kostya. Look, I know I haven't been in touch for a while. Been renting a place in Boston. Don't actually have a phone, so I can't give you a number, but...well, I just wanted to let you know I'm fine." I hung up and wiped my palm on my shirt.

From there I walked out into the sun, crossed the street, and sat down at the bus stop. Took out the envelope and looked at it.

I pictured Forché walking through the orange grove on the postcard, some palm trees on a beach off in the distance, warm waves rolling in. She looked lonely there, and a little bored. Maybe Flaherty would take my advice, get a dog, tell her about it on the phone: Sabine, I got this mutt here, I don't know what to do with him. You understand dogs at all?

I saw myself on a crowded sidewalk in a place full of tall buildings and bridges and lights, on my way to see Ruth. But that's as far as my imagination would take me. I'd missed her at first, but now it was just a familiar ache, like the one in my hip, a part of me.

I liked this bus stop. It was as good a place as any to watch the world go by. I'd gotten to know a fair number of people in the neighborhood, had figured out who was selling and who was buying, where you could fence whatever you stole, who would sell you a weapon with the serial number filed off. I knew women who caught the bus early in the morning to clean houses in Newton and came home exhausted but ready to do battle with anyone who got between their children and a future. Old ladies in hats who dressed up just to go to the market and wore their dignity like a suit of fine clothes. All they knew of me was that I cashed a disability check at the Redi Cash every couple of weeks, bought the cheapest brand of whiskey at the liquor store, ate my breakfast at Antoine's. If I had any change in my pockets when I passed someone rattling a few coins in a paper cup I usually dropped it in. A harmless slacker. Nobody in particular.

I finally tore open the envelope and laughed. The letter was in the stilted language of police reports. Some federal funding had become available; a new position had been created in the department, requiring someone with extensive experience in criminal investigation. I was encouraged to submit my name for consideration. And scribbled below Joe Cobbett's signature, translating the typed part for me just in case: "Get your ass back up here, Slovo."

The letter, with its formal phrases, reminded me that I had a contract to draw up. It needed some of those stiff words, a sense of importance, a promise that could be folded up and tucked away in some secret place and looked at from time to time. I could ask Faron to keep it going for me, keep an eye on the kid. Dewayne could do worse than have a cop like him in his corner.

The sun felt good. I often sat on this bench, watching people get on and off the buses, for some reason always looking up as they step off onto the sidewalk, checking out the sky to see if there had been any change in it while they crossed town. Old women carefully arranging their bags so that the weight of a half dozen oranges won't topple them over into the gutter as they reach for the bar beside the bus steps, kids chasing around, full of energy. Faces all shades of what is called black but which ranges from bronze to mahogany to roan and more variations; recent Russian immigrants whose conversation sounds like slightly warped and harsh Ukrainian; an Indian woman in a sari shot with gold threads, elegant over her battered, sandaled feet with horny, chipped toenails. A drunk, talking to himself, explaining to everyone that would listen that he was a professional writer, trying to show them crumpled pages covered with scribbled writing to prove it.

For fourteen years, I thought I knew who I was. And if anyone else needed to know, I'd flash the tin. I'd spent the past few months being nobody, thinking it over, figuring it out.

Still me, even without that shield.

I looked down at the letter in my hand, that scribbled note.

Should I?

Fuck, what do I know?